THE GREAT
SWITCHEROONIE

ALEX SHEARER
THE GREAT
SWITCHEROONIE

Bill, Benny's boots and bling!

Hodder
Children's
Books

A division of Hodder Headline Limited

A Catalogue record for this book is available
from the British Library

ISBN 0 340 88403 7

Typeset in NewBaskerville by Avon DataSet Ltd,
Bidford-on-Avon, Warwickshire

Printed and bound in Great Britain by
Bookmarque Ltd, Croydon, Surrey

The paper and board used in this paperback by Hodder
Children's Books are natural recyclable products made from
wood grown in sustainable forests. The manufacturing
processes conform to the environmental regulations
of the country of origin.

Hodder Children's Books
a division of Hodder Headline Limited
338 Euston Road
London NW1 3BH

1

Twenty Things I Don't Know (About Football)

I suppose in some ways it was a bit of an unfortunate coincidence that I should get kidnapped on the same day as Benny Spinks.

Of course, whoever kidnapped Benny Spinks got quite a good deal, really, as Benny Spinks is worth squillions in ransom money, as everybody knows.

I, however, am worth about fifty pence in ransom money, as the people who kidnapped me didn't know.

Now why, you may ask, should anyone bother to kidnap somebody who was only worth fifty pence in ransom money, when they could have had Benny Spinks?

Well, the truth of the matter was that the people who kidnapped me thought I was Benny Spinks. Only I wasn't Benny Spinks, as Benny Spinks might have told you, only he couldn't, as he'd been kidnapped too – by somebody else.

Now, you might well wonder how it came to be that any self-respecting kidnapper with a modicum of brain should mistake me for Benny Spinks.

And that's where it starts to get complicated.

Personally, I usually have a little lie-down round about now.

In fact, I think I might go and have one.

I'll get back to you later.

Right.

That's better.

Now then.

It all started with the hairdryer.

As far as I am concerned, there are two periods of history: there is BTHD (Before The Hairdryer) and ATHD (After The Hairdryer).

If it hadn't been for the hairdryer, none of this would have happened, and it wasn't even mine. (The dryer that is, though the hair was.)

Before I get on to that though, I had first better tell you what I know about football, as that will be important for later.

Basically I don't know anything about football at all. Except the following.

Here is the list of *Things I Know About Football:*

1) It is played with a ball. (And a foot.)

2) There is also a field involved. (And some nets.)

3) Twenty-two people take part, two of whom are

goalkeepers. (More if you count the linesmen and referee.)

4) There is something complicated called the Offside Rule.

5) Nobody understands it.

6) An awful lot of people are football fans. Many of these are fat blokes who eat pies and quite a few of them are also bald blokes.

7) A lot of the pies are pork ones, though some of them are kebabs.

8) When you play football, you can win, lose or draw. But even when you draw you can still win or lose due to something called Aggregate.

9) Aggregate is like the Offside Rule. Nobody understands it.

10) Some footballers are famous and marry pop stars and get paid loads of money. But most of them aren't and don't.

11) A lot of people want to be footballers. They want to be the sort who get paid loads of money. Nobody wants to be the sort of footballer who nobody's ever heard of and who doesn't get paid loads of money, as that would be stupid.

12) When somebody on your team scores a goal, you kiss them.

13) When somebody on the other team scores a goal, you thump them when nobody's looking.

14) Football is a game of two halves and each half is forty-five minutes long; when somebody gets tired

or injured you can bring on a substitute.

15) If his team loses, the manager always feels right gutted. When it wins, he is over the moon. But only at the end of the day.

16) The referee has red and yellow cards in his pocket. These are good for playing snap with. When he is in a mood, he will show his cards to people and blow his whistle.

17) The idea of football is to get the ball into the other team's net and the team with the most goals wins. (That is unless the Offside Rule and Aggregate are involved, when it is possible to win the game by not even turning up for it.)

18) If you are a football manager, you get to have a nice overcoat.

19) If you are the bloke who takes care of the injuries, you have your own bucket with a yellow sponge in it. But you don't get an overcoat.

20) That is all I know about football. (Which is why I'm not much good at it.) I also have two left feet. (Which is a bad idea. If you want to be good at football it is best to have one left foot plus a right one.)

So those are the twenty things I know about football. It might seem like a lot, but it isn't. I bet that if you are a football fan and if you sat down and made out a list of all the things you knew about football, it would come to a lot more than twenty. Most of the twenty things I know about football are what are known as 'confessions of ignorance'.

In other words, I don't really know anything about it at all.

Sometimes I used to feel a bit out of it, due to not knowing anything about football. People would come up to me at school on Monday mornings and say, 'What did you do over the weekend, Bill? Did you see any matches on Saturday?' And I'd say things like, 'Yes, I did. We've got a big box of matches in the kitchen, and I think I saw those when I was getting my cereal.'

Then they'd walk off, looking disgusted, and not want to speak to me any more.

Or maybe somebody would come up to me and say, 'So tell me, Bill, what team do you support? Are you a Manchester, a Chelsea, or an Arsenal fan?'

I wouldn't really know what to say, so I'd just mumble something along the lines of, 'Yeah, Manchester. I'm a real big Manchester Wanderers fanatic, myself. I used to support Arsenal City All Stars, but I stopped following them when they lost on Aggregate to Birmingham Dynamos, or "The Sparrow Legs" as we call them, who I believe (if I'm not mistaken) are now languishing at the bottom of the Thursday League. I think they fell foul of the Offside Rule and got relegated due to the number of yellow cards they'd collected.'

People would start backing off and edging away round about then, and they would look at me as if I were a nutcase who didn't really know what he was talking about. (Which was half true.) They would point their fingers at their heads as if they were thinking of shooting themselves, and then make circling motions with their hands, as if there were loonies about. Only, when I looked to see where the loonies were, I couldn't spot any.

On other occasions, some of the kids in the class might be chatting about our chances in the World Cup, and I'd try to take part so as not to feel left out and say, 'Well, for my money we've got a pretty good chance of winning the World Cup and Saucer this year and possibly even the World Tea Spoon as well, what with good old Imran in the team. With him as fly-half-centre-forward, I don't see how we can lose. He'll kick those googlies into touch in no time.'

I didn't know that Imran only played cricket. But nobody can be expected to know everything. I guess I'm just not really the sporting type. Mostly I'm best at being useless – and that's only because I practised and got a lot of personal tuition.

The one thing I was good at though, was running in straight lines. When it came to running in straight lines, there was no one in our class to touch me. I would slow down a bit on the curves, but always made time up again on the straight lines. I was also pretty good at swimming, cycling and at throwing the discus.

But team games weren't really made for me and I wasn't made for them. I suppose they don't suit everybody, and there's nothing wrong with that. Yes, it's being in a team that doesn't suit me. I'm all right left to myself. I'm better off on solitary activities like eating or any sports where you don't have to get balls in nets. If it was a question of getting balls into living rooms by means of kicking them through windows, I would be your man. But I seem to have an aversion to nets and for some reason they don't agree with me. It's the same with teams. Whenever I am put in one by Mr Barster the sports teacher, all the others say things like, 'Oh no! It's him!' and 'Heaven help us now!' and 'We're doomed!'

None of it would ever have mattered really except that once a week we all had to play football, want to or not. We chose our own sides then. And guess who always got picked last when the teams were being chosen?

You're absolutely right.

Yours truly.

It would go a bit like this.

Two captains would be appointed, and they would take it in turns to select their teams.

First off, they would select their best mates to be on their teams.

Next off, they would select anyone who was a good player (though not necessarily best mates) to be on their teams.

Next, they would select anyone who was just about reasonable to be on their teams.

Next, they would take it in turns to have a fat bloke.

Next, they would take it in turns to choose an asthma sufferer.

Then it would be anyone with bad eyesight.

After that, they would take anybody with a pulse.

Then it would be anyone with a nice coffin, who wasn't too dead.

Once they had their quota of deprived minorities, registered medical conditions and dead people, they would look around to see who was left.

That would usually be Rosemary Cottins and me.

The only thing Rosemary Cottins is good at is flower arranging, and that's only after she's been in hard, rigorous training for a few weeks.

So they would choose Rosemary Cottins.

And then, finally, when the dregs had been emptied and the barrel had been well and truly scraped, somebody would have to have me, as there was nobody left.

It was all right in the summer, of course, when athletics were on. People always wanted me to be on their running teams and relay teams as I could run fast in straight lines. But winter meant football and football meant misery – at least it did for me.

Then one day, everything changed.

And it was all due to the hairdryer.

* * *

Now normally, I don't get involved with combs. I'm against stuff like brushing and combing. I don't mind a bit of toothbrushing, as it keeps you out of the dentist's, but hairbrushing, I'm not so keen on. It's my opinion that it weakens the scalp and can be the cause of bald blokes, especially in men.

My mum, on the other hand, is very big on combing. Quite often, after I'd had a bath, she would wait outside the bathroom with a comb in her hand, or she would hide in the airing cupboard. Luckily though, it is a straight line from our bathroom to my bedroom and so she was never able to catch me, as I am very fast over straight lines, as I have said.

At one time I had my hair cut so short there were just bristles. It was all right like that as it couldn't even be combed, but my little sister, Debs, who was then two, seemed to think that I looked like a boiled egg, and she would sit in her high-chair at the breakfast table, tapping my head with a spoon and saying, 'Yummy!' and waiting for the top of my head to come off and for the yolk to come out.

When that didn't work, she would try to stick bits of toast into my ears to get the yolk out that way. Only I got the blame, of course, and my mum would come into the kitchen and criticise me for having toast in my ears and a spoon up my nose, though anyone could see I was an innocent party and it wasn't my fault at all. My sister is a bit older now, but it is a habit she has never grown out of.

Anyway, I decided to keep my hair long after that and had no more to do with the number one cutters. I never had more than a trim.

Now, this particular day at school it had been very wet and cold outside. Our team had just lost by seven goals to nil. What made this even worse was that I had scored six of them.

People were giving me hostile looks as we made our way back to the pavilion changing rooms. I even heard some muttering about how some people 'had had enough' and were 'going to get him' afterwards. I didn't know who 'him' was and who they were talking about, but they seemed pretty upset with 'him' and I was just glad that it wasn't me.

Now, normally I don't bother with showers after football if I can avoid it as I prefer to stay as I am. There's nothing wrong with a bit of mud and some grass stains up your legs. On this occasion though, I was so wet and cold from the weather that I decided to have a shower to warm myself up.

There are two changing rooms in the school pavilion, one for Home and one for Away. When we are not playing Homes and Aways, the Home becomes the girls' changing room and the Away becomes the boys'.

Once Rosemary Cottins came into the boys' changing room by mistake (so she said) when everybody was taking their trousers off. She claimed that it was all an accident, as she had got her Homes and Aways confused, and that she was only looking for her flower-arranging catalogues, but it seemed to me that she was hiding a digital camera up her sleeve and that there was a lot of giggling going on outside in the corridor. Fortunately Mr Barster came along then and told her to get back to the other changing room before there was trouble.

Two days after that, a photo of Derek Spoot without his trousers on appeared on the school web-site. Underneath it was a caption which said: 'Full Moon This Month'. Personally I think that Rosemary Cottins had something to do with it, though she denied all knowledge. Derek Spoot said that it wasn't him anyway and that it was a forgery and that his head had been pasted on to somebody else's body. I think that this was probably true as in the photograph Derek Spoot's head and his bum were not the same colour.

Myself, I have never been prejudiced and have friends of all shapes and sizes as well as colours, but I have never known anyone whose bottom was a different colour than his head. But I still think that Rosemary Cottins had something to do with it, forgery or not. The Headmaster ordered the photo to be removed from the web-site immediately, and he said that if anything like that ever happened again, he wouldn't rest until he got to the bottom of it. (No matter what colour it was.)

Anyway, in some ways that's all by the by, but I thought you just might be interested.

The showers in the changing room aren't actually all that private. They aren't in individual cubicles, but are communal, and stand in a long line, one after the other. Some people are bold as brass and stand there showering away, not wearing a stitch. Other, more shy, reserved and sensitive souls (such as yours truly) prefer to have a shower with all their clothes on, or they might bring along a pair of swimming trunks, or possibly even a rubber wet suit. Paul Martley, who has an aversion to water, always has a shower under an umbrella marked Alton Towers. I believe it is a souvenir of when he went there.

When you see a boy going into the Away changing rooms for a shower, you will usually see that he is carrying no more than a towel and a bottle of shower gel.

It is different when you see a girl heading for the Home changing rooms for a wash though, as she will have much more equipment. She may possibly be pushing it all along in a wheelbarrow.

For a start she will more than likely be carrying about twenty-five bottles of smellies, several towels, some tins of talc, two or three styling brushes, a large hairdryer (the kind you sit in at the hairdresser's), a couple of pots of skin conditioner, some tubes of anti-wrinkle cream, some lip-salve, some deodorants, a packet of emery boards, some tweezers, a magnifying mirror and five or six bottles of nail varnish. She will also more than likely not be on her own, but will be accompanied by someone from the beauty parlour, a personal trainer, her best friend (so she'll have someone to talk to), Mr Cecil from Snippers and Claudia from Happy Nails. She may also be carrying a sun-bed, along with a replacement bulb for the lamp.

Getting back to the boys though, Mr Barster is not in favour of people having showers with all their football kit on, even though – as I have pointed out to him numerous times – it saves on washing it when you get home. I tried to tell him that I was only having a shower with all my football kit on to save my mum from having to put it in the washing machine. He said that it was not a good idea to wash your kit in shower gel and I wasn't to do it.

The following week, therefore, I brought a packet of washing powder along instead, but he still wasn't satisfied. He said it was not a good idea to wash your hair in Persil, even though I could see nothing wrong with it, as the water felt about the right temperature for cottons and delicates. But he said that either I had to have a shower properly or not have one at all.

I didn't bother having showers for quite a while after that, except for once. But even then Mr Barster wasn't satisfied and demanded to know why I was standing under the shower wearing my rucksack and football boots, though I would have thought that it was obvious to anyone with a bit of common sense that I was doing it to be ready in case the fire alarm went off and we all had to flee from the building.

Anyway, on this particular afternoon – the cold and bitter one, when I needed warming up – there I was there under the shower with the lovely hot water pounding down on my head. I was trying not to think of the six own-goals I had scored, though I did wonder if it was some kind of record, when Mr Barster shouted from out in the corridor that time was pressing on and we needed to be moving.

I hurriedly finished my shower and got dressed, but my hair was still pretty wet, even though I'd towelled it hard enough to rub a hole into my brain. I didn't want to go out into the cold with wet hair, so I went and stood under the hairdryer.

Strictly speaking, the changing room 'hairdryer' isn't a hairdryer at all. It's a big electric fan which pumps out cold air in the summer and hot air in the winter. It's set in the ceiling and you normally can't get under it for everyone else doing the same thing. But today I was lucky. There was only me left in the changing room by then. Mr Barster was outside, counting everyone up. I knew he'd start shouting for the missing person in a moment, or come in and check, but for now I just wanted to get my hair dry.

So there I stood, right under the fan, with the warm air blasting at me. I rubbed my hair with my fingers to help it dry faster, and I suppose that in doing so I must have frizzed it up.

'Will whoever is left in the changing room come on out now!'

'Just coming, Mr Barster!' I called back.

'I mean *now*!' he said. 'As in *this very instant*!'

I grabbed my stuff and headed for the door.

I opened it, and there everyone was. The girls were waiting, the boys were waiting. They were all talking and laughing and elbowing and joking and then –

Then I appeared.

They all fell silent, one by one. And they all stared at me. Derek Spoot's mouth fell open. So did Rosemary Cottins's, as she raised her finger, pointed at me and said the fatal words.

'Benny Spinks!' she said. 'Benny Spinks! Look, it's Benny Spinks!'

Other voices were saying the same name, and people were nudging each other; they were all laughing and smiling, and saying, 'Benny Spinks! Hey, it's Benny Spinks!'

But they weren't saying it like it was terrible; they were saying it like it was really cool. Like *I* was really cool – me. The one who always got picked last for football, the very last in line, after Rosemary Cottins and all the dead people.

Yes, that's right, me. Me, in person. They were gawping at me as if I were some kind of really cool dude, the kind of cool dude you'd want to hang out with.

'Benny Spinks!' they kept saying. 'Benny Spinks! It's the spitting image of Benny Spinks.'

It was great, it was tremendous, and all I could think was that it couldn't possibly last.

Well, that and one other thing.

The other thing I kept thinking was, 'Who the heck is Benny Spinks?'

For my mind had gone blank and I couldn't think who they were talking about. I knew I'd heard the name from somewhere, I just couldn't quite place it. But then it came to me. Benny Spinks. Oh yes. Benny Spinks. I know who Benny Spinks was all right.

The most famous boy in the world.

2

Elvis, Benny, Derry and Snosh Ketchup
(Also Known as Mimsy Tosh)

Now I'm not saying I'm against people who are rich and have lots of money and the royals and such and people like that who live in palaces, but I never thought it was fair that they should have these big houses with all these bedrooms and space when I have to share my room with a pig called Elvis. Strictly speaking my brother Elvis is not a pig, but in all other ways (except strictly speaking) he is. He is basically nothing but trotters.

Our mum called him Elvis as she was a fan of Elvis Presley. His full name is Elvis Presley Harris. My other brother (who is never in) is called Kevin, which coincidentally is also the milkman's name, and I was called Bill because I apparently arrived on the same day as the gas bill. Fortunately they called me Bill rather than Gas; though Elvis says that was a mistake on their part and that Gas or even Gas Works would have been better.

What made it worse was when it turned out that the gas bill hadn't arrived on the same day as me at all – it was actually the sewage bill. So when Elvis found this out he said I should have been called Sewage, which is not, however, a good name in my opinion, at least not for a boy. It would be different if you were something like a DJ or in a pop group though, or were an actor, as then you would be entitled to have whatever funny-sounding name you like.

It seems to me that if you are in show business, the odder your name the better, as then people are more likely to remember it and producers will say things like, 'Get me Sewage Harris on the phone. He's the kind of type I want to play the serial killer in my next movie. I was also thinking of some other guy, but I can't remember his name. So get me Sewage.'

Also, if you were a DJ or an MC or a rapper or something like that, people would probably not bother turning up to see you if your name was Vernon Dudger or Roger Spoony. But if your name was Jazzy Sewage or Puff Sewage or Mel D. Sewage then you would be packing them in in no time. Or at least that is my opinion.

Sewage would also probably be a pretty good name if you were a plumber, especially if your surname was Problems. For then your full name would be Sewage Problems and when people had any, they would look you up first in the phone book.

Now Elvis and Kevin are older than me, and Elvis can't wait until Kevin leaves home so that he can get his room. Dad is also waiting for Elvis to leave home, so that he will be able to have what will by then be Elvis's room (formerly Kevin's) as his study.

There are a lot of people in our house waiting for other people to leave home so that they can get their rooms.

I am also waiting for Elvis to outgrow his mountain bike so I can have it. Elvis is waiting for Kevin to outgrow his moped and get a car so that Elvis can ride Kevin's moped around. Mum is waiting for Dad to re-tile the bathroom. Dad is waiting for a chance to get round to it but he doesn't have the time. Our cat, Munster, is waiting for the dog to die so that he can get his kennel. I don't know what a cat wants with a kennel, but I reckon that is what he is up to, as he keeps giving the dog funny looks, as if he were willing him to drop dead. Dad is waiting for his numbers to come up on the lottery. When that happens, he says he will re-tile the bathroom, but otherwise, being rich won't change him. I don't know what my sister is waiting for, but you can bet she's waiting for something, like for the next boiled egg to come along, or something like that.

So you can see for yourself the sort of pressure I

am under and what I have to put up with, living with people who are eyeing each other's rooms and kennels up all the time, and why I don't think it's fair that some people should have big houses with hundreds of rooms when I am stuck in a bunk bed with Elvis Presley.

Now what's all this got to do with Benny Spinks, you might ask, and the answer would be that Benny Spinks was the complete opposite of all this, as Benny Spinks had everything I didn't.

For starters, Benny Spinks lived in a great big house with masses of garden and he went to a private and posh school, while I went to a leaky-roof school with no decent central heating. The only time it was ever warm in our classroom was the day somebody set fire to the desks.

The reason that Benny Spinks was so well off was simple – he was the son of Derry Packham Spinks. If you don't know who he is, I can only assume you are an alien from another planet, or that you have been in prison for a long time.

Derry Spinks is probably the most famous footballer in the country, or even in the whole, entire world. People who've hardly even heard of feet, let alone football, still know who he is. In fact, he is probably so famous that there are nomads in deserts and strange life forms in distant galaxies who've still heard of him. Which isn't bad really, considering he's only a footballer. I mean, it's not brain surgery, is it? And if I ever needed my brains operated on, I'd rather a brain surgeon did it than a bloke with a football and a pair of boots and a shirt with the name of a well-known brand of beer on the front.

Anyway, for the benefit of those who possibly don't know who Derry Spinks is (as they have indeed just come out of prison after serving long sentences in solitary confinement without TV sets) then Derry Spinks is the best-known footballer in the country – and in several other countries besides.

Derry Spinks is not only famous, he is rich as well, and he makes more money in a week than my dad is likely to make in several lifetimes unless he wins the lottery. But even then, he would probably only win it once, whereas Derry Spinks earns so much money, it is like winning the lottery every week.

'It's all right for him!' my dad says, whenever Derry Spinks turns up on TV (which is often). 'Getting millions for kicking a ball around and what have you. They pay him two million a year just to wear that brand of boots!'

'How much do they pay you, Dad, to wear your uniform?' I asked him.

'Not a penny,' he said. 'Though I do get to keep the trousers when I retire.'

My dad works for an internet company installing broadband – which is a fast kind of internet access. He gets free trousers and a van which he parks in the drive. My mum doesn't like it as she says it lowers the tone, to which my dad says, 'What tone? I didn't know we had one.'

She isn't all that keen on his trousers either, even though they are free. The van is free too and Dad gets to use it at the weekends to drive Mum down to the supermarket, but she makes him park it miles away from the entrance as she says it is embarrassing to be seen in a big blue and white van with 'Inter-Netty' written on the side. But I don't see that it is embarrassing at all, and it is certainly a lot better than the van our neighbour has. He runs a mobile dog-grooming business and his van has 'Doggy-Dogs' on the side, along with 'Full Grooming Service' and 'Fleas Removed'.

Personally, I think that 'Fleas Removed' is a lot more embarrassing that 'Inter-Netty', but that is just my opinion, and as I am only young nobody pays any attention to me and my opinions and they always say, 'Shush!' and 'You'll learn,' and 'You'll find out one day,' whenever I express them, so mostly I keep them to myself, except when I am writing things in my diary like now when I can say whatever I like.

Anyway, there we were. And there, living only a few miles away from us, but almost in another world, was Derry Spinks, the famous footballer, and his wife, Snosh Ketchup.

Although Mrs Spinks's real name is Mrs Spinks, most of the newspapers call her Snosh for as well as being married to Derry Spinks, she was also famous in her own right for being a singer in a pop group called the Ketchup Girls.

If you are very old, you will probably remember all about the Ketchup Girls, and you might have heard some of their records – or, even worse, bought one of them.

My mum was a big fan of the Ketchup Girls, but my dad was against them. Mum said that they were good singers and that they were all about 'sisters doing it for themselves' and stuff like that. But Dad said that they were terrible and sounded like somebody trying to flush a very large walrus down a very small toilet, while banging it on the head with a spoon. He also said that all that 'sisters doing it for themselves' stuff was a big con, and that it was just about them showing off and swanking about and trying to get attention.

My mum still has all her Ketchup Girls CDs and sometimes she gets them out and plays them.

I think this is part of the reason why Kevin intends to leave home soon, and why Munster the cat keeps eyeing up the dog kennel.

Well, for quite a few years the Ketchup Girls were everywhere, so my dad says. You couldn't open a newspaper without the Ketchup Girls being in there. When they started off, there were six of them altogether. As well as Snosh Ketchup (who is also now known as Mimsy Tosh – the name she chose to launch her solo career) there was Spooky Ketchup,

Skinny Ketchup, Saucy Ketchup, Little Ketchup and Sumo Ketchup.

After about five big hits though, they started to have differences, and Saucy Ketchup left the band and went solo with her own album called *Saucy Ketchup Shakes the Bottle*.

The other five Ketchups went on to have a couple more hits, but then Skinny Ketchup left as well to become an actress. But she turned out to be not a very good one. She did make a film but the critics said that they should have given the part to a plank of wood instead. They said it wasn't right that planks of wood should be standing around idle while Skinny Ketchup went and stole their work.

The remaining Ketchups still made the occasional record, but not many. Spooky, Saucy and Sumo sort of faded away, but Snosh went from strength to strength, especially after she got married to Derry Spinks and said that from now on she would be known as Mimsy Tosh, to distance herself from the past.

You were always seeing the Derry Spinkses in the glossy magazines like *Hi!* magazine and *Gimme Five* and *Okey-Dokey Weekly*. My mum is very fond of these magazines and likes to read them in doctors' and dentists' waiting rooms. She doesn't have appointments, she just goes in for a sit-down to read the magazines. Sometimes she even buys them. My dad is not so keen, however.

'Never mind *Hi!* magazine,' he said once. 'When is that Snosh Ketchup Mimsy Tosh woman going to turn up in *Goodbye, Cheerio and Good Riddance* magazine? Or in *Thank Heaven, We've Seen the Back of Her At Last* magazine. I'm sick to death of the woman. If I see another photo of Snosh Ketchup, I'll give up eating chips.'

But he didn't.

When Snosh and Derry got married, there were cameras everywhere, so my mum said. Of course, I hadn't even been born then, as I was born later, round about the same time as Benny Spinks. My mum told my dad that it was really exciting that Benny Spinks and I should have been born within a few days of each other, but I think that my dad found it hard to get too excited about things like that.

Benny Spinks soon got to be as famous as his mum and dad. First he was getting christened, then he was having his first birthday, then it was Benny Takes His First Step and Benny Says His First Word, and although I was also saying words and taking steps, nobody seemed particularly interested in that, though it was just as remarkable, at least it was to my mind.

It was Benny Spinks this, and Benny Spinks that, and Benny Spinks the other. Then it was Benny Spinks Gets His First Football Lesson, and there he was, out on the field with his dad, dressed in a cut-down version of the team strip, with his little boots on, having a bash at kicking a football, which wasn't much bigger than he was.

Then it was Benny Spinks Goes To Nursery, and the newspapers were full of photos of Benny Spinks being taken to some expensive and exclusive nursery school in a chauffeur-driven car, with his mum sitting next to him, holding his hand.

I always wondered if he called her Snosh, and if, when he went to bed, she said, 'Night, night, Benny,' and he said, 'Night, Snosh.' But I expect he didn't. He probably called her Mum, same as everyone else. Or maybe it was Mimsy.

After that it was Benny Goes on Holiday! and there he was, with his mum and dad, in some exclusive resort in the sun-kissed Caribbean, on a beautiful island with lovely blue water. I remember seeing that photograph; I remember it really well. We were stuck in our caravan down at Rainstorm Sands at the time, watching the sleet hammer against the window as the gale-force winds blew up the beach. I can remember it like yesterday. The locals said that it was very unusual for the weather to be that bad in August, and that they hadn't had a tidal wave that size since 1972. I think that was the summer when the man with the donkey rides lost three of his donkeys to the hurricane, though fortunately they turned up later in somebody's back garden, half a mile away. One of them was up a tree.

What I could never figure out about Benny Spinks was what he had actually done to be so interesting. I mean, all right, his dad was famous for being a great footballer, and OK, his mum was famous for singing, but what had Benny ever done? Nothing, as far as I could tell. I mean, he hadn't done any more in life than I had.

So why wasn't *I* famous? Why wasn't *I* in *Okey-Dokey Weekly*, along with my mum and dad and my little sister, as we sat in our rented caravan at Rainstorm Sands, watching the postman go by in his rowing boat?

It didn't seem right to me at all. In fact, I even asked my dad about it.

'Dad,' I said. 'Why is it that some people live in big houses with no worries and loads of dosh, whereas here we are, living in a little terraced house with not enough bedrooms to go round and a cat who keeps eyeing the dog's kennel up all the time?'

'Could be worse, Bill,' my dad said. 'We could be living in a mud hut.'

'Would that be a big mud hut, Dad?' I asked. 'One with lots of bedrooms and a big double mud garage and a mud attic with a pool table?'

'All I'm saying, son,' he said, 'is that there're millions worse off than us and we should count our blessings. At least we've got a roof over our heads and plenty to eat, and a nice van to drive around in at the weekends, and two weeks every summer at

27

Rainstorm Sands. In fact, I was even thinking that this year we could go abroad for a change. I've heard about this nice place in Spain, on the Costa del Sol. Quite cheap it is. Called El Halfo-Finished Building Sito Apartmentos y Middle of Nowhereos, I think. Very reasonably priced. We could have a fortnight there. So, far from being hard up, see, we've got quite a lot. We've got our health, our strength, jobs, holidays—'

'And a brother called Elvis,' I reminded him, in case he might have forgotten.

'It's all relative,' Dad said. 'Some might have a lot compared to us, but we've got a lot compared to others. There're some people in this world who don't even have trousers.'

'Who are they, Dad?' I asked.

'Trouser-less people,' he said. 'You find them in remote parts of the world. They just get by with underpants. But they probably don't go out much, at least not to restaurants and places like that. So we should count our blessings, like I say.'

'Yes, Dad,' I said, 'I can see that. But all the same, why is it that someone like Derry Spinks gets paid all that money for kicking a football and his wife, Mimsy Snosh Ketchup Tosh makes a fortune for sounding like a walrus stuck in a toilet being hit with a spoon, when there's you and Mum working all hours, and you still have to borrow money off Grandad?'

'It wasn't a borrow,' Dad said. 'It was a gift.'

'But why is that, Dad?' I said. 'How come Derry Spinks gets paid millions for kicking a football?'

'Search me,' he said. 'Because people will pay him a lot for doing it, I suppose.'

'Would people pay millions to see you kick a football, Dad?' I asked.

'No,' he said. 'I shouldn't think so.' He thought for a second and then said, 'They might pay a few quid to watch me swallow a football though.'

But I don't think he was entirely serious.

So I was none the wiser really. I didn't understand it and I still don't. In some ways it seems to me that the more unnecessary a thing is, the more you get paid for doing it. Because really, kicking balls and singing like a walrus aren't actually *necessary* – not like being a doctor or driving an ambulance. But not even a doctor gets paid as much as Derry Spinks.

Maybe it's one of those things that you get to understand as you grow older, but I'm not banking on it.

Some nights, as I lay on the top of the bunk bed, listening to my brother Elvis as he snored away downstairs on the lower bit, I used to wonder what it would be like to be Benny Spinks and to have a rich dad and a famous mum and all the money you could spend and a house the size of Buckingham Palace set in grounds the size of Devon.

I thought, if I could just have a little taste of that

29

for a while, I'd be happy. I wouldn't want it for ever, because I'd miss my mum and dad and my sister and brothers – even Elvis, probably, strange as that may seem – but it would be nice to try it, just for a while.

Just imagine that, I thought, to be the most famous boy in the country, with your photo in *Hi!* magazine, and everyone wanting to give you presents on your birthday and to be your friend.

It would make such a change, I thought, from being me, who wasn't really all that good at anything, except at running in straight lines. And although I got on sort of all right with most people, I wasn't exactly a celebrity. I mean, I wasn't Mr Popularity or anyone like that.

But when I came out of the shower that afternoon, with my hair all frizzed up and curly for a change, instead of flat like I usually have it, I got a brief taste of what popularity could be. Because instead of everyone saying things like, 'Come on, Harris, last again!' and 'Oh, look who it is, it's the man with the two left feet,' and 'Six own goals, Harris. Good going!'; instead of all that I got, 'Hey! Cool, man!' and 'Get a load of the hairstyle – it's Benny Spinks!' and 'Oi, Benny, my son, gimme five!'

For once in my life, people were actually glad to see me.

Even the girls. Even Vicky Ferns. Vicky Ferns is the most beautiful girl in the school. (At least she is now that she has had her teeth straightened and that her spots have eased off.)

When she saw my brand new hairstyle, she actually gave me a smile with her newly straightened teeth (she'd only just had the braces removed) and she wrinkled up her nose (where the spots used to be).

'Hey Bill,' she said. 'You're not as ugly as I thought, after all.'

Which was quite a compliment indeed.

Even Mr Barster was gawping at me.

I turned to see what they were all looking at, and there it was, my own face, staring back at me from the old chipped mirror in the corridor of the pavilion. Only it wasn't my face, it was someone else's. It was Benny Spinks's face. It was him – his nose, his teeth, his hairstyle.

But more than anything, it was the hairstyle, the brand-new, frizzed up hairstyle. I was so like Benny Spinks, I could have been his identical twin. (Apart from not having the designer labels, of course. He probably had Gucci, whereas Mum got most of my clothes from Primark.)

I just laughed to see it really, old Benny there, in the mirror. I felt really pleased to see him, almost like he was a long-lost friend.

'Come on, Benny,' someone said. 'Stop admiring yourself. Let's get back to class.'

So we left the pavilion and crossed the fields and headed back to the main building.

Quite a few people seemed to want to hang back and talk to me, and they kept making jokes and calling me Benny. One or two of them even asked me what I was doing on Saturday – though they had never asked me before. When they heard that I wasn't doing anything, they suggested that I might like to hang out with them, and when some of the others heard, they said, 'Yeah, that'd be cool!' and 'Why don't you?' and they told me where they'd be, so I could come along if I wanted to.

'We'll be waiting for you, Benny!' Dave Porter called, as I left school to get the bus at the end of the day.

'See you, Benny!' Vicky Ferns called. 'Hope you can make it!'

I knew then that I would make it, that I would go and hang out with them on Saturday, down at the Green, where they all do the skateboarding and rollerblading and ride their bikes.

When I got in at home, Mum was already back, and so was Elvis. (Kevin was out, same as usual.)

'What have you done to your head?' Elvis said. Then he got closer, until we were eyeball to eyeball (well, he's a lot taller than me; to be more exact, we were standing eyeball to Adam's apple.) 'You remind me of someone,' he said. 'Only I can't think who it is. But I'll remember. And when I do . . .'

He didn't specify what would happen when he did, but he sort of implied that it wouldn't be pleasant.

'Well, I like your new hairstyle,' Mum said, when Elvis had gone. 'And it does make you look like someone – someone really familiar. Only who is it now?'

It didn't take long for her to find out, because Dad came in then, still wearing his free trousers and his sweatshirt with 'Inter-Netty' on the back.

'Flipping heck!' he said. 'Benny Spinks! Benny Spinks in the house – that's all we need.'

'Of course!' Mum said. 'That's it! That's who you are! Just like in *Okey-Dokey Weekly*! It's amazing, Bill. With your hair like that – you could be his twin.'

'Quick,' Dad said. 'Go and have a shower and flatten it back down again. I liked you better when you looked like a wet dog in a thunderstorm.'

'Leave him alone,' Mum said. 'He looks fine. Wait till the neighbours see it. What'll they think when they see we've got Benny Spinks in the house?'

'They'll think his dad's bought our place for a holiday home,' Dad said. 'Or possibly to keep his boots in.' (I think he was being sarcastic.)

Anyway, I wasn't going to go and have a shower, not like he suggested. I was going to keep my hair as it was. I'd never been popular in my life before, and I wasn't about to let it stop, not two minutes after it had started, anyway.

I was going to enjoy it while it lasted, even if that wasn't for long.

3

Plug Uglies

The novelty soon wore off.

It was all well and good to begin with, going around looking like Benny Spinks with everyone saying, 'Hi, it's Benny,' and 'Hey, Benny, tell your dad to put one in the net this weekend,' but after a while, I have to admit, it began to get tedious.

It got to the point where I simply wasn't Bill Harris any more, I was a sort of local substitute for Benny Spinks. People seemed to have forgotten that I had my own name and identity. It was Benny this and Benny that all the time. I was even tempted to go and flatten my hair down, like my dad had suggested. But after a few weeks had gone by, I quite simply daren't do it. Everyone was so used to me being the local Benny Spinks, that if I'd gone back to being just ordinary me, I might have got lynched.

I started getting invitations to things like parties

and barbecues, and even garden fêtes and little kids' football matches.

'We'll get Benny round to kick the ball and start the game off,' they'd say. So there I would be, too stressed out and worried to refuse, while hordes of little kids shouted, 'It's Benny! It's Benny!'

I often suspected that nobody had explained to them that I wasn't the real Benny at all. Sometimes they even came up to me for autographs, and I had to sign the books with Benny Spinks's name. Once I signed my own name, and the little boy got so hysterical that his dad came over to see what the trouble was. When he saw that I had signed the book Bill Harris, he told me to do it again properly and to apologise.

'But I'm not Benny Spinks,' I tried to explain to him. 'I'm just a look-alike.'

'You'll be who I say you are,' he said. 'And don't you go upsetting my Justin by saying otherwise.'

So I had to write 'Benny Spinks' or I'd have got hammered. No wonder I was starting to get a bit tired of it.

After a few weeks of that, I began to feel that being Benny Spinks wasn't all it was cracked up to be, and I might well have packed the whole thing in there and then, and gone back to my old hairstyle, if it hadn't been for my brother Elvis, who came home with the local newspaper one day (he had his chips wrapped in it; he wasn't big on reading) and said,

'Here you are. That's what you want to do. You could make some money.'

He left me the newspaper and I sat down to read it. There – among the chip stains – was an article on an agency for look-alikes, with pictures of their clients; people who looked like famous film stars and TV celebrities and members of the royal family and pop stars and all the rest.

Apparently they got paid for it. People booked them up for advertisement photos and publicity shoots and for modelling clothes and all sorts of events, and they made loads of dosh out of it – which was just what I wanted. Dosh was always in short supply in our house, and if you got a chance of making any, it was as well to take it.

'*Do you look like a celebrity?*' the article went on. '*If so, there could be money to be made. Talent agencies are always searching for celebrity look-alikes. If you feel you have what it takes, why not send your photograph to the address at the bottom of the page?*'

But then I started to have my famous second thoughts again. It was the name of the look-alike agency that put me off.

It was called Plug Uglies Ltd.

Now I'm not saying I'm the best-looking person in the world, but Plug Ugly was pitching it a bit strong. I mean, OK, so I wasn't handsome (not under normal lighting conditions) but with the wind in the right direction and the sun in other people's eyes, I could easily pass for passable. I could even pass for Benny Spinks, and he wasn't ugly at all. Some girls at school actually thought he was handsome. (But that might have been due to him being famous. Somehow, the more famous you are, the better looking you get. Even when you really look like a bag of spoons, people just don't seem to see you that way.)

As well as supplying look-alikes, Plug Uglies Ltd also had a load of weird and wonderful people on its books. It had ladies with beards and big fat blokes and amazingly skinny people and people who looked like parrots or fence posts. Quite often they would be wanted to stand behind models while they advertised clothes, or to be in the background in TV programmes when the hero visited dens of iniquity in the underworld.

Anyway, I wasn't that keen on the Plug Ugly bit, I have to say. It wasn't much of a prospect in store, if people were going to ask me who I was, and I had to tell them that I was a Plug Ugly. But on the other hand, money is money, and if you have money, you can get stuff.

It's always very useful for getting stuff, is money, and in my experience, there is never any end to the amount of stuff you can get.

It is not that I am especially concerned about stuff, but a bit more stuff would have come in handy. Being in a big family with not much dosh, I didn't really have a lot of stuff at all, and most of the stuff I did have was second-hand and hand-me-down. I wanted some new stuff for a change, stuff that didn't have Elvis's name in it already, or stuff that he had played with when he was younger, and had more than likely dirtied up or broken.

Some people say that happiness does not lie in the realms of stuff, and that stuff is all an illusion, and that true peace and tranquillity cannot be found in stuff, but only in prayer and contemplation. The vicar is always saying that when we go to church. Not that we go that often, which is maybe why he feels he has to say it when he sees us coming in.

It is all well and good though, saying that too much emphasis is placed on stuff, but when you have to wear your brother's old underpants with his name tag still in them, you suddenly feel (even though they have been boiled) that there is much to be said for new stuff after all.

So I used to think that it was all right for the vicar to go on about stuff in the world today, but he probably had his own underpants, and didn't have to wear old ones, handed down to him from the bishop. So I decided that I would send my photograph in to Plug Uglies after all, and then maybe some work and some money might come of it, and I would be able to get some stuff.

Elvis took my photograph with the digital camera he had got for Christmas (Elvis always had loads of stuff, for some reason; he seemed to have stuff galore). I then wrote a letter in my best longhand, and sent it off to Plug Uglies with the photograph enclosed, explaining that I was the new Benny Spinks and that I would be available (for a small fee) for parties, exhibitions, photo-shoots, weddings, christenings, and corporate events (whatever they were; I had seen them referred to in the newspaper article).

I enclosed a stamped addressed envelope, as requested, and then I sat back and waited for a reply.

In the meantime, I had a date with Vicky Ferns. And if that surprised anyone, it didn't surprise them as much as it surprised me. For Vicky Ferns (now that she had had her teeth straightened and her spots had gone) was one of the best-looking girls in the school.

The weekend after the arrival of my new hairstyle, I had gone down to the Green on Saturday afternoon, as invited, and had hung out with all the people who had never had five minutes or a good word for me back when I was Bill Harris, but who couldn't get enough of me now that I looked like Benny Spinks.

I'm not much at skateboarding as I have a tendency to fall off skateboards and to break various bones, including the ones in my head, but not everyone had a skateboard anyway. Those who went down to the Green but didn't have skateboards used to do posing and looking cool instead, so I decided I would do a bit of that. I also decided to borrow Elvis's mobile phone cover (the Union Jack one) and to bring my phone along, so that if nobody talked to me, I could pretend to be having long and interesting conversations with people they didn't know. I decided that I would talk to these unknown friends on the phone and say things like 'Cool, dude!' and 'No way, man!' and 'Get out of here, you're kidding me!' and that I would laugh occasionally as if sharing various jokes, and that way I wouldn't look like a total divot. As well as Elvis's phone cover, I borrowed his dark glasses and his silver-plated toothpick.

Well, I felt a bit hesitant and apprehensive as I made my way across the Green, but I had no need to really, for as soon as they saw me coming, everybody called out and said 'Hey, Benny!' and 'It's Benny – cool!' and they seemed really pleased to see me.

Some other people stared when they saw me coming, and it was clear that they'd recognised me, and they thought I was the genuine article, the real Benny Spinks in person, and that these were my friends. So everybody thought that I was really cool and I even got a go on someone's skateboard – though I did fall off.

Vicky Ferns and a couple of her friends turned up after a while, and they came over to where I was standing, looking cool in the borrowed shades. To make things even cooler, my phone rang as they were walking over, just to let them know that I was a sought-after person with contacts. Unfortunately it was Elvis ringing, wanting to know where his phone cover was and whether I had seen his sliver-plated toothpick. When he realised that I had borrowed his stuff without asking him, he threatened to 'come over there right now and sort you out'. But as I refused to tell him where I was, he couldn't. So he said he'd get me later. But I couldn't worry about that for the moment, as Vicky Ferns was on her way across.

'Hi, *Benny*,' she said.

'Hi,' I said. (I thought that would be a good thing to say and not too controversial.)

'How're you doing?' she said.

'Great,' I said. 'How're you doing?'

'Great,' she said too. And then her friends started giggling, though I didn't think that anyone had said anything funny.

'Cool shades,' she said.

'Cool shades yourself,' I said. (For she was wearing shades too.)

'Neat phone,' she said, taking a look at Elvis's phone cover.

'Neat phone yourself,' I said. (For she had a neat phone cover too.)

There was a bit more giggling after that, and then one of Vicky's friends said, 'I wonder what's on at the cinema this afternoon?'

'It's that film,' Vicky said. 'The one I wanted to see. Only I don't have anyone to go with.'

But I didn't really see that that was true, as she had all her friends to go with, and I was just about to explain to her that she could go with one of her friends, when I realised that maybe . . .

'Oh,' I said, 'I was thinking of going to see that film myself this afternoon.'

'Were you, *Benny*?' she said. (Everyone called me 'Benny' now.) 'Were you really . . . ?' Then she sort of trailed off.

'Maybe we could go together,' I suggested, hoping that she wouldn't expect me to pay for her ticket, as I didn't have the money – unless I sold Elvis's phone cover, but if I did that, he'd probably kill me.

'Yes, right, OK,' she said. (As if she could take it or leave it and it was all one way or the other to her.) 'That would be cool.'

But if I'd thought that it was just her and me going together, I was very much mistaken. Her friends came as well, though I did get to sit next to her. I noticed that as we queued in the cinema to get our tickets, people started pointing at us and whispering, muttering things like, 'That's Benny Spinks, the footballer's son, isn't it?' and 'Hey look, that's Benny Spinks; and that must be his girlfriend!'

I didn't like being the centre of attention all that much, but Vicky Ferns appeared to enjoy it no end. She kept calling me Benny all the time too, in a voice that seemed louder than it had to be. When the film was over, we all went to a hamburger place to have a cola. Everybody turned and stared at us as we came in, and they all plainly thought that I was Benny Spinks and that this girl next to me was somebody special. We sat and had a drink and Vicky and her friends did a lot of whispering and giggling. It was odd really, it was like I was there, and yet I wasn't; part of it, yet not part of it at all.

I walked back with them to the Green afterwards, then told them that I had to go home now, as I needed to charge up my mobile phone as I was expecting important phone calls. (The truth was I wanted to get back before Elvis moved from being plain angry to livid.)

'Bye, Benny!' Vicky called. 'See you Monday!'

People turned when they heard the name Benny and they stared at us again.

I waved and went on my way, not quite sure what to make of it all. I took my baseball cap out of my pocket and pulled it down over my eyes. I was fed up with being Benny Spinks for the moment, and wanted to be myself, and for people not to stare at me. In my heart of hearts, I wanted Vicky Ferns to like me for who I was – Bill Harris. But in that same heart of hearts, I knew she didn't. She only liked me because I looked like Benny Spinks, and she got a kick from being seen with him. But if a fall of rain had come and flattened my hair, and I had gone back to being Bill Harris again, she'd have vanished like a rainbow; she'd have gone, without a backward glance.

It was odd to be liked because you looked like somebody else; you almost felt as if you had stolen something. You felt like a fraud, an impostor, as if you were walking around in borrowed clothes.

So there I was, walking home on a Saturday afternoon, with Benny Spinks's hairstyle under my baseball cap, and the name Elvis sewn into the underpants I was wearing. It seemed that it was hard to be yourself, sometimes; and sometimes it was difficult to even know who you were.

About a week later, a letter came. It was franked with a logo reading Plug Uglies Ltd.

Elvis brought it up and threw it on to my bed.

'Here you are,' he said. 'They've caught up with you at last. It has to be for you. It's got "ugly" on it.'

(Which I thought was quite an unnecessary remark to make. But that is Elvis for you, he's full of unnecessary remarks. In many ways, he is a very unnecessary person. To be honest I thought he was jealous of me for looking like the spitting image of Benny Spinks when all he looked like was a fat rat. In fact if Elvis were ever to win any look-alike competitions, it would be for having a face like Frankenstein's monster. The only difference between Elvis and Frankenstein's monster being that

Elvis's face would probably look like the monster's bottom. But I decided not to tell him any of that, as he is a lot bigger than me, and I didn't want it to lead to controversy or to anybody getting their nose punched and doing things that they might later regret.)

I opened up the letter and read what it had to say.

'Dear Mr Harris,' it began (that was me). 'Thank you for your letter and photograph. We have deemed you suitable to be included on our books as a Benny Spinks look-alike, and have retained your photograph to that effect. We will circulate your details amongst our various clients, and should your services be required, we will be in touch. Our commission rates are as outlined, and you will need parental permission before accepting any work. We will be in contact immediately should any work opportunities arise. Thank you for your interest.

Yours sincerely,

Mr J. Mugg

Prop. The Plug Ugly Agency Ltd.'

I ran downstairs and showed my letter to anyone willing to look at it, including the cat. Not that he could read, of course, but he could do a nice job of staring at things and trying to look intelligent and as if he understood them. (Somewhat like Elvis.) I have to say that nobody else was as excited as I was.

'It's not actually an offer of any work though, is it,

love?' my mum pointed out. 'Don't get your hopes up too high. Why not be more realistic and set your sights on a paper round or something like that? Or you could be a butcher's boy.'

'I'm trying to be a vegetarian,' I pointed out.

'You could be a vegetable boy then,' Elvis said. 'I mean, you've already got a cabbage for a brain and a cauliflower ear and a nose like a carrot, so you're more than halfway there already.'

I just ignored him as I could tell that he was only jealous of my good looks and being a celebrity.

'Just don't get your hopes up too high, that's all I'm saying,' my mum said, then she put some more toast in the toaster.

But I didn't think there was much chance of that with my family. They seemed to look on my hopes the way people with shotguns look at clay pigeons.

'If they do get me a job will you let me do it?' I asked.

'I suppose so,' she said. 'As long as it doesn't mean time off school.'

'Promise?'

'Yes, OK, promise.'

'Thanks.'

I went back upstairs and spent several hours admiring my letter from all angles. I'd never had a proper letter before, not one that called me Mr Harris.

The only other letters I'd ever had were for

overdue library books. Oh, and I once got an anonymous letter which had been made up with words cut from newspapers. It said, 'You are a fat bum. Signed, A Friend.' The smudged and semi-literate handwriting on the envelope made me suspect that it had been sent by someone of poor academic skills and limited intelligence, but when I asked him, Elvis denied having anything to do with it.

Although it was great to get the letter from Mr Mugg of Plug Uglies, saying that I had been accepted as a client and put on the books, it was with growing impatience that I waited for something more concrete to arrive.

I mentioned this to Elvis, but he just acted stupid and said, 'Why are you waiting for more concrete to arrive? I didn't know that you had any concrete? What are you doing with it? Making a new patio? Ha, ha!' And then he went out, calling to Mum as he left, saying, 'Hey Mum, Dimwit –' (that was supposed to be me) '– is waiting for some concrete. So if a big lorry with a revolving tub turns up, it's for him.'

But personally I thought that that kind of thing was quite unnecessary.

At school things remained a whole lot better than they had been BTHD. (Before The Hairdryer.) I was unofficially Benny Spinks the Second now, and that was what everyone called me.

'Hiya, Benny!' they'd shout, the moment I appeared in the playground. And instead of being amongst the last to get picked for teams during Games, now I was one of the first to be chosen. It felt strange not to be left there with all the rejects and the spurned and unwanted and the kids with two left feet or three right ones.

I felt a bit sorry for them now. I was glad I wasn't one of them any more, but I had known what it was to be amongst their number. The fact that I wasn't being chosen for myself, but only because I looked like somebody else, didn't really bother me – well, not that much, not to start with.

It was just a relief to be popular.

Even my football improved. I still wasn't that good, but I'd stopped scoring own goals. And even when I missed a cross or fluffed a pass, instead of everyone groaning and saying, 'Come on, nerdy boy, pull yourself together,' they'd just be sympathetic and say, 'Bad luck, Benny,' or 'Good try. Never mind,' and the game would go on.

It was strange really. It seemed to me that if you were popular, you could make all sorts of mistakes, and get away with them. But if you were unpopular, you could make absolutely no mistakes at all, and you'd still get blamed for everything.

Still, as my dad never tires of repeating, whenever I complain that things aren't fair: 'Who said life was fair?' And I don't know the answer. But I do know that even if life isn't fair, it still feels to me that it ought to be, and that if it isn't, somebody ought to fix it.

As well as getting picked for the teams now, I had a large and serious dose of Vicky Ferns to contend with. She was coming on a bit strong, it seemed to me, a bit overpowering even, like one of those extra-strong deodorants that you put on your armpits in hot climates.

I had noticed, when we had gone to the pictures, that although she liked to be seen with me, she wasn't all that keen on talking to me much. In fact, whenever I offered any opinions on anything, or tried to keep up a conversation, she was inclined to roll her eyeballs.

I didn't really take this in properly at the time, or think all that much of it. I just assumed that this was a habit of hers, a sort of twitch or something. Many people have their own little personal habits, including Elvis, only I won't mention what his are, as they might put you off your food.

Vicky Ferns was very keen on being seen with me, but not so keen on talking. She liked us to walk down the street together with a couple of her friends in tow, with all the heads turning and people nudging each other, saying, 'Did you see who that was? That was Benny Spinks, wasn't it?' and, 'Who's that good-looking girl with him?' or, 'Who's that gorgeous girl with Benny Spinks? Do you reckon she's anyone?'

Then, 'Must be,' someone else would say. 'Must be a film star or a model, or a singer in a babe band.'

Yes, Vicky seemed to love all that, but whenever we were alone together – which wasn't often, or for long – and I tried to talk to her about 'us' and 'our relationship' and 'where we were going' (which was all the stuff girls were supposed to like talking about, according to a book I'd read called *How to Understand Girls* – a very thick book in several volumes) she would either change the subject or start yawning or have to go to the toilet to check her make-up or she'd get her nail file out. Generally though, Vicky always had her friends with her.

One day, one of the girls in my class called Sandra Debbings – who sits at the back and never says much – came over to me in the playground as I was hiding round the back of the Portakabin to get a break from having to be Benny Spinks all the time. I don't know if she had been looking for me or had just come upon me by chance, but either way, instead of calling me Benny, like everyone did now, she actually said, 'Hi, Bill,' which came as a bit of a shock.

I was so used to being Benny by then that the sound of my own name unnerved me; it brought back all the bad old days of when I'd been unpopular and unwanted. In fact, when I heard my own name, I almost flinched.

'Hi, Sandra,' I said.

'What are you doing round here?' she asked.

'Oh, just – you know – having a break,' I said. I didn't elaborate. I hoped she wouldn't ask me what I was having a break from. She didn't.

'Me too,' she said. 'Can I join you?'

'Sure,' I said.

She sat down next to me on the back steps of the Portakabin. I could hear the noise of break-time leaking round from the other side of the building. As usual, it sounded as if a riot were going on. Possibly even two or three riots, all happening simultaneously, and a couple of small wars.

'Nice to get away from it for a minute,' Sandra said.

'Yeah,' I nodded. (My brother Elvis had told me that girls like it if you agree with them. I didn't know if this was true or if he was lying to me to put me wrong and so as I would look stupid, but I decided to give it a try.)

'You know, Bill—' Sandra said, but then she stopped, as if she had changed her mind about something.

'Know what?' I asked.

'Oh, nothing.'

'No, go on,' I said. 'What were you going to say?' (As I felt that somehow it was going to be important.)

'Oh, nothing really,' she said. 'Just – well – you know . . . I just wanted to say . . . the way it is now and how you look so much like Benny Spinks and everything, and how everyone says that, and I've noticed how things have changed for you, ever since you frizzed your hair . . .'

'Oh, have you?' I said, wondering what was coming next.

'Yes, and I'm really pleased for you, Bill,' she said. 'I am. Because I know that – well – maybe you weren't quite so popular before your hair got frizzed up and you started looking like Benny Spinks. I've noticed the way everyone talks to you now and wants to be your friend and they invite you everywhere and you're even going out with Vicky Ferns who is the best-looking girl in the school now that she's had her braces off and her spots have gone . . .'

'Yes, it's been a great improvement,' I agreed.

'But . . .'

I'd known there was going to be a 'but' somehow. You can usually tell when they're coming.

'But what, Sandra?' I said.

'Oh . . . I don't know – I just wanted to let you know – that maybe some people – in the class – they maybe . . . sort of . . . kind of . . . preferred you . . . as you were. The old you, you know.'

'Oh,' I said.

I sat there on the step, a bit stunned, not really knowing what to say. In fact I was shocked. It was astonishing to find out that certain people had actually preferred me as plain old Bill Harris and not as Benny Spinks.

'Do – did – you have any idea of who it was?' I asked. 'Who sort of . . . preferred me as I was?'

Sandra Debbings seemed to change colour a bit, but it was probably due to the sun.

'No,' she said. 'I didn't get their names. I just overheard some people talking – while I was doing something, somewhere – and I heard these voices say that they thought the old Bill was better . . . than the new Benny.'

'Ah,' I said. 'Right.' Before I could say anything else, a football came shooting round the corner of the Portakabin, with a dozen people after it. When they saw me sitting there, they all yelled, 'Hey, it's Benny!' and 'Come on, Benny! Have a game!'

So I had to go and join them, and be popular again. I don't think any of them even noticed Sandra, there next to me, and somehow I didn't want to draw their attention to her.

I stood up and made a sort of 'I'd better go then' kind of face, and Sandra gave this faint kind of smile in return, which wasn't really a complete smile, but a bit sad and wistful. A part of me wished that I could have stayed on the step and just sat there with her, maybe not even talking, just sitting there and saying nothing at all. But I had to keep my fans happy.

'Come on then, you losers!' I said. 'Let's get with the game!'

I ran after the ball, and a moment later it was at

my feet and everyone was after me. I didn't even know which side I was on, but it didn't seem to matter. I was away around the other side of the Portakabin and back on the tarmac. I saw the two sweatshirts on the ground which made the goal and headed for them. I took a long kick – which was meant to be a pass – and although it went wrong, luck was with me, for the long kick turned into a cross and it went straight into the goal. The keeper just went one way and the ball went the other.

'Nice one, Benny!'

'Good one, Ben!'

The voices were all around me, their arms were around my shoulders and their hands were at my back.

'Good one, Benny boy! Good one!'

I got a glimpse of Sandra, walking away from the Portakabin. What she had said came back to me, with a terrible pang. But I turned away from her, as the game was starting up again.

The trouble was, as far as Sandra went, that I already had a girlfriend. I had Vicky Ferns, the best-looking babe in the school. I mean, Sandra was all right, nice enough in her way, and quite pretty too, and what was really special about her was she was somebody you could talk to. And not only that, someone you could be quiet with, someone you didn't feel you had to talk to, you didn't have to make any effort with her at all. She was nice, she really was. And she would have done fine for somebody like old Bill Harris. But as far as Benny Spinks went, she just didn't make the grade. Benny Spinks needed somebody different on his arm: a looker, a fashion accessory, that kind of thing.

That was what Benny Spinks needed. Good old Benny Spinks. All-star, all singing, all dancing, washing instructions attached, manual enclosed, lifetime warranty and batteries included – Benny Spinks, babe magnet.

4

Mr Mugg

Things remained very quiet on the Plug Uglies front and I was disappointed that there had, as yet, been no demand for my look-alike services.

I did have something to show for it though. A week after receiving the letter from Mr Mugg (head of Plug Uglies) saying that he was putting me on the books, a copy of the books themselves arrived, and there I was, in person.

The book was an agency catalogue titled: *Plug Uglies – You Name 'Em, We've Got 'Em*, which wasn't entirely true, as I could have named several characters such as Dracula, the Loch Ness Monster and the Incredible Hulk, and who wouldn't be in the book at all.

However, when I opened the catalogue up, I saw photographs in there of all sorts of weird people, many of whom made the Loch Ness Monster appear positively handsome.

There were look-alike pictures of loads of famous people. There were ones who looked just like members of the royal family, or well-known pop singers, or famous movie stars. They didn't always look *much* like them though: sometimes you had to use a little imagination; sometimes an awful lot.

I took the catalogue up to my room (Elvis was out, fortunately) and pored over it for ages. I found my own photo – the one Elvis had taken for me – at the back, under *Look-Alikes (Junior)*. There I was, every inch the Benny Spinks. In fact, the more I looked at myself, the more I realised that I looked more like Benny Spinks than Benny Spinks did.

I went down to the garage and searched through the pile of newspapers which were waiting to be taken to the recycling skip, until I found a photo of the Spinks family. It was some special charity event and they'd all gone to it. There was Benny's dad, Derry Spinks, and there was his mum, Mimsy Tosh (formerly Snosh Ketchup of the Ketchup Girls) and there was Benny himself.

I took the newspaper photo upstairs and placed it next to my own photo in the Plug Uglies catalogue. It really was uncanny, the way I looked like him. But then, while I was thinking this, another thought came into my mind.

I didn't look like Benny Spinks at all.

The truth was that Benny Spinks looked like me!

Well, that was right, wasn't it? I wasn't just his look-alike; he was mine. And if things had been a tiny bit different, if I had been famous and not him, it would have been Benny Spinks going around with *his* photo in the Plug Uglies catalogue, pretending to be my look-alike, and then Vicky Ferns would be all over him like a swarm of midges just because he looked like me!

It was weird, and the more I thought about it, the weirder it got, because in a way, what it all meant was that it didn't really matter what or who you were – it was who people thought you were that was important. Or at least it was to them.

I kept the catalogue hidden underneath the wardrobe so that Elvis wouldn't come across it. Knowing him, he would take the mick something terrible – even though Plug Uglies had been his idea. So I decided not to give him any ammunition or let him get the opportunity.

Every now and again, when I was sure he was out, I would get the Plug Uglies catalogue and turn to my photo and read the caption under it.

'Genuine Benny Spinks-Alike,' the blurb said. (Mr Mugg referred to all his clients as 'Alikes'.) 'Available for Social Events, Advertising & Promotions. Can be booked solo, or along with Derry Spinks-Alike and Snosh Ketchup-Alike. Discount available for triple booking.'

The Derry Spinks look-alike in the catalogue was fairly convincing, but he looked as if he had dyed his hair. There was a photo of him in full football kit, wearing a shirt with Derry's number on it. As for the Snosh Ketchup-Alike, she wore the right clothes, but as far as I could tell she looked about as much like Snosh Ketchup as a bamboo pole did. Mind you, my dad is of the opinion that Snosh Ketchup really is a bamboo pole, as she is very much on the slim side. Not only does she look like a bamboo pole in Dad's opinion, she also sings like one.

'Dad,' I pointed out to him once, 'bamboo poles can't sing.'

'Exactly,' he said. And he gave me one of his 'Go figure it out' looks, then went off to take the newspapers down to the paper bank.

While I was leafing through the Plug Uglies catalogue one afternoon, wondering if I would ever get some work as a look-alike and if the phone would ever ring, the phone did just that – it rang, downstairs in the hall.

I let it ring a bit to see if someone else would answer it, but when they didn't, I ran out of my room and down the stairs and just grabbed it on what sounded like its final ring before the person calling gave up.

'Hello?' I said. 'Who's calling, please?'

'Hello?' a voice replied. 'Who's answering?'

'You tell me first,' I said.

'Why should I?' the voice demanded.

'Because if you don't tell me who's calling,' I

pointed out, 'and what number you rang, I won't be able to tell you if it's the right number.'

There was a pause for a while then.

'All right,' the voice said. 'It's Mugg here and I'm looking to speak to Bill Harris.'

'Speaking.'

'That you, Bill?' the voice said.

'Yes,' I said. 'It is.'

'Can you talk?' the voice said. (Which I thought was a rather stupid question.)

'Of course I can talk. How else could I have answered the phone?'

'I meant, are you free for a chat? I'm not interrupting anything?'

'No. Not at all.'

'It's Jeff Mugg here, of Plug Uglies. You sent me your photo, right? You're the kid who looks like Benny Spinks, aren't you?'

'That's right,' I said, getting quite interested now and wondering what was up and if he might have a job for me.

'Bill Harris, that's you, isn't it?' Mr Mugg said. 'Benny Spinks look-alike, right?'

'Right.'

'Right. Well, listen, kid,' Mr Mugg said. 'Going by your photo here, you may look like Benny Spinks all right, but there's something I have to tell you – you sure don't sound like him.'

I was a bit offended at that. The way Mr Mugg put

it, it sounded as if I'd been trying to deceive people and to put one over on him.

'I never claimed I sounded like him,' I pointed out. 'I said in my letter that I was a look-alike, not a sound-alike. Or even a smell-alike, come to that,' I added for good measure, just to let him know that I wasn't the kind to be pushed around and that I knew my rights and was ready to stand up for them.

'All right, kid,' Mr Mugg said. 'Take it easy. No offence. The job I've got in mind for you won't involve any talking anyway. Now, how are you fixed?'

'What do you mean, fixed?' I said. 'I was never broken, so how could I have been fixed?' (I was starting to wonder a bit about Mr Mugg by now. He seemed to be under the impression that I was held together with superglue.)

'Now listen, kid,' Mr Mugg said, his voice getting growly, 'don't mess me about, I'm a busy man. I've got fingers in more pies than a ten-toed octopus in a pie factory. I need to know how you're fixed for next Saturday. Can you be at the Marshfield Studios in Culpepper Road or can't you? If so, there's a job waiting for you; if not, I'll have to try and find somebody else. You're first choice as you look like him, but nobody's indispensable.'

I covered the phone with my hand and yelled at the top of my voice.

'Mum! Am I free on Saturday?' No reply. 'Dad!'

Nothing either. He must have gone out and Mum was probably in the garden, killing weeds.

I put the phone back to my ear.

'Well?' Mr Mugg was saying. 'Is it all right? Did you ask your mum?'

'It's fine,' I lied – though it wasn't *really* a lie. Maybe it *would* be fine. I just hadn't had the chance to ask anyone.

'Can you go?'

(Well, nobody had said I couldn't.)

'Yes. Sure. What do I have to do?'

'What do you think?' Mr Mugg said. 'You have to be Benny Spinks.'

'Yes but – I mean – who for? What for? What do I . . . ?'

'They'll tell you when you get there,' Mr Mugg said. 'I'll post you the information and confirm in writing. I should be able to get you about three hundred quid. Less my commission, of course.'

Three hundred quid!

I nearly dropped the phone. Three hundred quid! That was probably more than my dad made in a year!

'D-did you say – t-three hundred q-quid?' I s-stuttered.

'That's right,' Mr Mugg said. 'Why? What's the problem? Don't you think it's enough?'

'N-no, it's n-not that, I-I . . .'

But Mr Mugg was in top gear by now.

'No, you're right, kid,' he said. 'It's pathetic. I

should never have let them get away with an offer like that. I'll go back to them, demand four hundred – and if they say no, the deal's off. You can't work for nothing, just because you're a kid, kid. They're taking advantage, that's all, trying it on because you're still in short trousers.'

'But I'm not in short trousers,' I said. 'I'm in joggers.'

'You know what I mean,' he said. 'You're in short trousers in principle. Stand by the phone,' he said. 'I'll bell you back.'

Before I could say another word, the phone went dead. I stood there in dismay, staring at the silent handset. A moment ago I'd all but had three hundred pounds in my hand (less Mr Mugg's commission) and now I was going to end up with nothing because he mistakenly thought I wanted more.

To be honest, I'd have done it for a fiver.

Brrng, brrng, brrng! The phone rang again. I grabbed at it.

'Hello. Bill Harris speaking.'

'That you, Benny?'

'That you, Mr Mugg?'

'It is. I said I'd bell you straight back and I have. Now, there's good news and there's bad news, kid. And the bad news is that they won't do four hundred.'

'And what's the good news?'

'We've split the difference on three-fifty.'

Three hundred and fifty pounds! The stuff I'd be able to buy with that!

'Are you still there, kid?'

'Y-yes, Mr Mugg. I'm here.'

'Three-fifty OK with you? Not too disappointed, are you?'

'N-no. Not at all. Well – maybe just a little bit. But no. It's fine by me.'

'OK. That's a deal then. Must go. I've a call waiting on the other line. I'll confirm in writing as I said and send you all the info. See you then, kid.'

'Yes but – but what do I have to do, Mr Mugg?'

'Just do a Benny, kid. Do a Benny. They'll explain when you get there.'

He hung up and the phone went dead.

I stood there in the hall, feeling alone and a little bit nervous, wondering what the Marshfield Studios in Culpepper Road might hold in store. What did they want me for, what did they expect, and what would I have to do for my three hundred and fifty pounds (less commission)?

It was easy for Mr Mugg to say that all I needed was to 'do a Benny', only what did 'doing a Benny' involve? How exactly did I 'do a Benny'? Why did they want me to 'do a Benny'? I mean, I didn't actually know Benny Spinks from a banana. He was just a picture in the newspaper, someone I had seen on the telly now and again, cheering from the sidelines as his dad scored a goal. Or I might have seen him on the news, checking in at some airport, as he and his parents set off for an exotic holiday on some far-flung island, where hotel room prices started at two thousand pounds a night, and a bed was extra.

No, I didn't know anything about 'doing a Benny' at all.

But I did wonder what it would be like not just to *look* like Benny Spinks, but to *live* like Benny Spinks, to have an enormous mansion like Benny Spinks, with its own Olympic-sized indoor heated swimming pool, to have my own chauffeur-driven limousine, to go to a posh school with the sons of the mega-rich and the mega-famous and the daughters of lords and ladies.

Three hundred and fifty pounds wouldn't be much to Benny Spinks at all. He probably got that for his pocket money. He probably spent that on CDs and sweets in a week.

I looked around the hallway at the inside of our little house. I'd seen a feature in one of my mum's *Hi!* magazines on the Spinks's family home. You could have fitted our whole house into their living room. So it was difficult, really, for me to imagine what 'doing a Benny' would be like.

My mum came in from the garden. She saw me standing by the telephone. Maybe I looked a bit lost.

'What's up, Bill?' she said. 'Got a problem?'

'N-no,' I said. 'Not exactly.'

I told her about Mr Mugg's phone call. I didn't say I'd already told him that I could go next Saturday and asked if it would be all right.

'I don't see why not,' she said. 'I presume they are going to pay you for this?'

'Eh, yes,' I said. 'I think so.'

'And what do you have to do, precisely?' she asked.

'Just – be Benny Spinks, as far as I know,' I said. 'Just "do a Benny".'

I went back up to my room and stood in front of the mirror, trying to 'do a Benny'. Elvis caught me at it. I didn't hear him come in and he must have crept up the stairs. He's always doing things like that, as he's sneaky by nature.

'Here,' he said. 'What are you doing?'

'I'm doing a Benny,' I told him. 'So mind your own business.'

'You looked more like you were doing a Wally to me,' Elvis said.

'Oh really?' I said. 'Well, if you ever want to see what someone doing a Total Pea-brain looks like, I suggest you look in the mirror.'

'Eh?' he said. 'Eh?'

By the time he'd figured it out, I was already downstairs, out of the house and on my way to the Green. Everyone was there, same as usual, with their rollerblades and skateboards.

'Hiya, Benny!' they called. 'How's it going?' I waved back and went to join them.

Vicky Ferns and her friends were there, but she was a bit on the cool side today, as if my looking like Benny Spinks was a novelty which was starting to wear off, and which needed another dimension to it to keep it fresh. That is, she was a bit on the cool side until I happened to mention to someone who happened to mention to her about me going to the Marshfield Studios in Culpepper Road the following weekend.

She came straight over then and sat on my bench.

'Hi, Benny,' she said. 'So I hear you're going to be a film star?'

She knew more than I did then, but I didn't like to disappoint her, so I just nodded and grunted a bit and tried to be modest and said, 'Something like that, I suppose.'

She suggested that we should maybe go for a smoothie at Starbucks, as it was quite a hot day and a nice, cold smoothie would go down a treat. So off we went for smoothies, just her and me and a couple of her friends. Seeing as I was apparently going to be a film star, it only seemed right that I should pay for them. As they'd all gone and sat down and left me at the counter, I didn't have a lot of choice. I had just enough on me, but it almost cleaned me out for the rest of the week.

I just hoped that it wouldn't be everyone who

wanted me to buy them a smoothie, now that I was a film star, or my three hundred and fifty quid (less Mr Mugg's commission) wasn't going to go very far.

It's funny that. What you once thought was a lot of money can suddenly seem like not so much money after all.

I calculated that after thirty rounds of smoothies it would all be gone. I would have to try and save some of it. I couldn't go frittering it all on smoothies. But I guessed that such is the price of celebrity and fame – you have to support your followers and entourage and to buy them smoothies or they'll think you're nothing but a stingy tight-wad who never puts his hand in his pocket.

I did wonder if maybe one day Vicky Ferns would want to buy *me* a smoothie, but I wasn't sure she would. I guessed that Vicky Ferns had strong views when it came to buying smoothies and that she was of the opinion that anyone who knew how to treat a girl right would be off buying her smoothies and no questions asked. I didn't want her thinking that I didn't know how to treat a girl right, so I didn't say anything about paying for all the smoothies.

When we had all drunk our smoothies, one of Vicky Ferns's friends said that her smoothie had been quite delicious, but it was amazing the way that one smoothie seemed to leave you a little bit empty and unsatisfied, and how you often yearned for another, and that a chocolate chip cookie would go down nicely too. Vicky Ferns agreed and said that in her opinion the only thing to have after a smoothie was another smoothie plus, if at all possible, a blueberry muffin. Then she and her friends all turned their heads round and stared meaningfully at the counter.

I was starting to get a bit worried then, and I was also rather amazed at how Vicky Ferns and her friends could put smoothies, muffins and chocolate chip cookies away as if they had been doing a day's labouring on a building site instead of just hanging around the Green and Claire's Accessories looking at styling brushes and earrings.

'More smoothies?' I said. 'With muffins and cookies! Wow! You girls amaze me, the way you can shovel it in. Still, what's a few more pounds after all? What's wrong with a few fat bits here and there? You can get too hung up on all that skinny stuff if you ask me. The bigger the better, I say. In fact, I read in our geography book that in some parts of the world great big girls full up with muffins and cookies are highly esteemed and considered to be almost as valuable as elephants.'

Strangely enough, once I'd finished telling them about big girls in other countries, they all went off the idea of more smoothies, which I don't mind telling you was a great relief. So I went up to the counter on my own and spent the last of my dosh on a flapjack for myself, to stay slim. I did offer it around, but nobody wanted any, not even when I insisted they have a bite.

Afterwards we went back down to the Green and I lay on the grass and basked in the sun and in the glory of looking like Benny Spinks and of being popular – which was still a nice novelty for me. I listened to the clatter of the skateboards and the murmur of voices and then I fell asleep.

When I awoke, everyone had gone and the sun was sinking. As I walked home, I got a glimpse of my reflection in a shop window. Lying on the grass had flattened my hair a little, and I didn't look like Benny Spinks as much as I had earlier. I quickly ruffled my hair up, so that I looked like him again in case I met somebody I knew on my way home.

Some friends of my eldest brother Kevin passed as I crossed the precinct. They saw me and called out 'Hello, Benny!' and 'How's it going, Benny boy!'

I waved and they laughed and it was pretty cool really. They were older than me, on their way for an evening out by the look of it, and they were all in high spirits and out for a laugh. It was great really, having a laugh and a joke with them like that. You felt like you were in with the in-crowd.

At the end of our road, I saw Sandra Debbings drive by in the back of her parents' car. I don't think she saw me, but I saw her. She looked a bit on her own, really, and when I thought about it, I realised that she often was. She was nice, but she was quiet.

She didn't have a lot of friends. She reminded me of me – of the old Bill Harris, before his amazing transformation into Benny Spinks. I felt a little sorry for her, to be honest. I thought it was a shame that she didn't look like somebody famous too – like somebody in a babe band, or some actress from a TV programme.

I just hoped for her sake that she too might have a 'hairdryer moment' and be transformed into somebody else. It was hard being an ordinary nobody. As I well knew from personal experience. After all, I'd been one for years.

5

Nigel and the Nicka Nackas

It turned out to be chocolate bars, which was all right by me, though it didn't turn out to be quite as straightforward as I expected.

A thick, brown envelope arrived on Tuesday morning, with my name on the front and with a 'from' stamp on the back reading, 'Plug Uglies Ltd. Prop: J. Mugg.'

Inside the envelope was a letter and a thick contract with a lot of small print in it. I gave it to my dad to read. He had a look at it and said that it seemed all right to him. I was pretty impressed at the way in which he managed to read and digest a whole two-hundred-and-forty-page contract while eating his Shreddies and still understand all the small print. There wasn't just small print either, there was also tiny print, for the small print had even smaller print of its own. When Dad got to the bit about the three hundred and fifty pounds, he almost spluttered his Shreddies all over the table.

'How much?' he said. 'For one day's work! Just for looking like Whatshisname Rinkydinks!'

'Benny Spinks, Dad,' I reminded him.

'Three hundred and fifty pounds!' he said. 'I can't believe it! Kids today! Easy life!'

'Less Mr Mugg's commission,' I pointed out.

'It's a scandal,' Dad said. 'Kids today getting paid money like that just for looking like other people. In my day, when I was a kid, if you wanted to make any pocket money you had to go out and slave over a hot paper round. Three hundred and fifty quid was the sort of thing you only used to dream about. Why, back in my day there were even millionaires who didn't have that much money! Well, I wish I looked like someone, that's all I can say, and then I could get three hundred and fifty quid for old rope as well. Easy life!'

It was on the tip of my tongue to tell Dad that he did look like somebody – he looked an awful lot like the bloke down at the corner shop who operates the lottery ticket machine. But obviously there was no money in looking like him as he wasn't famous, so I didn't mention it.

'I don't know,' Dad said. 'And what are you planning on doing with all this money?'

'Oh – save some, spend some, I suppose,' I said.

'I should think so,' Dad said. 'You make sure you

73

do save some. I'll help you open a savings account, if you like, and you can put your cheque in there. I don't want you going squandering it all on fast living and loose women and expensive fruit smoothies round at Starbucks.'

I got a bit worried then, when Dad mentioned smoothies, and I wondered if maybe he had been spying on me and knew all about my private life, or if he was just psychic. Or maybe he was only guessing.

Mum came into the kitchen then and wanted to know what was going on, so Dad told her all about my three hundred and fifty pounds (less commission) and naturally she had to say the same thing about it being a lot of money for a boy of my age (it wasn't enough that I'd heard it once already, no, I had to hear it again) and how I had to be sure to save it.

Then Elvis came down and he got in on the act. But he didn't want me to save my three hundred and fifty pounds at all, he wanted me to give it to him. I told him not to hold his breath waiting as he'd probably suffocate, but he just said that wasn't very brotherly, and if he'd had some money, he'd be sure to give me half of it at least. Which was news to me as I'd never had a penny off Elvis and nor had anyone else, not even the bloke who came to the door collecting for the lifeboats. Elvis told him that he never went sailing and was therefore unlikely to drown and wouldn't give him anything.

'So what exactly do you have to do for all this money?' Mum wanted to know. 'Apart from look like Benny Spinks? Or is that all you have to do?'

I still didn't know. I didn't imagine it could be that simple. There had to be more to it than that. And there was, as I discovered when I read through Mr Mugg's letter, which accompanied the contract.

'Please present yourself at the Artistes' Entrance at Marshfield Studios in Culpepper Road this coming Saturday at 8.00 a.m. prompt. You will be required to stand in for Mr Benjamin Spinks for lighting and rigging set-ups and rehearsals, for long shots and back shots and for some action sequences. Filming should not go beyond 6.00 p.m.; should it overrun, an additional fee will be paid. Chaperone/Minder will be supplied by film company.'

The letter went on to explain that the sequence being filmed was an advertisement for 'the brand new, soon to be launched, Nicka Nacka Chocolate Bar'.

'What a stupid name for a chocolate bar,' Elvis said. 'I'd never buy a chocolate bar called Nicka Nacka.'

'You never buy chocolate anyway,' I reminded him. 'You just pinch other people's.' (Which was why I had taken to hiding mine in waterproof bags in the toilet cistern.)

'Nicka Nacka chocolate bars, eh?' Mum said. 'They sound nice.'

Nice or not didn't really matter to me. Just as long as I was getting my three hundred and fifty quid (and to be honest, I was starting to resent paying Mr Mugg his commission) I didn't care if Nicka Nackas were made out of horse dung and sawdust.

As far as I could understand from the rest of Mr Mugg's letter, the deal was that Benny Spinks had been signed up by Nicka Nacka to advertise their new chocolate bars.

As he was such a well-known face – possibly even the most famous boy in the country, even more famous than the boy who'd stood on the burning deck, who was sort of famous, but nobody really knew what his name was – the advertisers reckoned that kids everywhere would want to try out Nicka Nacka bars, just as long as Benny Spinks was recommending them.

'I just don't get it,' my dad said as he looked at the letter, shaking his head. 'I never have and I never will. I mean, this Benny Spinks – I'm sure he's a decent enough sort – but what has he ever actually *done*? Absolutely nothing, that's what. He just happens to have a famous mum and dad, and so he ends up famous too. But famous for what? Nothing. Just for being famous. And now they pay him a load of dosh to sell chocolate bars. It's beyond me. It really is.'

Well, in some ways, it was beyond me too. But if Benny Spinks was getting paid a load of dosh just for having a famous mum and dad, who was I to criticise, when I was getting paid dosh too, just for looking like Benny Spinks?

'Pay no attention to your father,' my mum said. 'Why look a gift horse in the mouth? Just make hay while the sun shines and don't put all your eggs in the one basket as tomorrow is another day.'

Which seemed fair enough as far as I was concerned.

The rest of the week dragged, as I waited for Saturday to come. I spent a lot of time looking in the mirror, worrying about a spot which seemed to be developing round by my left nostril. I was concerned that it might spoil my close-ups (if there were any) and jeopardise my career as a stand-in for Benny Spinks.

It occurred to me, while I was standing in the bathroom, wondering whether to squeeze my spot with the tweezers or to let sleeping spots lie, that although I looked the spitting image of Benny Spinks today, it might not be that way tomorrow. Faces change as people grow older, shaped by experience as much as genes. Mum was right. I had to make the most of it while I could.

What if his face changed as he grew older, or mine did? What if he started to look like a carthorse, whereas I just got more and more handsome and distinguished? My career as a Benny Spinks look-alike wouldn't last long in those circumstances and I'd soon be unemployed.

Elvis said he would get the bus with me to Marshfield Studios to see I arrived there safely and then he would meet me later at six o'clock to go back home, even though it meant up getting early on a Saturday morning, which he didn't usually like to do. Mum said it was kind of him, but I wasn't so sure. For a start, the sound of me getting up would probably have woken him anyway, and also I suspected that he just wanted to get inside the studio in the hope that there would be famous actresses there and he could get their autographs which he would later sell to impressionable people at inflated prices.

As it turned out, the security guard took one look at him and wouldn't let him past the gate. This is quite often the case with Elvis and security guards. I have also noticed that when we go into shops, the security people start muttering into their little walkie-talkies, and quite often someone who looks like a little old lady (but who is probably a beefy store detective in a dress) starts to dog our footsteps until Elvis is out of the shop.

So Elvis reluctantly went away from Marshfield Studios, muttering something about being back at six, and I sat down in reception to wait for somebody to come for me. A lady turned up a few minutes later, took one look and said, 'Wow! You do look like him, don't you? It's amazing. You could be his brother – his twin! It's uncanny. It really is.'

'It was all due to the hairdryer,' I explained to her as we walked along a long, long corridor, on our way – I presumed – to the studio.

'The what?' she said.

So I told her the story about the shower and the changing room and my hair getting all frizzed, and how my life had altered for ever beyond recognition and how new vistas had been opened and pastures new, and now here I was making movies (well, advertisements anyway).

'Well, well,' she said. 'What fun. Down here and left at the end.'

'Have you ever met him?' I asked, as we walked down another long corridor. I was starting to wonder if maybe we shouldn't have got a taxi.

'Benny?' she said. 'Yes. I have. A couple of times.'

'What's he like?' I asked.

She smiled.

'Look in the mirror,' she said.

'No,' I said. 'I don't mean that, I mean, what's he like – you know – as a person?'

'Oh, right—'

But before she could answer, we were at a set of double swing doors. We pushed our way through them, and on through some heavy fire doors, then through a thick, sound-proof door, and at last we were in the studio.

79

There were cables everywhere – cables and cameras and blokes with tools and hammers in holsters, looking like gunslingers about to beat each other to the draw with pliers and screwdrivers. There were electricians and carpenters; there were people shouting into walkie-talkies and gabbering into mobile phones and others listening to them.

'This way,' the lady said. 'I'm Caroline, by the way. The director's PA. His personal assistant, that is.'

'Oh, right,' I said. 'I'm Bill.'

'I know, Bill,' she said. 'You're down on the call sheet as Benny Number Two, OK? So if you hear the director or anyone shout for Benny Number Two, it's you they want.'

I was very glad then that they hadn't let Elvis into the studio. I could just imagine what he would have said if he'd found out that I was down on the cast list as a Number Two. The fact that it was a Benny Number Two wouldn't have mattered to him. I'd never have lived it down or heard the end of it for the rest of my days.

'I'll take you to meet the director. Over here.'

Caroline led the way across the studio. It was a huge place, the size of an air hangar. There were lights everywhere, massive banks of them hanging from the roof, or standing on great tripods. There were several film sets in the studio; you could see the backs, with chalk marks and wooden batons all over them, as well as the fronts – the part the cameras saw.

The carpenters were still working on them, screwing them together and banging in nails. As far as I could make out, the sets seemed to represent different parts of a factory – a chocolate factory, I guessed. In fact it had to be. One set was of a long metal gantry. Underneath it was a vat of dark brown liquid which I presumed was supposed to be chocolate. Not real chocolate, of course, pretend chocolate, for the purposes of the advertisement.

'Nigel! Benny Two's here!' Caroline called.

A man looked down at me from a gantry. He had spiky hair and several earrings – one of which was in his lip, another of which was in his nose, and a third of which was in his eyebrow. I guessed that he had probably got dressed in a hurry.

'I'll be right with you, darling,' Nigel called, and he returned to the agitated conversation he was having with somebody else.

'That's the lighting designer Nigel's talking to,' Caroline explained. 'He arranges the lights for the cameras.'

'Ah,' I said. 'Right.'

I tried to look cool.

My looking cool was interrupted by the clattering of cowboy boots coming down metal stairs. It was Nigel himself, the main man, the director. He looked like he hadn't shaved for a couple of days and like his T-shirt had come out of the dirty-laundry pile, but he was friendly enough. Too friendly if anything.

'Benny Two, darling,' he said. 'So you got here unscathed?'

'Eh – yeah,' I said. It maybe wasn't much of an answer, but it was the best I could come up with at short notice.

'Well, darling, shall we get to work?'

'Eh, right,' I said.

'This way then, darlings,' Nigel said, and he strode off rapidly; Caroline and I followed on behind, trying to keep up. It turned out that Nigel called everyone 'darling', even the security guard's Alsatian.

We sat down on some sofas which were part of one of the sets and Nigel put his boots up on the arm.

'OK, Benny Two, darling, so you know what to do?'

'Eh – not really,' I said.

Nigel looked a bit cross.

'Didn't you get a script, darling?' he said.

'Eh – no,' I said. 'I didn't.'

'That Mugg!' Nigel said, raising his eyes to the heavens. 'Useless! Mugg by name, mug by nature. All he needs is a handle and you could drink your coffee out of him. Here.' He threw a script over to me. 'Take a quick look at that while I talk you through it.'

'Eh, right.' I opened the script.

'OK, Benny Two, here's the deal. Benny One will be in later to do his bit and strut his funky stuff – right, Caroline, darling?'

'Yes, Nigel, darling,' Caroline nodded. 'As you say.'

I could see now that not only did Nigel call everyone else darling, but they called him darling too. I decided to bear that in mind and to act accordingly. It is always a good idea, when in Rome, to do as the Romans do. That way you do not come across as stupid and provincial and not very cool.

'OK, Benny Two, darling, are you paying attention?'

'Yes, Nigel, darling,' I said. 'I am.'

I may have been mistaken, but I thought I saw a small vein start to twitch underneath Nigel the director's right eye just then. But it was probably my imagination, or a trick of the light.

'OK, Benny Two, sweetheart,' he said. 'Shall we get down to what you have to do?'

As Nigel had moved on from darling to sweetheart, I presumed that we had broken the ice now and were getting on to informal terms and that it would be as well if I made the effort to be as friendly as he was.

'Right you are, Nigel, lovikins,' I said. 'Ready when you are.'

Oddly enough, his other eye seemed to twitch now as well.

'OK,' he said. 'Benny Two, my little cutie . . .' and he also appeared to be grinding his teeth a bit – which is not very good for the fillings.

'Yes, Nigy-Poohs?' I said.

Caroline intervened then and asked if anyone would like a cup of coffee. Nigel said he would have one – which I thought was a good idea, as it might help stop his eyes from twitching – and I asked for a diet cola as I am watching my figure, so I don't drink the sugary stuff.

'Right,' Nigel said. 'The scenario is basically this. We're in a chocolate factory – the one where the Nicka Nackas are being made. There is a thief on the prowl – the villain, who is stealing all the Nicka Nacka bars.'

'So he's nicking the Nicka Nackas?' I said, just to make sure I had it right.

'That's correct.'

'He's the Nicka Nacka nicker?'

'That's it, darling. Can we press on?'

'Right.'

'OK. Now Benny Spinks is our hero. He is a private eye, hired to track down the Nicka Nacka thief.'

'Right.'

'He sets a trap – a trail of Nicka Nackas. The thief can't resist them. A chase ensues through the Nicka Nacka factory, with Benny after the thief. They race through the factory. They get sprayed with toffee, they get covered in crunchy biscuit crumbs, they get dipped in fudge, they get drenched in caramel, they get sprayed with sultanas, raisins and crispy rice, and soaked in cream.

'It all ends in a stand-off at the end of a gantry.

Benny and the thief tumble into a vat of chocolate. It's not a deep one, don't worry. Nobody's going to drown. We cut to the vat, first Benny, then the thief, appear. They're both covered in chocolate by now. Benny nabs the thief with his handcuffs. Then, in the final shot, we see Benny all cleaned up with the thief being taken away in the background. Benny has a magnifying glass in one hand and a Nicka Nacka bar in the other. He turns to the camera and says: "Nicka Nickas – only one safe place to keep them: in here!" He points to his stomach, unwraps and takes a bite of his Nicka Nacka bar, makes a "Oh, it's so delicious I could die, darling" face and holds his magnifying glass up to his eye. Then he says, "Keep an eye on your Nicka Nackas!" Then we have the jingle going "Nicka Nacka, Nicka Nacka, Every mouthful is a cracka!" as Benny holds a Nicka Nacka up to camera. And that's it, darling.'

'I see, sweetie-kins,' I said.

'Any questions, darling?' Nigel asked.

'Just one, deary-poohs,' I said.

'Being, darling?' Nigel said, sounding a bit tetchy and looking at his watch. 'We have to have this all done by six, you know.'

'My one question is this,' I said. 'What does Benny Spinks do? Because I seem to be doing it all.'

'Benny One?' Nigel said. 'What does Benny One do, Benny Two? Didn't I make it clear? He does the piece to camera, of course. At the end.'

'The bit with the magnifying glass?'

'That's right. Is there a problem, sweetie-pie?'

'All nice and dry and all cleaned up – Benny Spinks does that bit?'

'Your point being?' Nigel said, sounding tetchier by the minute.

'Just trying to get it straight,' I said. 'So all the getting sprayed with sticky toffee and syrup and honey and getting coated with biscuit and raisins and sprayed with fudge and all that, and then having to fall into a vat of liquid chocolate – that's me?'

'That's right, darling. You have it. So shall we press on?'

'So basically, munchkin,' I said, 'I get to do all the dirty work?'

'Correct, Benny Two, darling,' Nigel said. 'You do. But you can have a shower after, and the soap is free and the towels are particularly fluffy.'

'Just out of interest, sweetikinsy,' I said. 'How much is Benny Spinks getting paid for staying nice and dry and just doing the last scene with the magnifying glass in one hand and the Nicka Nacka in the other?'

'Well, I'm scarcely at liberty to disclose the financial arrangements we have made with our star. But I shouldn't think that Nicka Nacka Ltd will be seeing much change from fifty thousand.'

I gawped at him. My chin must have landed on the floor and then bounced back up again. Fifty thousand pounds! For eating chocolate bars! And Benny Spinks was the same age as me! He was getting fifty thousand pounds for endorsing Nicka Nackas, and he was going to stay nice and dry and clean. I was going to get sticky and gooey and covered in fudge and raisins and all I'd get was three hundred and fifty lousy quid (less commission). My big cheque suddenly seemed like very small potatoes. In fact, to be perfectly honest, I was starting to dislike Benny Spinks.

No, I wasn't.

I was starting to hate him. I was beginning to resent him big time. Deep grudges had opened up inside me. Deep grudges and lakes of resentment.

I'd been quite happy with my fee until I found out what Benny was getting. It just didn't seem right. Here I was, doing all the dirty work for a pittance, while all he had to do was to breeze in at the last moment, say his piece, pick up his fifty thousand quid, say, 'Cheerio, Nigel, darling,' and go home to his Olympic-sized swimming pool with wave machine. He probably even had his own performing dolphin in it, for all I knew.

There was no justice. I could see it clearly now. My dad had been right all along. The whole Spinks family were a pampered lot of overprivileged celebrities who got paid a fortune for doing next to nothing, whereas honest, humble, hard-working sorts (like me) had to sweat and toil just to make a crust and earn a pittance and had to get covered in toffee and raisins in the process.

If I hadn't already signed a contract, I'd have gone home.

Only I had signed it, and I may have my faults, but I do keep my word, and when I make a promise, I stick to it if I possibly can.

So I'd see the Nicka Nackas through to the very end – all the way to the vat of chocolate. But I wasn't happy about it, and I resolved that if I ran into Benny Spinks that day, then I would tell him exactly what I thought of him. I would give him the biggest dressing-down he had ever had. Yes, I would give him a piece of my mind all right. One he wouldn't forget in a hurry. (Elvis says I don't have much mind to spare so I shouldn't go giving pieces of it to anyone. But he only says that because his brain is made out of mushrooms.) Yes, I'd put Benny Spinks straight on a few things if I ran into him. No doubt about that.

'OK, Benny Two, darling,' Nigel said, taking his cowboy boots off the sofa. 'Shall we make a move? Caroline will take you over to costume and they'll get you ready. Then you can meet Morris, who's playing our Nicka Nacka thief. Caroline, darling, if you would?'

We headed off towards costume and make-up. I decided then that I *would* run into Benny Spinks that day, no matter what. I'd make a point of tracking him down. Even if I had to hide in his dressing room inside an old laundry basket, I was going to confront him and tell him a bit about the real world, as it was high time he found out what a pampered and overprivileged life he was leading. It was time he learned about the sufferings of the poor and the deprived – people like me, who had to share their bunk beds with brothers called Elvis and who probably would have died, some nights, if they hadn't managed to get the window open in the nick of time to let the smells out. It was high time that Benny Spinks came face to face with the real world.

I followed Caroline to the costume department where they fixed me up with a 'Benny Spinks, Boy Detective' type of outfit, consisting of a trilby hat and a trench coat. It all seemed a bit old fashioned to me, but what did I know, I was just a Number Two.

They took me to make-up then where they didn't do much really apart from powder my face a bit to take the shine off. The make-up lady did notice my spot, however, the one by my left nostril.

'Got a spot,' she said.

'I know, darling,' I said. 'It's such a fret! But what can one do?'

'I could cover it with some make-up if you want,' she offered. 'But it's probably not worth it. They won't be doing any close-ups.'

'Won't they?' I said, feeling a mite disappointed.

'Not of *you*,' she said. (And the way she said it put me in mind of toads coming out from under stones.)

'Benny *One* will be in the close-ups. You're basically there for falling in the muck, aren't you?'

'You don't think that spot by my nose will endanger my film career then?' I said.

She looked a bit puzzled. 'What film career is that then, love?' she said. 'Have you got more work lined up?'

I had to admit that I didn't. So we left my spot as and where it was.

A man I vaguely recognised wandered into the make-up room then, dressed up as a burglar, in striped jersey, mask and black tights. He had a bag with him with the word SWAG written on it.

He saw me sitting in my trench coat and with my trilby hat on the arm of the chair. He looked from me to his reflection in the mirror to me again.

'They're going for realism then, I see,' he said.

(I think he was being sarcastic.)

'Take a seat, Morris,' the make-up lady said. 'With you in a moment.'

That was when I remembered who he was and where I had seen him. He was an actor called Morris Trewitt and he had once been in a TV series for very young children, playing a character called Mr Pie Crust.

He had always frightened the daylights out of me when I had been small and whenever he had appeared on the telly I used to run from the room screaming and sobbing uncontrollably, yelling for my mum and shouting, 'Mr Pie Crust is after me! Mr

Pie Crust is out to get me! He wants to turn me into a pie!'

Seeing him now though, he looked perfectly harmless. He looked as if he'd have trouble taking his trousers off, never mind turning people into pies.

'Are you the real B. Spinks, young man?' he said. 'You certainly look like him.'

I had to confess that I wasn't.

'Ah, you must be the substitute then,' he said, 'who has the privilege of falling in the goo, along with myself.'

I had to admit that I was. It didn't seem like much of a job though, being a substitute for somebody else and falling into the goo with Morris Trewitt. Why couldn't Benny Spinks do his own falling in the goo? What was he – stuck up or something? I felt a bit like own-brand, economy cola; I wasn't the real thing. And as for who I really was, nobody cared about that. They weren't interested in the slightest.

I think I earned my money several times over that day, chasing Morris Trewitt round Marshfield Studios in Culpepper Road, falling into vats of pretend chocolate, getting sprayed with glue coloured to look like toffee, and being pelted with crispy rice, crumbled-up biscuit, and sacks of sultanas and raisins.

It all stuck to me something chronic, not just to my trench coat, but to me personally. It all went down the back of my neck too, all the fudge and raisins and all the rest, and when I fell into the vat of chocolate for about the forty-ninth time I was so soggy and chocolate-logged that I needed help to get out again. My trilby hat was full of liquid chocolate and so were the pockets of my trench coat and both my shoes.

'We'll just get a nice shot of that splash again, darlings,' Nigel said. 'Doesn't matter that you're already mucky. It's the splash we're after and a nice shot of the two of you surfacing, covered in goo. And I'd like to see that bucket of soft toffee again, Benny Two, darling, tipping over your head. And props – oh, props – another can of syrup, darlings, for rubbing into Benny Two's hair when his hat comes off. There's a sweetie.'

As for Morris Trewitt, he got as wet and sticky as I did, maybe even more so. But at least Morris Trewitt was Morris Trewitt. At least it was *him* playing the burglar. I was playing Benny Spinks playing a detective. I was sort of twice removed.

'We must soldier on regardless,' Morris said to me, as we hauled ourselves out of the chocolate vat yet again and as Nigy-poohs the director called, 'Loverly, darlings, but I think we'll go once more on the surfacing-from-the-gunge shot. A bit more pizzazz this time, darlings, if you would.'

So off we had to go once more, ducking down into the gunge and popping out again, with soft toffee and syrup trickling on to our heads.

'Pizzazz!' I heard Morris mumble. 'I'll give him pizzazz! I'll pizzazz him right into this chocolate vat, first chance I get.'

And though I didn't like to encourage him, I didn't *dis*courage him either, because Nigel was getting on my nerves too and I felt that a taste of the chocolate vat would do him no harm at all.

By about half-past three in the afternoon, we had it all done to Nigel's satisfaction apart from the very last bit where, after bobbing up from the chocolate vat, I had to arrest the burglar with the handcuffs. I had chocolate everywhere by then, in my hair, up my nose, dripping out of my ears, and down the back of my pants.

'Once more, darlings, if you would. Just get the cuffs on Morris again, would you Benny, lovikins.'

'It's not Benny, it's Bill!' I snarled.

'Sorry – Benny Two, I meant to say,' Nigel said. 'OK everyone, positions please, and action!'

So once again Morris and I had to duck down into the chocolate, and then we had to pop up and I had to snap the handcuffs on him when we surfaced and snap the other part around my wrist and that would be it.

Finally Nigel was satisfied.

'OK everyone,' he yelled. 'Thank you, darlings. That's a wrap.'

'So what do we do now then?' I asked.

Nigel peered down at us from his lofty perch up on the gallery.

'I'd have a good wash, if I were you, darlings, and get some clean clothes on.'

'Typical,' I heard Morris Trewitt mutter. 'You give them all your craft, all your years of experience, all your heart and soul, and what do you get in return for it? "Go and have a wash!" That's what you get. Oh, it's a heartbreaking profession, acting is. I should have listened to my mother and opened a cheese shop instead.'

Morris and I climbed out of the chocolate vat and walked, wet and dripping, across the studio floor, heading for the dressing rooms and the showers.

'Oh, darlings!' Nigel called after us as we went. 'Try not to drip so much, if you would. Thank you, darlings. Ever so kind. Love you both to death!'

Morris went a bit pale under his coating of imitation chocolate.

'That man,' he said, 'is a Philistine!'

'Right,' I said. 'He is.'

I wasn't really sure what a Philistine was, but I knew from the way Morris had said it that it wasn't a good thing to be, so I decided to agree with him on that basis alone. It was enough for me.

Morris pushed the dressing-room door open and I went to follow him inside. As I did, I heard Caroline calling across the studio to Nigel, the director.

'Oh, Nigel!'

'Yes, Caroline, my sweet?'

'Reception just rang. Benny One is here for his close-up and speech to camera.'

'Then go and fetch him immediately,' Nigel said. 'We cannot keep our star waiting.'

That was pretty rich, I thought. He'd kept Morris and me waiting for hours, all standing around covered in goo with sultanas and raisins down our underpants. But when it came to Benny Spinks it was all different. As soon as the real Benny turned up it was all *Yes, Benny* and *No, Benny* and *Benny, three bags full, Benny*. It was *Mustn't keep Benny waiting* and *Get a chair for Benny* and *Perhaps Benny would like a nice drink and a biscuit and a soft cushion to sit on and some fresh batteries for his MP3 player?*

Oh yes. Benny Spinks didn't have to waddle about soaked in half a ton of goo with about six pounds of raisins, biscuit crumb and crispy rice in his underwear and a couple of pints of fudge in his socks.

Oh no. Benny could just stroll in at the last minute when he felt like it, do his couple of lines in a nice dry part of the studio, pocket his fifty thousand and clear off home in his chauffeur-driven limousine back to his Olympic-sized diving boards and his deep end and his monogrammed swimming trunks.

Very fair that was – I didn't think.

The door to the dressing rooms closed behind us.

'I'm off for a good long soak,' Morris Trewitt said, 'to get this goo off. Though to be honest, I suspect I shall still be finding the odd raisin in two or three weeks' time.' He went off to his dressing room. I headed for mine.

I have to be fair and admit that the dressing rooms were pretty good. You got your own personal bathroom, complete with bath and shower attachments. I wouldn't have minded a good long wallow in a nice hot bath myself by then, but no, I had other plans, because the old Bill Harris fighting spirit had been roused by now and my dander was up big time.

My dad always says that you don't want to mess with a Harris when his dander is up. And he's right. To be perfectly truthful, danders are a bit like Philistines to me, in that I'm not really sure what they are. It might have something to do with dandruff, I don't know. But I know that a Harris with his dander up is a person to be taken seriously. There's no doubt about that.

No. No long baths for me. It was going to be a quick shower, back into my own clothes, and then out into the studio to catch Benny (Number One) Spinks before he shot off home to his life of luxury. I wanted to have a word with him. I wanted to mark his card for him and to let him know what life was like for the poor and downtrodden who had to slave for hours under mega-hot studio lights while the crispy rice and the raisins in their underpants got slowly roasted.

I was going to give him that piece of my mind.

I got under the shower and poured on about half a litre of shower gel to get all the goo off. It took me ages to get clean and I was worried that Benny might already have gone. I turned the shower off, got dressed, quickly dried my hair with the hairdryer there – making sure it went frizzy – then I headed back out towards the studio, leaving my sodden trilby and trench coat in a plastic bin marked DIRTY.

Somehow, I got lost. I must have opened the wrong door. Instead of finding myself back in the studio, I ended up in a corridor. So I retraced my steps – I thought – and tried another door. But I still wasn't in the studio, nor was I back in the dressing-room area. I was in some sort of storage place where they kept old props and bits of scenery. And so it went on: I walked further and further and got loster and loster, until finally I found myself all alone in a long, empty corridor. I just didn't have a clue where I was.

Then I heard footsteps, and they were coming my way. Thank heavens – it was someone who would know the way out. At the far end of the corridor I saw a distant figure. I heard the sound of his shoes as he slowly drew near. They squeaked a little, like new trainers.

I stood and watched as the figure approached.

Soon it was near enough for me to make out its features. It was someone I knew, I thought; someone I knew really well. But, for a moment, I couldn't place who it was. The person looked so familiar and yet somehow so foreign and strange and—

Then I realised that I was having some kind of out-of-body experience. Or maybe I'd died and come back as a ghost and hadn't really noticed.

Because the person approaching me . . .

Was me.

I stood there, the fear and the horror growing inside me as I watched myself walk nearer and nearer. I would have run away if I could have, but I was stuck, rooted to the spot, like there was superglue on my shoes. I knew what was going to happen. There'd been some kind of a time warp or a time slip. I was going to meet myself. And when I did – I'd probably explode. And it would be the end of the universe. I'd done it in Physics at school.

I took a step forwards. Then I stopped. I stopped and I stood there and I stared at myself.

And I realised that it wasn't me at all.

It was Benny. Benny Spinks. Benny Spinks himself.

He stared back at me. Not with fright or fear, just incredulity, I suppose, and curiosity. Then he sort of smiled and said, 'I c-can't b-believe it. I-I look j-just like y-you. I could b-be your double.'

I realised then that I'd just discovered something

about Benny Spinks that I'd never known. I now knew why I didn't sound like him.

He had a slight stutter.

'Hi,' I said, putting my hand out. 'Bill Harris.'

'H-hi,' he said. 'B-Benny Spinks.'

'Nice to meet you, Benny,' I said, all thoughts of telling him off forgotten.

'N-nice to meet you too. W-what are you doing h-here?'

'I'm lost,' I said.

'That's f-funny,' he said. 'So am I.'

So we had more than appearances in common.

6

Benny Spinks

He wasn't such a bad bloke after all. I knew he was all right when he said, 'I look just like you.' Lesser blokes with bigger egos wouldn't have seen it that way. They'd have said, 'You look like me,' putting themselves up as the standard against which others had to be compared.

'W-who are you?' Benny asked. His stutter was easing off already and it soon wore off completely.

'I just told you – Bill Harris,' I said.

'No, I m-mean – you know – what are you doing here?'

'I was standing in for you,' I told him. 'I'm your look-alike. They had me doing all the dirty jobs, like getting covered in toffee and having raisins stuffed down your underpants – well, *my* underpants, to be precise.'

'Oh,' he said. 'Sorry about that.'

But I could hardly blame him. Nobody had made me do it, and I was getting three hundred and fifty quid.

'Have you done your bit?' I asked.

'Yes,' he said.

'How did you get on?' I said.

'Fine,' he said.

'What about saying, "Keep an eye on your Nicka Nackas!"?'

'No problem,' he said. 'Why?'

'Oh, just wondering,' I said.

'You mean my stammer?' he said.

'Stammer?' I said, acting surprised and not wanting him to think I had noticed it or that I was one to discriminate against stuttering minorities. 'What stammer's that?'

'I've got a bit of a stutter sometimes,' he said. 'Only when I'm under pressure. But I managed to say "Nicka Nackas" all right, as I'd been practising it.'

'Ah, good,' I said.

Just then a voice came bellowing down the corridor, soon followed by a spiky head and a torn T-shirt and many earrings (not all of them in ears). It was Nigel.

'Benny!' he was calling. 'Benny, darling! Are you there? The limo's at reception for you! Benny, is one there?'

He saw the two of us standing chatting and he stopped like he'd suddenly slammed the brakes on.

'Good grief!' he said. 'Benny . . . ?'

He couldn't tell the difference. Benny Spinks started to smile, so I smiled too, just to maintain the confusion.

'What . . . which . . . ?'

We stood there, both grinning at him, waiting to see if he could get it right.

'Now, don't tell me, it's you, isn't it . . . or no . . . maybe it's – no – now that I think about it . . .'

He stopped looking at our faces and began to study our clothes. It was the only thing that could tell him. I knew that, and I knew why. It was because Benny's clothes were all better than mine, and his labels and logos had probably cost about ten times as much.

'Benny!' Nigel said triumphantly. 'I always know the real thing!'

Lying fibber, I thought. You don't know it's him at all. If it hadn't been for his top-of-the-range, state-of-the-art trainers compared to my old, falling-apart, bog-standard ones, you wouldn't have known one of us from the other, or your head from a hole in the wall.

'Well,' Nigel said. 'It's nice that you've met.' (But he didn't say it as if he meant it much.) 'Shall we get back now?'

'Yes, sorry,' Benny said. 'I got lost.'

'Oh deary,' Nigel said. 'Poor you.'

'I got lost too,' I told him.

He didn't say 'Oh deary' to that though. There was no 'Poor you' for me. He didn't seem bothered about me getting lost at all. If anything, Nigel gave me the impression that he wished I *would* get lost – permanently.

We followed him back along the warren of corridors. He seemed a bit keen to talk to Benny Spinks, but Benny just wanted to talk to me.

'Where do you live, Bill?' he asked.

I told him.

'Is it nice?' he said.

'It's all right,' I said. 'But our whole house would fit into your sitting room.'

'Where did you see our sitting room?'

'In *Okey-Dokey Weekly* or something,' I said.

'How many bedrooms have you got?' he said.

'Three,' I said. 'And a loft extension. You've got twenty-four, haven't you?'

'Twenty-five,' he corrected me.

'Sorry,' I said. 'I wasn't trying to make out your house was small.'

'How do you get to school in the morning?' he asked me.

'Walk or bus,' I said. 'Why?'

'I get taken in the limo—'

Then we simultaneously said the same thing.

'That must be nice!'

I stared at him.

'Nice?' I said. 'What do you mean, nice? It's getting

103

taken in the chauffeur-driven limo that's nice. What's nice about having to walk in? Or stand in a crowded bus?'

'I don't know,' Benny said. 'But I'd like to try it once – it sounds nice to me. Being free, you know, to make you own way, and dawdle around if you want – stop off in a shop, hang around, go through the park – all the things I can't do . . .'

'Why can't you do them?'

'Well, we live too far away from my school to start with.'

'What sort of school is it? Posh?'

'I don't know. I suppose they might think so – the people who run it.'

'Do you have to pay to go there?'

'I suppose so. Do you pay?'

'No,' I said. Then, 'What with?' I added. 'There's four of us,' I said. 'Altogether. They could never pay for four of us.'

'Four!' Benny said.

'Two brothers and a sister.'

'Do you have to share a room then?'

'Yes.'

'That must be nice,' Benny said. 'Being able to share a room.'

I just had to stop at that. I stopped and stared at him.

'Nice?' I said. 'Having to share a room? With Elvis? The king of the pigs? Nice? It's about as nice as having to share a room with a six-foot wart.'

We walked on, still following Nigel.

'You've got somebody to talk to though, haven't you?' Benny said.

'Believe me,' I said, 'all you want to do with Elvis is ignore him and pretend that he doesn't exist.'

'I'd quite like to have a big brother,' Benny said.

'You'd be better off with nits,' I told him.

'No, I'd like it,' Benny said. 'It sounds like you've got a great life to me.'

I had to stop again. In fact I practically had to have emergency oxygen and a lie-down.

'Great?' I said. 'Benny – you're the one with the great life. Not me. Your dad's the most famous footballer in the country, your mum's Mimsy Tosh, a celebrity in her own right and an ex-member of the Ketchup Girls. You've got more money than most people ever dream of, you've got a big house, you get driven round in limos and get to go on fantastic holidays and people pay you zillions of pounds to advertise Nicka Nackas and clothes for kids and, well, basically, you name it – so how come you think that I'm the one with the great life? Are you ill?'

Benny had stopped too. Nigel hadn't realised that we had both stopped and he had gone striding on, shouting, 'This way, darlings,' without a backward glance.

Nigel was one of those people who always assumed that everyone else was following him.

This can often be a mistake in my opinion, because usually, they aren't.

'Well – you can be yourself though, can't you?' Benny said. 'You don't have people staring at you all the time and wanting to be friendly with you just because you've got a famous dad and have your photo in the paper. I mean, your friends like you for who you are, don't they? Not for who your mum and dad are and what they've got.'

I didn't like to tell Benny that the only reason I was popular was because I looked like him, and that before I'd started looking like him hardly anyone wanted much to do with me at all. (Apart, maybe, from Sandra Debbings, but she didn't really count.)

'Well, Benny,' I said (and not without a touch of bitterness), 'if you think it's so great being an ordinary nobody, going to ordinary school and having an ordinary life and being ordinary from the moment you wake up in your ordinary bed until the moment you get back into it, then you ought to try it, just once, that's all I have to say. And then you'd know what being ordinary is all about, and you'd want to get back to your twenty-four bedroomed house—'

'Twenty-five, actually.'

'That was what I meant, your twenty-five bedroomed house – you'd be dying to get back there and back to posh school in no time.'

'Well, if you think it's so great being rich and famous, Bill, maybe you ought to try it, too.'

'I wouldn't mind,' I said.

'Well, neither would I mind,' Benny said. 'In fact, if I could, I'd even swap with you. If only for a day. Just to have your life for a while, and you could have mine.'

'Any time, Benny,' I said. 'Any time you feel like it. You just name the day!'

We were joking, of course. Or we seemed to be. Because even if we hadn't been, it would have been impossible. How could I ever have passed myself off as Benny Spinks in his own house, or he in mine? Fooling and confusing other people was one thing, but your own brothers and sisters, your own mum and dad – you'd never fool them, they'd smell a rat in no time.

Wouldn't they?

I said as much to him, asking him the same question.

'Well, wouldn't they, Benny?' I said. 'Wouldn't they?'

Nigel was coming back. He'd discovered that we'd stopped following him and was retracing his steps, trumpeting down the corridor like a dainty elephant.

'Bennies, darlings!' he was calling. 'Do keep up!'

Benny Spinks was taking a pen from his pocket. It wasn't an ordinary old biro with the cap missing like people usually have; it was titanium and gold. It had probably cost somebody about two thousand quid.

'Give me your mobile number,' he said. 'And your e-mail address.'

I hesitated, but then I told him. He wrote it all down on his arm. Then he told me his mobile number and e-mail address. I wrote that down on the palm of my hand and hoped I didn't start sweating before I got home.

I couldn't believe it.

I had Benny Spinks's mobile number. If Vicky Ferns knew I had that, well, what wouldn't she have given to get it. I could probably have sold it to her for fifty pounds a digit.

'Come along now,' Nigel was insisting. 'The shooting's all wrapped up and they need to close the studio.'

We were soon in reception. Benny Spinks's driver was waiting for him. Elvis wasn't waiting for me. I found him outside, leaning against the wall of Marshfield Studios and playing with his Gameboy. (Well, more accurately, it was my Gameboy and he'd helped himself to it without asking.)

'What kept you?' he said.

'I thought you were meeting me inside.'

'No,' he said. 'Outside. They wouldn't let me in, remember? I was too good for the place.'

A big stretch limo eased by. Elvis was in the way a bit and the driver parped his horn.

'Hey!' Elvis said, as the car drove off. 'Did you see

who that was? In the back of that limo? That was Benny Spinks, wasn't it? In person? The real, live, Benny Spinks.'

'Was it?' I said, acting casual. 'I didn't really notice.'

'He was waving at somebody too,' Elvis said. 'Who was he waving at? There's only me and you here.'

'Dunno,' I said. 'Maybe it was someone up at a window in the studio.'

'Well, well,' Elvis said. 'So I've seen the real Benny Spinks in person, in the flesh.'

'Do you think he looked like me then?' I asked.

'No,' Elvis said. 'Not in the slightest. You look like him though. I wonder who he was waving at?'

'Yeah, me too,' I said. 'I wonder.'

We went home then, Elvis walking too fast as usual, and making it difficult for me to keep up with him.

So Benny Spinks thought it would be nice to have a brother, did he? And to live in an ordinary house on an ordinary street and go to ordinary school and lead an ordinary life and be ordinary until the day he finally died – of something ordinary – and then they buried him in an ordinary coffin in an ordinary hole in an ordinary cemetery.

That was what he thought, was it?

I looked down at my hand, at the phone number and the e-mail address written there. I decided that when I got home, I might get in touch with Benny Spinks and maybe drop him a line or two.

I had a small suggestion to make.

To Benny Spinks.

As it turned out, I didn't even need to make it. He made it first. There was an e-mail already waiting for me when I got home, sitting there in my inbox. The sender was one B. Spinks by name. I made sure that the bedroom door was closed and that Elvis wouldn't come barging in. To stop him doing so, I jammed a chair under the door handle. Then I went back to the computer and double clicked on my e-mail, to see exactly what my new mate and look-alike Benny Spinks had to say to me. Because that was me, you see, good old Bill Harris, friend to the rich and famous and on first-name terms with the stars.

I wondered if maybe his e-mail was to invite me round to his house for a visit. Which it was; and it wasn't. That is to say, he was inviting me round to his house for a visit, only he wasn't planning on being there when I arrived.

Oh no. He was planning to be somewhere else entirely.

He was planning on being round at my house.

Great minds, you see (as the saying goes) think alike. (I believe the rest of that saying is, 'And fools never differ.' But we'll ignore that for now, as I don't think it's relevant. Or, at least, I didn't then.)

7

The E-mail

Hi, Bill. After meeting you today, on my way home in the limo, I started thinking about what we'd been talking about – you know, about being ordinary and being famous and all that and the difference between them. *'If you think it's so great, you ought to try it,'* right? Did you say that? Or was it me? Either way, it got me wondering.

When I got back home tonight Mum was out at a film premiere (I couldn't go too as it was over-18 only) and Dad's off in Germany playing in the international. So it was just me, really, and Joe (who drives the limo) and Alice and Dave (who look after the house) and George (who does the garden) and Tony and

Steve (who're in charge of security) and Liz (who helps Alice) and Alberto who does all sorts of stuff.

I had a bite to eat and then went up to my room. I ate on my own. I bet you ate with your mum and dad and brothers and sister. I bet you were all making a racket too and arguing and you wished you had some peace and quiet. But me, I just wished I had someone to talk to – apart from the people who work here. I mean, they're all really nice, but they still work here, they're paid to be here, you see. It's not the same, somehow. At least I don't reckon so.

I could have had a friend round from school, I guess, but you wouldn't believe the arrangements it takes, all the telephoning and the fetching and driving and getting picked up and dropped off and all that. It just doesn't seem worth it somehow when all you want is a bit of a chat – it all seems like too much trouble.

So anyway, I went on my computer and had a chat in the chat-rooms for a while. I belong to several and have different names. People don't know it's me, which is great, as I can say what I like then, and so can they. When people do know it's you though, and who you are, it's different. They're all over you, hoping for an invitation round to meet Dad or something, or they get nasty and say he played badly last Saturday and was rubbish, or they say my mum can't sing or something like that.

(I felt a bit bad then, when I read that part of Benny's e-mail, because my dad is always going on about Mimsy Tosh sounding like a load of spanners falling on to a tin roof. It had never occurred to me – nor to Dad either, I guessed – that if something like that got back to Mimsy or someone in her family it might actually hurt their feelings. I suppose that when it's somebody famous, you feel you can say what you like, you don't really think they have any feelings at all.)

So anyway, I had a chat for a while and then I got fed up with the chat-rooms. I mean, I don't know what you reckon, but I think they're all right for a while and then you get tired of them after that. So anyway, I played some on-line games for a bit, then I sort of wondered what you might be up to and whether you'd got rid of all the raisins yet! I hope so. I hope they paid you a lot too, for being my stand-in and having to get dirty and sticky. I hope they paid you the same as I got, or even more, as you deserved it.

(If only you knew, Benny, I thought. If only you knew.)

So anyway –

(I noticed that he wrote that a lot. I decided it had to be a sort of nervous habit of his, writing, 'So anyway.' Maybe it was the e-mail equivalent of stammering.)

So anyway, I got to thinking again about what we'd talked about – and you know something Bill, the more I thought about it, the more it seemed to me that it could really be done. I look so much like you, and you like me, we really could do it – we could swap places. We could. We could swap places, couldn't we, just for a little while, just to see what it really was like? I'm sure if we did it properly we could fool them all. Then we'd know, wouldn't we, who was right? Me or you? You think it would be great to be rich and famous, and I think it would be great to be just the opposite, which is all I've ever really wanted since I can remember.

So what do you say, Bill? Are you up for it? Just say no if you think it's too risky.

Maybe you don't think it would work.
Maybe you feel it would be too dangerous—

('Dangerous!' I heard myself say out loud. 'I don't think it's dangerous. Even if I did, it wouldn't stop me. Us Harrises thrive on danger. Well known for liking a challenge, we are.' Then I told myself to be quiet, and read on.)

But, in my opinion, it needn't be dangerous in the slightest. As long as we plan it properly and send each other lists of information and plans and maps of each other's schools and houses, and things like who we know and what we usually say to them – I reckon we could get away with it. We could do it, Bill. I could be you and you could be me – if only for a day. Wouldn't it be great, Bill? We could have a taste of each other's lives and nobody but us would be any the wiser. We could fool them all. You could have my house at your disposal, all twenty-five bedrooms! You could swim in our Olympic-sized pool and get to meet my mum and dad. I'm sure we could fool them too. And I could be you – and meet your brother Elvis, I'm sure I'd like him . . .

(You think? I thought.)

And your other brother and your little sister – I bet she looks up to you and thinks you're great. Mum and Dad are always saying they're hoping for a brother or sister for me one day, but one never seems to arrive. I don't know why.

So what do you say, Bill? Shall we do it? I mean, you don't have to. Just say it's a stupid idea if that's what you think and tell me to forget about it. It doesn't matter. But if we could do it, it would be great – wouldn't it?

Let me know what you think. No hurry. Either way, it was nice to meet you this afternoon. I can't tell you how freaky it was to see myself walking down the corridor towards me. For a second there, I'd thought I was walking towards a mirror. Crazy. I think I nearly freaked out, which was what brought my stammer back. So anyway, let me know what you think and e-mail me back some time.

All the best.

Your new friend,

Benny Spinks

I sat there and read the e-mail over again. The downstairs door slammed and I supposed that it was maybe Elvis coming back, but it was only him going out. There didn't seem to be anyone else around, or if there was, they were keeping quiet. It was as if I had the whole place to myself; and maybe I did, or maybe I didn't. It didn't matter. It just felt that way.

Mine, all mine. Our house. I thought of Benny Spinks and his house, which was *his, all his* and how it could be *mine, all mine* for a day, and our house would be *his, all his* then.

I wondered what he would make of it. He'd think it was small and cramped and poky, I guessed. Well, he was bound to when he was used to twenty-five bedrooms and Olympic-sized swimming pools with foot bath, sauna and jacuzzi. We had a bath though, so that was something.

I looked around the bedroom, eyeing the wardrobe where Elvis's and my clothes did constant battle. Elvis was always trying to encroach into my half, and so I'd retaliate by shoving my clothes over into his bit.

'I'm older and I've got more clothes so I should have more space!' he'd say. Mum told him he had to share it equally with me, but he was always trying to get a bit more for himself when she wasn't looking.

Then there was the bunk bed – him on the bottom and me on the top. I wondered what Benny Spinks would make of that, and how he'd enjoy having a big brother lying down there underneath him, kicking him up the back of the mattress when he felt like it, just to be mean and spiteful. He wouldn't like that either.

I carried on looking around the room for something Benny Spinks *would* like. I couldn't see anything. There was nothing that would do for him at all. He'd hate it, I reckoned, every inch of my house and every moment of being me. Yes. Maybe I should take him up on his offer. Maybe I should let him try it – give him a taste of what life for Bill Harris and all the thousands (or was it millions?) like him was like.

It would come as a shock. I was sure of that. But then again – if he wanted to try it . . . After all, fair dos to him, at least he was interested, at least he was curious. And it would be a good swap from my point of view, because I'd find out what it was like to be him – not just *look* like him, but *live* like him as well.

If we changed places, if only for a day, *I'd* be the one getting driven around in the big limo, and *I'd* be the one jumping into the swimming pool, and *I'd* be the one getting waited on hand and foot, with people catering to my every whim.

I could just picture it. There I'd be, lounging back on comfy cushions, and all I'd have to do would be to ring a little bell and Brian the Butler or Mavis the Maid would appear and it would be, 'You rang, sir? Can I be of assistance?' 'Yes,' I'd say. 'Could you just shift the telly round a little bit? I'm having trouble seeing it without moving, and I'm far too comfy for that. And while you're at it, a long cool drink and a couple of chocolate bars wouldn't go amiss – shaken, not stirred on the drink, and wrapper off on the chocolate.'

Yes, that would be the life. Benny Spinks didn't know how lucky he was. But then a day of being me might tell him. I was almost tempted to say yes. To be honest, I was more than *almost* tempted. I was sorely tempted. Sorely, seriously tempted.

But I had to be realistic. It would never work. Benny Spinks was a nice enough sort, you could tell that. His heart was in the right place – in his chest somewhere, same as mine. And he couldn't help being rich and having twenty-five bedrooms, but he didn't really have a clue. Being rich and having twenty-five bedrooms (and maybe about sixteen toilets as well) does that to people. They lose contact with reality, they get out of touch, they don't know what's happening out there in the real world.

It was all well and good him saying we should swap lives for a day, but how? You can't just swap lives the way you can swap stamps from a stamp collection, or picture cards of famous footballers, or stuff like that.

No, it seemed to me that Benny Spinks was overlooking one or two things – maybe even one or two hundred things. For starters, how exactly did we swap places? Where or when did our paths ever cross? We lived in different areas and went to different schools. He went to an amazingly posh and unbelievably expensive school, with the children of pop stars and lords and ladies. I went to an ordinary, not bad, bog standard, let-anyone-in school, along with the children of other people who worked for Inter-Netty.

I knew the school Benny went to. It was about three miles away from mine. It had big gates and a long driveway and private grounds. It looked like a stately home, from what you could see of it, half hidden behind great, huge, leafy trees. When you walked past you'd see Rolls Royces and Bentleys and big stretch Mercs with tinted windows ferrying their charges to school. Nobody ever seemed to do anything as simple as walk there.

My mum said that they'd made films at Benny's school, using it as a backdrop for historical dramas which they showed on the telly after I'd gone to bed. (Or at least I hoped it would be after I'd gone to bed or Mum would have made me sit down and watch them too.)

And outside of school, where did our paths ever cross? Nowhere, as far as I could tell. Benny had his own swimming pool, so he wasn't likely to turn up at the public baths for the splash-about session, when they had the inflatable octopus and the plastic treasure island in the water. He had acres of garden too, so he wasn't likely to turn up at Flowerstones Park for a kick-about of an evening. He also had his own skateboarding ramp – I'd seen it in a feature in *Okey-Dokey Weekly* – so he wouldn't be heading down to the Green for a spot of skateboarding either. He had his own private fifty-seater cinema at home too, for inviting all his friends round to, when it was his birthday – so he wouldn't be turning up at the local Showcase to see the latest James Bond.

There were other problems to take into consideration too. Benny might look like me and I like him, but that didn't mean he had my mannerisms or gestures or my tone of voice. You might fool other people as long as you didn't open your mouth, but how could I be at Benny's house, pretending to be him, and not saying a word to his mum and dad when I was spoken to?

Unless . . .

Bad throats.

Yes. Maybe. We could both pretend to have bad throats, or laryngitis, and we could speak all croaky, then no one would get suspicious. Yes. Bad throats, there might be something in that.

And bad legs. It was only a thought. Just came into my mind, really. I was only half serious. But it was worth considering. Because if anyone who knew you wondered why you weren't walking or standing or sitting in the usual way and they asked what was up with you, all you'd have to say was . . .

Bad leg.

Bad leg might just do it. Especially if you said it in a croaky sort of voice – which you would, due to your bad throat. And, of course, people would be more willing to accept a bad leg if you had a bad throat, because they'd think you were coming down with something, in which case, they wouldn't bother you too much, and if they thought you weren't your usual self, they'd put it down to your bad leg and your bad throat and to you coming down with something.

I decided that I might e-mail Benny Spinks with a few constructive suggestions on the bad leg front, just to see what he thought of it. Because we definitely looked like each other, and if we both had bad throats, we'd sound like each other; and if we had bad legs, we'd walk like each other.

In which case, we'd get away with it!

So I checked that the chair was still jammed under the door, and then I jammed another in under it, to be on the safe side. (I always have to be careful as Elvis is the sort of person who reads other people's e-mails if he gets the chance. I knew this because I had found a reference to one of my e-mails in one of his e-mails which I happened to read by accident.)

Then I got to work.

Hi, Benny,
Thanks for your e-mail. Nice to hear from

you. I've got rid of the last of the raisins, I think, though I did find a couple in my shoes. About what you suggested. I think we ought to keep this secret and just refer to it as 'the project' or maybe 'the suggestion' from now on, or how about 'the great switcheroonie'? That way we'll know what we're talking about but nobody else will.

It seems to me that it's not a bad idea and it could be done. There are a few problems though – I guess most of them are pretty obvious, and you'll have thought of them already. I may have found a way around them though, with something like bad legs and/or bad throats; that way anything unusual about anyone could more easily be explained away.

Some of the other problems are a bit more complicated though, and not so easy to deal with. The main one is the switch around, and after that, the switch back. I don't know how this can be done. Do you have any ideas?

But the biggest problem is knowledge and information. I'll need a map and a plan of your place and you'll need one of mine. I'd also need everyone's names and pet names and family jokes and in-jokes and a bit of personal history and likes and dislikes and all that – or we'll never be convincing otherwise and the cats will be out of the bags in no time.

So I suggest we make lists, like you suggested – one each. And let's take our time. List all the things I ought to know and I'll do the same for you. Tell me how you eat, for example. Do you use a knife and fork together, or do you tend to cut things up first and then just mostly use the fork? Anything you can think of like that. Do you take a shower or a bath? Do you brush your teeth from left to right or right to left? When you sit down, do you put your feet up on the chair or what? You might be left handed for all I know, Benny. Are you? I'm not.

So let's make those lists up then and send them to each other. If one misses something out, the other one can tell him, and if that one misses something else out, the other can tell him too.

Let's do that then, and take our time. We can't hurry this as bad planning will wreck it. And try to think of how and where we can do the switch. Right now, I just can't think of anything, but something might come to mind soon.

I'll be in touch then, when I've made up my list. This is going to call for big thinking, so don't expect anything in a hurry. Give it a week – OK?

All the best.

Your double,

Bill

I clicked on Send and Receive and off it went. I heard the front door open downstairs. Elvis was back. He'd probably nipped out down to the corner shop to buy himself a lottery ticket. He always got a lucky dip on a Saturday. I didn't know why he bothered. He had *loser* written all over him, as I used to tell him – until he threatened to strangle me if I said it again.

I moved the chairs away from the door, then hurried back to the computer. I was about to close it down, when there was the 'ping' of an e-mail arriving.

It was from Benny Spinks. He'd done a quick Reply to Sender. It was short and to the point.

OK, Bill, you're on. Get back to you in a week with my list. Will spend some thought on the great switcheroonie. Write you soon. Benny.

The door opened and Elvis walked in.

'What are you doing?' he said.

'Nothing,' I told him.

'What's that e-mail you're reading?' he said.

'It's mine,' I told him. 'Mind your own business.' And I logged off, so he couldn't see it.

'I'm going to find out your password one day,' he said. 'And when I do—'

'I already know yours, as a matter of fact,' I said.

He stared at me, looking mean, not believing me, but in a state of doubt just the same. His eyes narrowed.

'What do you mean – know my password? How did you find my password out?'

'I guessed it,' I said.

'How?' he said.

'It was obvious,' I said.

'Oh yeah,' he said. 'So what is it then, according to you? What is this oh-so-obvious password of mine then?'

'There's only one thing it could be, Elvis,' I said. 'One and no other.'

'So what is it then, clever guts?' he said. 'You tell me what my password is.'

'OK,' I said. 'I may be wrong, but I don't think so. I think I'm right in saying that your password . . .'

'Yeah?'

'Is none other . . .'

'Yeah?'

'Than moron. That's m-o-r-o-n, Elvis – in case you're too stupid to spell it. I think it's case sensitive too. In fact, I think it ought to be in capitals. That's you, Elvis, a capital M-O-R-O-N!'

Oddly enough, he didn't actually say anything in response to that. Though I have to admit that it hurt a bit, when he hit me with the bean-bag and then sat on it, with me underneath.

It was a long fifteen minutes, that was.

I was glad when it was over.

8

Job Description

If there's one person you know everything about –
and, in some surprising ways, *nothing* about – it's
yourself. Making up that list of things which Benny
Spinks needed to know about me in order to pass
himself off convincingly as me was one of the
hardest things I've done.

It took ages. I spent hours there tapping at the
computer keyboard, or sitting in class, sucking on a
Biro, trying to pay attention to the lesson with one
half of my mind while the other half mulled over all
the things he had to know.

I started off with Likes and Dislikes. They were
easy enough. But when I got into things like
Favourite Sayings and Nervous Ticks and Unusual
Personal Habits and How I Eat My Dinner, it all
began to get complicated. Because most of those
things you seldom bother about. You never ask

yourself how you do them, you just do them without thinking, they're first and second nature to you.

How I Walk, for example.

I wrote, 'One foot in front of the other', but that wasn't much help, as one foot in front of the other is how everyone walks. You don't get many people walking with both feet together at once – unless they're kangaroos. Which isn't walking anyway, it's jumping.

The trouble with little personal habits (which can be extremely irritating to others) is that often you simply don't know you have them. There isn't really a mirror you can hold up to things like that. You have blind spots about how you seem to other people.

Mrs Campbell, who takes us for English (although she is Scottish), is always quoting Rabbie Burns to everyone. (He was Scottish too and is Scotland's national poet. They celebrate his birthday in Scotland every year by getting drunk on whisky and eating haggis while listening to the bagpipes. My dad says this is the only way to listen to the bagpipes. He says that if it wasn't for whisky you would never be able to listen to the bagpipes at all and would probably go mad, and that the Scottish invented whisky as the remedy for bagpipes and as a means of putting up with them without committing suicide.)

So anyway (as Benny Spinks would have put it – I was getting into being him already), Mrs Campbell was fond of quoting a line of Rabbie Burns's which went, *O wad some Pow'r the giftie gie us To see oursels as others see us*! (Or something like that.)

She even translated this for us too, as she spoke both English and Scottish quite fluently. She said it meant, *If only we could see ourselves as others do*. Which I thought was pretty true, really. If only Elvis could have seen himself the way I did, with all his faults and disgusting personal habits. If he could just have done that for a few minutes, he'd have realised what a low and despicable person he was, and he would have changed his ways immediately. I dare say he'd have sworn off sticking his finger up his nose when he thought nobody was looking (but everyone could see him) for starters, and as for the noises he made in the bathroom, well, it was no wonder the vicar stopped coming round.

It was a problem really. Maybe self-knowledge always is. I felt that left to my own devices I would never know enough about my own little quirks and mannerisms to be able to pass the information on to Benny Spinks. So I decided to ask around, but to be discreet about it. I started with Sandra Debbings. I found her round at the back of the Portakabin during break-time, hiding from the tumult. She was reading some girly book (judging by the cover) about lurve and that kind of thing.

'Hey, Sandra,' I said. 'Can I ask you a question, if I'm not interrupting you too much?'

'Of course you can, Bill,' she said. 'I'm never too busy to talk to you.'

(I just tried to ignore that. It makes me nervous when people are too friendly. I prefer it when they're irritated that I've turned up and are anxious for me to go away – it's more what I'm used to.)

'Sandra,' I said, 'could you answer a question for me? Truthfully, that is. I don't want you to be polite to spare my feelings or anything.'

'I'll try, Bill,' she said. 'What's the question?'

'Well,' I said, 'have I got any funny habits?'

'Funny habits? You mean funny ha-ha? Or funny peculiar?'

'Either. Anything I'm always doing but I'm not aware of. A sort of trade mark, you know – if you saw somebody else doing it, you'd think, Well, well, that's Bill Harris all over again.'

'Ah, I see,' she said. 'Why do you want to know?'

'No special reason,' I said. 'Just curious – that is – I'm getting into self-improvement and trying to be a better person and stuff. I thought that if I could find out what my irritating quirks and annoying little habits were, I could try to iron them out a bit. So do I have any?'

'Well, yes, you do have some habits,' she said. 'I dare say I have too. But I wouldn't ever want you to get rid of them, Bill. I mean, I wouldn't have called them annoying, I'd have said that some of them were quite charming in their way. They make you *you*.'

She was making me nervous and getting me worried again, saying things like that. My philosophy, however, is that when faced with girls it is always best – whatever the circumstances – never to show fear. You should never panic and run away when faced with girls, as this is the wrong thing to do, for there is always the danger that if they see you panicking, they might take it as a sign of weakness and come after you in hot pursuit.

I stood my ground therefore and just said, 'So what sort of things do I do then, Sandra, that I might not know about?'

'Well,' she said, 'I don't know if you realise, but you're always fiddling with your ear lobe.'

'Am I?' I said, surprised to find – even as I said it – that my hand was fiddling with my ear lobe, my right one.

'But don't feel you have to stop,' she said.

I didn't know if I could. It was like a comfort blanket to me, that ear lobe. But I'd make sure that I told Benny Spinks about it. He'd have to take up ear-lobe fiddling himself, if he was to pass himself off as me.

Looking at Sandra, I guessed that she was the acid test. If Benny Spinks could fool her, he'd be able to fool anyone in the school. As for my family, I wasn't so sure. Your family know you better than anyone, but on the other hand, nobody takes you for granted like your family either. You could grow another head and it could be several weeks before they noticed, and even when they finally did, they probably wouldn't be particularly bothered about it. Or, if they were, it would only be as to how it affected them.

I could just picture Elvis coming down to breakfast one morning, finally noticing that I'd grown another head.

'Mum,' he'd go, 'Bill's grown another head.'

'Oh, so he has,' Mum would say. 'That's annoying. I'll have to get him some new shirts now, ones with extra collars. That is a nuisance, and more expense as well.'

'You'd better get him another baseball cap while you're at it,' Dad would say. 'To keep the sun off. Though where he thinks we're getting the money for extra baseball caps and double haircuts, I can't imagine.'

Then my little sister would start banging me on the heads with her spoon going, 'Oh look, dwubble boiled eggs!' and she'd try to stick her toast soldiers in all four of my ears.

Then my eldest brother Kevin would look in on his way out and go, 'Oh great! Now we've got a two-headed freak in the family!' And he'd be off, instantly forgetting about it, all wrapped up in thoughts of where he was off to that evening.

Elvis, meantime, would be looking for injustices and things to moan about.

'I hope fat face – or should I say fat faces – isn't

133

going to get twice as much to eat just because he's got twice as many faces to stuff now.'

'Of course he isn't,' Mum would say. 'All because you've got two heads, it doesn't mean you've got two stomachs.'

'Just as long as he hasn't got two bums,' Elvis would say.

'Now, now,' Mum would tell him. 'No need for that sort of talk, especially at the breakfast table.'

And that would be it. They'd just carry on as normal, and there I'd be, with this extra head I'd grown, and they wouldn't even take me down to the doctor's.

So that's the thing about families – they know you better than anyone, and they take you utterly for granted.

I stopped fiddling with my ear lobe for a minute.

'Do I have any other habits, Sandra?' I asked.

'You wrinkle your nose a lot,' she said. 'And furrow your eyebrows when you're thinking.'

'I never knew that.'

'I mean, you don't do it often.'

'What – think, or furrow?'

'Furrow, of course!'

'That it?'

'More or less.'

'Nothing else at all?'

'Not that I can think of.'

134

'OK, well thanks, Sandra,' I said. 'I appreciate you being so frank and everything.'

'I hope you don't think any of it matters, Bill,' she said.

'Sorry?' I said.

'I mean . . . they don't matter – a few little faults. Nobody's perfect.'

'No,' I said. 'Right.' I edged away. It's my experience with girls that as well as not showing any fear, it is best to clear off while you're still ahead. 'OK, well – my – look at the time,' I said. 'Best get moving. Break'll be over in a few minutes.'

'Bill . . .' Sandra said. 'Before you go . . . I've told you your little faults and habits – tell me mine.'

I stared at her.

'Yours?'

'Yes.'

I went on staring. I felt my brow furrow in a thoughtful way. It was that habit of mine, and I'd never been aware of it before.

'Well?' she said.

'Well . . .'

The strange thing was that I couldn't think anything, not one single thing wrong with Sandra Debbings at all. Not one. I mean, someone like Vicky Ferns, I could have found a million things wrong with her. She was vain and pushy and superficial and only interested in looking good and coming first and being the best and getting one over on other people and getting taken to the pictures and having free smoothies.

But Sandra . . . she was – I mean, I know nobody ever *is* – but to me, she seemed – at that moment, just then, round at the back of the Portakabin – sort of . . . perfect.

So after a long furrow, I said, 'You chew your hair.'

'I'll try to stop.'

'N-no!' I blurted out. I don't know why. I almost sounded in a panic. 'No! You mustn't.'

'Why not?' she said.

'Because,' I said, 'if you did, well – you wouldn't be you any more. And you wouldn't want that, would you – not to, well . . . be who you are.'

She looked at me thoughtfully.

'No,' she said. 'Maybe not.'

'I gotta go,' I said.

'See you, Bill,' she said.

I made to leave.

'Bill . . .'

'Yes?' I said, turning back for a moment.

'Nothing,' she said. 'It's all right.'

So I left her to her book.

I went looking for Dave Spencer – who tells everyone what's wrong with them, even when they don't want to know – and asked him if he thought I had any distinctive features.

'Yes,' he said. 'You take ages to pay your debts. You owe me a pound.'

I'd forgotten all about that and I gave it him back.

'Anything else about me?' I asked.

'Yeah,' he said. 'You don't owe me a pound any more.'

I could tell he was in one of his stupid moods so I left him to it.

I found Vicky Ferns holding court over by the wall. I collared her for a quick word.

'Vicky,' I said, 'do I have any faults or personal habits that I might not know about?'

'You have one fault and one fault only, Bill,' she said.

'What is it, Vicky?' I asked, intrigued.

'You aren't the real Benny Spinks,' she said.

She flounced off to rejoin her friends. I called after her. 'What if I was?' I said. 'What if I actually was the real Benny Spinks, not just a look-alike, but the real Benny Spinks, standing right here in this yard?'

She stopped and looked back at me.

'If you were the real Benny Spinks, Bill Harris – you wouldn't need to ask. I'd know the difference immediately. And then you'd see.'

That was it. She was off.

We'll maybe see about that, Vicky, I thought. If me and Benny can find a way to do it, he might be standing in this very playground one day soon, and I'll be round at his posh school, pretending to be him. And I wonder if you will know the difference.

I wonder if you really can tell instant from percolated, and margarine from butter, and Coke from Pepsi, and me from Benny Spinks, like you think. Perhaps we'll see one day. Maybe we will.

That evening, when I was up in my room, I asked Elvis if he thought I had any distinctive personal habits that I might not be aware of.

'Yes,' he said. 'You stink.'

Which I didn't think was very helpful, to be honest.

Later on, when we were both in bed, I leaned down, just after he had put the light out, and said, 'Elvis—'

'Shut up,' he said. 'I'm going to sleep.'

'I just wondered if you could answer a question for me – for my homework.'

'What?'

'Are skunks native to this country, Elvis?'

'No, of course they aren't. You only find them in zoos.'

'Oh.'

'Why?'

'Because I just wondered what you were doing with a skunk in your bed.'

'I haven't got a skunk in my bed, thicko.'

'Oh, well, if it's not a skunk in your bed, that horrible disgusting smell must be you then—'

To be honest, there are disadvantages to sleeping in the upper bunk bed. He must have kicked me up the mattress for a good twenty-five minutes. The only comfort I could take from it was that he was keeping himself awake as well.

Over the following days, I compiled a complete and comprehensive list of my personal habits and general lifestyle. I also compiled a detailed timetable of all my waking hours. Then I made a list of all my interests, likes and dislikes, my hobbies, pet sayings, favourite swear words, and a whole ream of personal stuff which Benny Spinks would need to know if he were to successfully pass himself off as me for five minutes, let alone a whole day.

I wrote down everything he ought to know about my family too – cryptic references, holiday anecdotes, what it meant when my brother Elvis said, 'Toolbox again!' and everyone started to laugh, and how he ought to react to it. I wrote down what my little sister meant when she pointed at the window and said, 'Parrot shoes!' and what you were expected to do about it. I racked my brains and memory for everything that he might need to know.

By the time I had finished, I had quite a few pages of close-written information on how to be me. I guess that it was the *Bill Harris Working Manual*, with all the facts and inside information on how to be Bill Harris.

I typed it all up on to the computer and e-mailed it to Benny Spinks as an attachment. I wrote a few words to accompany it, and to ask how he was getting on with the *Benny Spinks Working Manual*, and whether he would be ready to send it to me soon.

There was still one outstanding, vitally important question, however, which needed answering, and I didn't know how to answer it. I just hoped that Benny did.

Dear Benny,

I've thought long and carefully in compiling this list and here is all – or at least most – of what you need to know to be me. It's all here, I think, from the things I like to eat to family in-jokes and about school and so on. I hope you'll be able to remember it all when the time comes. But if all else fails, at times of danger, I think our rule should be to say nothing and act dumb. It's a rule that's never let me down before.

I hope the attached makes useful reading. I'll look forward to getting all the info on how to be you when you've had a chance to do it.

Any luck yet on working out how to do the big switcheroonie? I'm afraid I've not been able to come up with anything. It's easy enough for me to get away, as I have plenty of opportunity for sloping off and nobody would notice. But it sounds different for you, what with your security guards and limo drivers and all the rest. It seems to me that someone's always got an eye on you. Well, let me know if you can work a way around it. Here's hoping.

You know, Benny, I'm starting to get quite excited about this, and think that maybe we can really pull it off and fool everyone. How many people ever get the chance to be somebody else for the day? Not many I don't think, though I bet a lot would like to.

Hope to hear from you soon.

Best,

Bill

I clicked on the Send icon and off the message and attachment went, away into the depths of cyberspace, to the frontiers of the internet and beyond – which was pretty good, really, considering that Benny Spinks only lived about fifteen miles away. I sat and wondered how long it would take for him to get back to me. The way it worked out, it didn't take him long at all.

9

The Switcheroonie

Hi, Bill. Here's the deal. I've worked out a way to do the old switcheroonie. We do it at my school at the end of the school day. Here's how the plan goes.

Joe, our limo driver, usually drops me off and picks me up at the school gates. The school doesn't like people being driven in up the driveway as it's a narrow, one-way road and causes traffic problems. So everyone gets dropped at the gate. They also think that as most of us get driven everywhere, then walking up the driveway (about half a mile) is good, healthy exercise – though personally I get enough of that in the pool.

(Well, he would, as there was only him in it. He

probably had his own personal shark to chase him up and down and make sure that he did his lengths.)

> There's usually a teacher or someone standing at the gate to keep an eye on us. There are security cams as well, linked up to the lodge house – so we're going to have to be careful and quick. By the gates is a high wall and just inside, a copse of bushy trees, and that is going to be our only chance. What I suggest is this.
>
> First, can you make it from your school to mine, so you can be near the gates when I come out? I know this might be difficult and that you might have to leave your school early and then get a bus across town or something.

(No problem, Benny. I can bus it or bike it. I could even jog it.)

> We finish school at four-twenty.

(That was good. I finished at four. Which gave me a twenty-minute start.)

> It takes me ten or fifteen minutes to get my stuff together and walk up to the gates. I can dawdle around and spin it

143

out to twenty minutes to give you more time. I daren't push it much longer though, or Joe will start to wonder where I am and come looking. So the latest I can leave it to get to the school gates is four-forty.

(That gave me a clear forty minutes to get to his school. I could do that. No problem.)

Now here comes the tricky bit. What'll happen on the day is totally unpredictable, so this is only an outline and we might have to play it by ear.

Joe, the limo driver, parks as near to the gates as he can. If he's early and gets a good spot where he can see me come out, he stays in the car. If he has to park around the corner, he gets out of the car and waits by the gates, to make sure I'm not left standing on my own, wondering where he's got to. I can't predict which one it'll be. Maybe, if it's too difficult, we'll have to call the switcheroonie off and do it another day. Flexible is the keyword here.

Now, if you can get to the gates just before twenty to five, here's what to do. First, you walk inside the grounds and turn right. I don't think anyone will stop you, because you'll be wearing school uniform and blend in – our blazers are pretty similar colours, I dare say. The only real difference is the badge on your pocket, and they probably won't even notice. If anyone does talk to you, or call you by my name, just grunt at them and make out you're in a hurry, or that you've forgotten something. If you're not there on the day we've agreed, I'll know something's gone wrong and we'll just have to rearrange it.

(OK, Benny. We'll do that.)

So anyway, you walk into the grounds, turn first right, and there by the wall is a huge tree, a willow I think, with leaves and branches down to the ground, almost like a cloak.

(Sounded to me like you couldn't miss it.)

You can't miss it. Walk under the canopy of branches. I'll be in there waiting. We switch bags and blazers and ties. Hopefully the rest of our uniforms will match. Ours is grey trousers, black shoes, dark socks, white shirt.

(Snap, Benny. Snap, and snap again.)

So we swap blazers and bags. We wish each other luck. Then you go out first. Joe sees you, he waves or calls you over. You get into the limo and off you go to be me. I wait a couple of minutes, I come out, walk into the street, and go off to be you.

A day later, we do everything the other way round. We meet back under the willow, swap blazers, ties and bags back. You'd better do my homework and I'll do yours, as it'll probably have to be handed in next morning. I know our handwriting won't be the same, so we'd better use computers for any written stuff. Numbers should be OK. If that proves impossible, we just don't do the homework, or pretend to have lost it or something. It's not going to kill anyone, missing one day's homework. Or just do it anyway. The teachers probably won't even notice our handwriting is different on the one occasion, or we can say we had bad fingers and did it with our left hands.

So what do you think, Bill? Is the plan watertight? Can you see any leaks in it? Let me know what you think. You'll see there's an attachment to this e-mail. It's my list of everything I could think of that you'll need to know about me to pass yourself off as yours truly. Thanks for the list you sent me. I've been studying it and trying to remember it all off by heart and have been practising furrowing my brow and pulling at my ear lobe.

I'm waiting to hear from you, Bill, and to hear whether you think the plan's a good one. If you see any snags, let me know, and once we've got them straightened out it's just a matter of setting a date and having the nerve to do it.

It's sort of scary, don't you think, and kind of exciting too. I get goose bumps and butterflies just thinking about it. Do you think we really can go through with it? I think we should both be able to change our minds, right up to the last moment. But once that moment is past, we have to swear to see it all the way through. Part of me's half terrified about this, Bill, and another part of me can hardly wait. Is that how you feel too?

(You bet it is, Benny. You can put all your dad's millions on that.)

I'm looking forward to hearing from you,
Bill. No rush – but don't take too long
either.

Yours truly,
Ben

It seemed all right to me. I couldn't see any holes in
it. But then, as my brother Elvis is fond of saying,
'You couldn't find holes in a fishing net.' Not that I
was expecting it to be easy, there were bound to be
some snags on the way, but as far as I could tell,
Benny's plan was doable. It was just a matter of
setting the date.

Meanwhile, there was his Things You Need To
Know About Me file to read. So I double-clicked on
the attachment he had e-mailed me, and waited for
it to open up. (Our computer is dead slow. It's been
like that ever since Elvis fixed it. Most things don't
work once Elvis has fixed them.) But finally the
document appeared on the screen.

Important and Vital Things
You Need to Know About Me
For the Great Switcheroonie
– by Benny Spinks.

1) Most important fact of all, number one
– I'm allergic to peanuts. So whatever you
do, don't eat anything that even looks as

if it might have peanuts in it, or it'll be an immediate giveaway.

So no chocolate, I'm afraid, if the wrapper says Caution, May Contain Traces of Nuts. Even tiny traces are enough to set me off. You're all right on Nicka Nacka bars, however, as they are guaranteed nut-free.

(Maybe. But there was no way I was ever eating Nicka Nacka bars – they held bad memories for me. I'd rather go without.)

2) Next thing, as you can see, I've scanned in a little hand-drawn map of our house and the grounds. You'd better try to memorise the layout, because if you get lost in the house and have to ask directions, people are going to get suspicious or think you've lost your memory due to some brain-wasting disease or because you've been knocked on the head.

3) Next thing is my goldfish. Full feeding instructions are enclosed. Same with the gecko, who only needs a locust every now and again. They are in the box marked Locusts. The gecko is in the cage marked Gecko.

4) Next thing is everyone's name and what they do. Joe drives the limo, Alice and Dave look after the house, George does the garden, and Tony and Steve are in charge of security – they work on shifts. Liz helps Alice and also does some cooking. Alberto does all sorts of stuff, and you can't miss him as he's got an Italian accent. In the mornings Paula comes in. She's a kind of secretary and helps Mum and Dad with their letters. They both get millions of them from people we don't know. They want autographs or signed photos or want to find out how to be a footballer or a pop star (or both, in some cases) or they want to know if you can spare some money. Sometimes we get invitations to something, like a party or a concert or an opening night. If we took up all these invitations, we'd never be at home.

Don't worry too much about putting faces to names. Most of the people in the house just say, 'Hi, Benny,' and I say 'Hi' back. So if you can't work out who someone is, just smile and say, 'Hi!' and they'll never notice.

5) School. I'm also enclosing a list of my friends and enemies at school and a

layout of the place, so you'll know where everything is there too.

6) Terrible secrets. Here's my terrible secret which I guess I'm going to have to tell you, or otherwise your not knowing might be a bit of a giveaway. But keep it to yourself, Bill, because it's the sort of thing that newspapers love to get hold of and if they did, it would be a big embarrassment. The fact is that I'm no good at football – or any ball games whatsoever. I know I ought to be, but I'm not. I can't kick a ball straight to save my life, although my dad must have shown me a million times. But it's no good, I just can't do it, so I don't reckon I'll be following in his footsteps or in Mum's, as I can't sing either. It is a bit of an embarrassment, like I say, only Dad doesn't mind really, he says you have to be yourself and do what you're good at – only I'm not quite sure what that is yet (if anything) but maybe something will turn up.

So anyway, whatever you do while you're pretending to be me, don't get involved in games of football, or if you do, make sure you play really badly –

(No difficulty there, Benny.)

> – and if you have to do any hymn singing
> in morning assembly or anything like
> that, make sure you're right off key.

(No big problem there either.)

> That's it for now. I won't burden you with
> any more. Too much information is as bad
> as too little and I wouldn't want you to
> get information overload.

I read through the lists he had made. There was no way I could take it all in at once, I'd have to go through it several times. I was distracted too and a little shocked at the revelation that Benny Spinks – the son of Derry Spinks, one of the highest paid and best soccer players in the world – was useless at football.

It was hard to believe. You'd have thought that he'd have been born with a silver boot in his mouth, with his shirt and shorts on, all ready to trot out on to the pitch and start banging them into the net.

But I suppose there's no earthly reason why you have to be good at what your dad's good at. As far as I knew, I didn't have any natural talent for installing high-speed internet broadband connections, like my dad. So why should Benny Spinks be any different?

I sent Benny a quick e-mail back, just to let him know that I'd got his and that I was 'reading, learning and inwardly digesting' (as Mr Jubber, our French teacher likes to say) the facts he had sent me and was 'committing them to memory'. (He likes to say that too.)

I also told him that I reckoned his school uniform was pretty much like mine too, but just to be sure, would he take a photo of his with his digital camera (I knew he was bound to have one) and send it to me so I could see for myself. If there was any problem, I would let him know. I then asked him to let me know what dates would best suit him and I fired the e-mail off.

Then I printed out all the information he had sent me, turned off the computer, and lay down on my bed, reading it through and trying to picture myself in his shoes, in his house, saying 'Hi' to the gardener – whose name was . . . don't tell me now . . . yes! It was George – and to Alice, who helped Paula out— no, no, that was wrong, it was Paula who helped Liz out, and Joe who did the cooking – no he didn't, he drove the limo – or was he one of the security guards?

I had to start again.

As I did, I heard Elvis coming up the stairs, accompanied by his big feet and his even bigger mouth.

I hid the pages under my pillow and lay there looking up at the ceiling. I could have reached up and touched it, if I'd wanted to, it was that close. Sometimes, if I woke up in a hurry, not quite knowing where I was, I'd bang my head on it as I sat up.

There was a little dent in the ceiling from all the banging over the years. My head was all right, I didn't have any dents in that, but there was definitely a dimple in the ceiling, from years of accidental head-banging.

Of course, it was all right for Elvis, he had plenty of room down in the lower bunk, he never banged his head at all.

He kicked the door open – as usual – and came in.

'What are you doing?' he said. 'Clear off. I want to change my shirt.'

'That's a first, Elvis,' I said. 'Clean shirts. Whatever else? You'll be having a wash next.'

'Shove off,' he told me. 'I want to get ready to go out.'

'I don't see why I have to clear off just because you want to change your shirt,' I said. 'It's my room as much as yours.'

'No it isn't,' Elvis said. 'It's my room and I just put up with you being here. But frankly, I'd rather have rats.'

I decided to ignore him. I had my private plans

and schemes, and he didn't know anything about them.

He stood on the lower bunk and looked at me. His nose was about five centimetres away from mine. It isn't a pretty sight either, not that close to you – Elvis and his nose.

'What are you up to?' he said.

'Nothing,' I said. 'Go away. You make the place look untidy.'

'I know you,' Elvis said, 'and you're up to something.'

'Push off, Elvis,' I said. 'Why don't you go and play with that nice roll-on deodorant Mum gave you for Christmas. You know, the one that's got "Please. Please Use Me" written on it.'

'You're up to something and I'm going to find out what it is,' Elvis said.

'I'm not up to anything,' I said.

'Then what are you doing lying there looking at the ceiling?' he said.

'I'm admiring the dent,' I said.

'You're a liar,' he said.

'Not as big a one as you,' I said.

'At least I haven't got a big dent above me,' he said.

'No,' I told him. 'I bet you've got a big dent in your mattress though, from years of farts.'

He got me by the nose then, squeezing it between two of his fingers, and giving it a twist.

155

'That's enough of your lip,' he said. 'Any more cheek from you and you won't just have a dent in the ceiling, you'll have gone straight through it and your head'll be inside the loft! Got it?'

I was sorely tempted to retaliate and to give Elvis a taste of my famous poke in the ear, but the trouble was he was a lot bigger than me, and if I'd got him really riled, he'd have hammered me something serious. So I let him twist my nose for a while, but inside I was seething, and I promised myself that one day I would be revenged upon him and then he'd be sorry.

Eventually he got tired of twisting my nose and he let it go.

'And let that be a lesson to you,' he said.

'It was, Elvis,' I said. 'It was a lesson in what a total bullying twit you are.'

'I'm in a hurry,' Elvis said. 'Lucky for you.' He got his shirt from the wardrobe (I noticed it was hanging on what was rightly my side) and went out.

I gently rubbed my nose with the flat of my hand, trying to ease the ache and to get a little life back into it.

I was worried, to be honest. Not about me, but about Benny Spinks. If he was going to be me for a day and a night, then he'd have to sleep in my bed, with my brother snoring away in the bunk beneath him.

I felt that maybe I hadn't given him enough warning about Elvis and what he was capable of. I could cope with a nose-twisting, as I was used to it. I could shrug it off and recover in a few minutes. But what would Benny do if my brother picked a quarrel with him, thinking he was me? (Which was the whole idea, of course.) Benny might not like having his nose twisted. Rephrase that. Benny *would* not like having his nose twisted. Nobody likes having their nose twisted. But what if he started to yell and scream? Or even to cry? What if he shouted, 'How dare you! Do you have any idea whose nose you're twisting? I happen to be Benny Spinks!'

Of course Elvis wouldn't believe a word of it, and he'd twist it even harder.

Yes. It was a problem really. If I didn't say anything to Benny about Elvis, then he wouldn't be ready for him. But if I said too much, it might put him off the whole switcheroonie idea completely. Forewarned was forearmed – but foreterrified was another thing entirely.

I decided I'd just warn him to be wary of Elvis, but I wouldn't go into details about the nose twisting or Elvis's other speciality, the Chinese neck burn.

After all, as Benny himself had said, once we were both committed, we'd just have to play it by ear. (Even if Elvis happened to be twisting it at the time.)

Adapting and improvising as we went along was going to be half the fun of it. It wasn't just a matter of us being each other for a day, there was the thrill of fooling everyone, and of actually getting away with

157

it. It would be like committing the crime of the century – like the perfect robbery, the greatest con-trick ever. We'd have fooled them all, and we'd have pulled it off, like a couple of master criminals. And, what's more, we'd have got away with it.

Or so I thought.

At the time.

10

Ready, Steady . . .

My cheque came from Mr Mugg of Plug Uglies –
three hundred and fifty quid (less his commission).
I'd never had so much money.

I went and showed my cheque to Elvis, just to
annoy him. First he said that it was nothing and that
if it had been him they'd have paid him thousands
of pounds for being a look-alike.

'A look-alike of what?' I asked him. 'As far as I can
tell the only thing you could ever be mistaken for is
a carthorse's bum.'

He went and stole my cheque then and made out
that he had ripped it up and flushed it down the
toilet. I had to get Mum on to him to make him give
it back.

Once I had paid it into my bank account, he tried
to borrow it off me – in cash.

'I've got a sure-fire investment for you, Bill,' he

159

said. (I knew he was up to something by the fact he was calling me Bill. Usually he calls me Blubber Face.) 'Let me have your three hundred and I'll double it for you in no time.'

'I think you're confusing the word "double" with the word "spend",' I told him. There was no way I was letting Elvis get his hands on my money. It would turn itself into a big pile of DVDs and computer games in no time.

It was nice to have some money in the bank. I couldn't think of what to spend it on, so I didn't spend it at all. There were so many things that I could have bought, many of which I had always wanted. But now that I could afford to buy them, I didn't seem to want them so much any more. I wanted other, more expensive things, that I couldn't afford.

I kept hoping that the phone might ring again and it would be Mr Mugg with more look-alike jobs for me. But he stayed quiet. It seemed that not all that many people wanted a Benny Spinks look-alike. I began to wonder if I should try to start looking like somebody else – like Marilyn Monroe or maybe Attila the Hun.

Elvis suggested that I should become an Elvis impersonator (Presley that is, not Harris) but I couldn't see the point as there are thousands of Elvis impersonators already, most of whom look nothing like him. I thought the world needed another Elvis impersonator like it needed a hole in the ozone layer.

All the time this was happening, while I was leading my ordinary, boring existence, my secret life was going on too, as the real Benny Spinks and I plotted the great switcheroonie.

Benny Spinks's dad was in the news quite a lot. First he was a big hero for scoring three goals in an international; then four days later he was a huge disgrace for missing a penalty, a week after that he was back in everyone's good books for scoring the winning goal in the closing minutes of a big match; then he was all over the front pages for twisting his ankle, then there was a rumour that he was giving up football for ever and becoming a monk; but Benny sent me an e-mail saying that wasn't true. So I had all the inside information.

Benny's mum, meantime, had a new record out. I heard it a few times on the radio. It was called *Never Get Over It*. It wasn't really my cup of tea, but then I don't suppose she was expecting people of my age to buy it. My dad disliked it on principle.

'Good idea,' he said, 'calling it *Never Get Over It*, because I don't think my eardrums ever will.'

I also saw her singing it on the telly. As I sat and watched her I practised saying 'Mum', because that was what I would have to call her, come the great switcheroonie.

Elvis caught me at it. He'd sneaked in without me noticing.

'What are you saying "Mum" to the telly for?' he demanded. 'Is the telly related to you then? Does it tuck you up at nights and read you bedtime stories?'

'No,' I said. 'I'm not related to the telly. But I suppose that whenever you see a chimpanzee, Elvis, you probably go up to it and say, "Hello, Dad", and it probably looks at you and says, "There's my boy!" in chimp language. Did you know that you'd been adopted by Mum and Dad because they thought you looked sad and all alone when they found you picking fleas out of your fur round at the Animal Sanctuary for Retarded Primates with Learning Difficulties and Personal Hygiene Problems?'

I have to say that those Chinese neck burns of Elvis's don't half hurt.

Then it finally came. The big e-mail. It was short, pithy, and to the point.

> Ready if you are. Don't think I'm ever going to get any readier. What do you say to next Tuesday? Meet me by the gates of my school at 4.40. We'll do the switcheroonie, then I'll meet you back there at the same time the day after, and we do the switcheroonie back again. It's then or never, I think, Bill. If we leave it much longer my nerve's going to go. What do you say?

I went cold. I don't mind admitting it. It had all been great up until then, all the scheming and dreaming and planning and thinking. But doing. Actually *doing*. That was a different thing.

Then I thought – what's the worst that can happen? (I like to picture the worst that can happen, because then if it does, you're ready for it, and if it doesn't, well, it's a bonus.) The answer to the question was, nothing much.

It was true. Nothing much could happen really. A few people might get annoyed and a bit angry, that was all. But it wasn't as if we were doing anything criminal. It was just a bit of fun. If the worst came to the worst and I had to confess to Benny's mum and dad that I wasn't actually Benny at all, but an impostor and a look-alike, well, it would only take a phone call to my mum and dad and everything would be sorted out.

They'd be livid, of course, and angry at being fooled, but there wouldn't be any real harm done. So what was there to be nervous about? Nothing really. If the worst that could happen was the worst that could happen, then what reason was there to worry?

So I reached out and I clicked on Reply to Sender.

Ready when you are, Benny. Let's do it.
I'll be there, next Tuesday, outside your
school, 4.40 on the dot. Take your mobile

and I'll take mine. That way we'll still be able to keep in touch, even when we're in each other's houses. If any sticky situations arise, we can ring each other up for advice. Can't believe we're really doing this. Yours, Bill

A reply came immediately.

Can't believe we're doing it either. But it looks like we are. If there's any last-minute news or information, let's get in touch. Otherwise, see you as arranged. Any unforeseen problems, we can always abandon mission, right up to the very last moment. Just phone or text or something. Looking forward to being you for a day. Hope you enjoy being me and aren't too disappointed if it doesn't live up to what you think. Yours, Benny

But I couldn't really see that at all. How could being Benny Spinks not live up to – well – being Benny Spinks? It was all your dreams come true, like getting to be a film star for a day.

I was going to be the richest boy in the country, with a world-famous dad and a world-famous mum. I was going to live in a house with twenty-five bedrooms and its own Olympic-sized swimming pool complete with diving boards, plunge pool, jacuzzi, sauna and steam room. On top of that, I was going to go to a posh school, and ride round in a chauffeur-driven limo which was the height of swank and which was so cool it was practically an iceberg on wheels. I was going to have a taste of wealth and luxury, of being waited on hand and foot and probably leg as well. How could that possibly be a disappointment? How could I not enjoy being the real Benny Spinks?

I was going to love every moment of it.

It was Benny I was worried about – how was he going to cope with the shock of suddenly having to be me? No limos for me. It was legs or the bus.

No Olympic-sized swimming pool round at my house; just my little sister's inflatable paddling pool that needed a patch on it as it had a puncture. No bedrooms the size of ballrooms, no enormous bathrooms; just the downstairs loo and the one bathroom upstairs that we all had to share.

And then, of course, Benny would have to cope with Elvis. My eldest brother Kevin wouldn't be a problem, he was usually out of the house, and even when he wasn't, it felt as if he was. But how a rich, pampered type like Benny was going to cope with a psycho thug and clot brain like Elvis, I didn't know. He'd probably have a nervous breakdown and run screaming from the house, yelling, 'I'm not really Bill Harris at all, I'm Benny Spinks!' And everyone would humour him and say, 'Of course you are, that's right. You're Benny Spinks, Bill, that's who you are,' as they waited for the van to arrive and for the men in the white coats to bring the special jacket and the stretcher.

But there was nothing I could do about it – except warn him, which I'd already done, several times over. But I didn't really know if any of it had sunk in. It's hard to explain to somebody who has no brothers or sisters exactly what having them is like. It's a bit like trying to tell someone what toothache is like, or what having a spear stuck through your head is like. The only way to get the full impact is to go and try it for yourself.

Tuesday. Next Tuesday.

I went through all the information Benny had sent me, over and over, until I knew it all off by heart – names, family sayings, things that had happened, stuff they might refer to: in-jokes, nicknames, what to say if his gran phoned, all that kind of thing. I knew the geography of the grounds and had a map of the inside of his house imprinted on my brain.

Tuesday, and I was ready already.

Six days to go.

I counted those days down the way they count the seconds before rockets take off for outer space. As the numbers went down, the butterfly quota went up; first it was just one butterfly in my stomach, but by the time Monday night came, it was a swarm.

I lay in bed, looking up at the dent in the ceiling, which I'd banged my head into a hundred times. I wondered if Benny would bang his head too, and whether I ought to warn him about it, or maybe I already had.

It was dark, but the glow of a streetlamp came in from the pavement. There wouldn't be the glow of any streetlamps in Benny's room. His room would be dark as a cave; no passing traffic for him; no lorries heading for the supermarket in the early hours of the morning; not for Benny, resting peacefully in his private estate. No disturbed sleep for him.

Elvis was snoring. It was a grunty sort of snore, that stopped and started, then was quiet for a while. He sounded like a didgeridoo.

I closed my eyes and waited for sleep to wash over me, but it didn't seem to want to do much washing that night. Meanwhile the insects fluttered away in my stomach, like moths trapped in a wardrobe, nibbling away at your winter woollies.

The alarm blasted me awake. Elvis woke up too, muttering and moaning, same as usual. This was it then, this was the day. The day of the great switcheroonie.

I got up and made a point of standing on Elvis's head as I climbed down from the upper bunk. He swore at me and made various threats, most of which he was too lazy to carry out. He got hold of my big toe though and twisted it, which hurt, but it was worth it just to get to stand on his ear.

I got dressed and had breakfast. Debs, my little sister, was already down. She was always an early riser. She was having boiled eggs and she wanted to play the game where she pretends that I am also a boiled egg and she gets to bang my head with a spoon and to stick toast soldiers in my ears.

Strangely, I felt a bit sad. I let her get on with it and I pretended to get monstrous angry with her, as she expected me to do, and I made ogre faces and did a deep ogre telling-off voice, to act scary. But I was a bit sad.

You'll be banging Benny Spinks's head tomorrow, I thought, and sticking toast in his ears. I wonder if you'll suspect that it's not really me.

I felt sad to be leaving. It was weird. There I was, off to be rich and famous at last, if only for a day, off for a taste of the highlife. But a little part of me – to be honest, quite a big part of me – didn't want to go any more. I wanted to call it all off.

It's just nerves, Bill, I told myself. Only to be expected. Benny's probably feeling the same right now too. It's nerves and cold feet. Once you get out the door and get going, you'll be fine.

I didn't eat much breakfast. When Mum wasn't looking, I put half my cereal down the sink. Then it was time to go. I looked around the kitchen as if I might never see it again. I don't know why I felt like that, I just did. I even gave Debs a kiss on the head. I think she thought I'd gone mad.

'Soppy!' she said. Then she rubbed it off with her hand. Then she called me back, and hugged my finger.

'Bye, Debs,' I said. 'See you soon.'

She gave my finger a bit of a bite, but it was a friendly sort of bite, I thought.

In a way, I felt there should have been something memorable to mark the occasion, something to shout out that today was a different day, a special day, that new and exciting things were about to happen.

But the kitchen clock went on ticking, and the fridge hummed and nothing was different at all. Then I was on my way. Out of the house and heading down the road. It was eight-twenty-five. In another eight hours and fifteen minutes, I'd be at the gates of Benny Spinks's school, getting ready for the great switcheroonie. A day after that we'd be switcheroonie-ing back again.

I was going to be Benny Spinks for twenty-four hours, and he was going to be me. Then we'd both get back to normal. I thought.

Because that was the plan; that was what was supposed to happen. But as another of Mrs Campbell's favourite Rabbie Burns sayings goes: *The best laid schemes o' mice an' men Gang aft a-gley*. Which she also translated from the original Scottish for us.

It means that it doesn't matter how well and how carefully you make your plans, something will screw things up.

She said that there was also an Irish version of this, known as Murphy's Law. Murphy's Law states that if anything can possibly go wrong, then it will. And it did.

11

. . . *Go*

As soon as the bell went for the end of school, I was off. I didn't run, but I moved quickly. I checked my phone to see if there were any texts or messages, but Benny hadn't sent me anything, which I assumed to mean that everything was fine. The traffic was bad so I didn't bother with the bus, I just walked swiftly, making good time, jogging a bit now and then.

I was across town in twenty-five minutes and heading along the wide, leafy roads that led to Cheadlehulme College for the Sons and Daughters of Gentlefolk (Established 1532). I slowed down and dawdled a little, I didn't want to get there too early. I could see all the expensive cars parked waiting for the children to come out. Most of the drivers looked like parents, but some of them were obviously chauffeurs – I didn't think many parents would be sitting there in uniforms and peaked caps.

171

Joe didn't wear a peaked cap. Benny had already told me. He just wore a T-shirt and jeans. I spotted him at a distance. The numberplate of the car was SPINKS, though I think some of the letters were really numbers – like a 5 made to look like an S.

I didn't want Joe to see me. When he, the teacher on gate-duty and the security camera were all looking the other way, I slipped through the gates and into the school grounds. I saw it immediately – there was the willow with the long, drooping branches and the leaves brushing the ground. I pushed the leaves aside, like parting a bead curtain, and stepped under the green canopy.

'Benny? Ben?'

He wasn't there. I checked my watch. I was bang on time – maybe a few minutes early. I heard voices. School was out. Children were walking up the long driveway from the school to the gates, where their rides home were waiting.

Come on, Ben, I thought. Before I lose my nerve and run. Come on!

There was a rustle of branches behind me. I turned and there I was. OK – there *he* was. But it was uncanny how much we looked like each other. I'd almost forgotten about that. We were like two copies of the same newspaper. Or maybe, to be more accurate, we were like one of those spot-the-difference cartoons. You've maybe seen them. You get two pictures of the same scene, one above the other, and the caption tells you that there are six or ten differences or whatever between the two pictures. Only you have to stare and stare sometimes to find them. You can't just tell from a glance. Sometimes you even have to get a magnifying glass out. The differences are always in the details.

Which was the same with Benny and me. There were differences, of course. But you couldn't readily see them. Not without getting the magnifying glass out. As long as nobody looked too closely, they wouldn't be able to tell us apart.

And why would they look too closely? People see what they expect to. Most people don't have to be fooled into believing things by anybody else – they're already fooling themselves. And they're generally quite happy to do so.

'Benny!'

'Bill!'

'We really doing it?'

He was as nervous as I was and having as many second thoughts. I could tell just from looking that the butterflies were at him too. We could have changed our minds, either of us. The other one wouldn't have minded. It would have been no disgrace.

'I don't know. Are we?'

A car horn blared from out in the street, probably an impatient parent, trying attract their child's attention.

It shook us into life.

'We'd better get moving.'

'OK. Swap blazers.'

'Right.'

'Make sure you've got your own stuff from your pockets.'

'Done that.'

'Got your phone?'

'Yeah. You?'

'Yeah. We'll call if there's a problem.'

'Yeah. Or text. Better swap bags and ties now.'

'Right. OK. Am I doing your homework or doing my own?'

'You'd better do mine and I'll do yours. Mine's got to be in by tomorrow morning.'

'OK. We're probably at the same levels. What have you got?'

'Maths and Spanish. What have you got?'

'Maths and Russian.'

'I don't do Russian!'

'Yeah, well I don't do Spanish!'

'What'll we do?'

'Let's just do each other's Maths homework and leave the languages. We'll just have to hand those in a day late when we've swapped back again.'

'OK.'

'Right.'

I put his jacket on. It fitted a treat. He was wearing mine already. Then we swapped bags and ties.

'OK.'

'Anything else?'

'Don't think so.'

'One thing, Benny . . .'

'What?'

'What do you usually say to Joe the driver, when you get into the car?'

'I told you. In the e-mail.'

'I've forgotten. Remind me again.'

'I wave as I get near. I sit in the front next to him. He always says, "Seat belt." I say, "I know." He asks me what kind of a day I've had. I say "All right." He says, "Benny, that's all you ever say." I grunt. We move off. I ask to change the radio station to Radio One as the one he always listens to is boring. He says, "I suppose so," and changes it. We don't say much after that – if anything. If he does say anything, I usually just grunt. And that's about it till we get home. Now, how do I get to your house?'

'I told you, Benny! I e-mailed you the map.'

'I forgot it. I left it in my room.'

'Flipping heck.'

I told him the way and made him write my address down so that he could ask for directions if he got lost.

'Or phone me,' I said. 'You can get a bus to my house or walk it in about half an hour.'

'OK. That it then?'

'That's it.'

'Right. You go out first.'

'See you back here tomorrow – same time. For the switcheroonie back.'

'Right.'

'Good luck, Ben.'

'I'm Bill now.'

'Good luck.'

'Good luck.'

'Give me a couple of minutes before you come out.'

'Will do.'

For some reason I put my hand out, and we shook hands. Then I picked up his bag and headed out from the canopy of the tree when he suddenly called me back.

'Wait!'

'What?'

'Watches! We forgot!'

I felt a bit embarrassed, giving him my cheap old watch in exchange for his Rolex. But he didn't seem to mind. I nodded cheerio, listened out to hear if there was anyone around, heard nothing, and pushed the willow branches aside.

I heaved Benny's bag up on to my shoulder and headed for the gate. I walked out into the street. Joe, his driver, was at the wheel of the limo, reading a newspaper propped up against the dash. He saw me and began to fold the newspaper up and put it away. I smiled, waved, and headed towards the car.

Click!

The door opened.

'Hi, Benny.'

'Hi, Joe.'

I sat in the front seat next to him.

'Seat belt,' he said.

'I know,' I told him, and I buckled it on.

I could feel him staring at me. Something was wrong.

It was my voice.

'Got a sore throat?' he said.

'Just a little,' I said, rubbing at my Adam's apple.

'Thought you sounded a bit different.'

He started up the car.

'Can we listen to Radio One?' I said. 'This station's a bit boring.'

He gave a sort of put-upon, exasperated sigh. But you could tell he didn't really mean it. He changed the station. He slipped the car into drive, indicated and pulled out into the traffic.

As he did, I saw a boy come out from the gates of the school. He was wearing a slightly different blazer from the others. But he looked vaguely familiar.

He turned and walked back the way I had come – heading back into town and towards the neighbourhood where I lived.

Joe and I, meanwhile, were driving towards the motorway. We took the first exit and followed a long, country road. Ahead of us, up on a hill, I could see a vast house, the size of a stately home, surrounded by landscaped gardens and fountains and acres of lawn and a maze created from hedges. Even from this distance I could see peacocks strutting about and in a nearby field there were horses and next to that stables and outhouses. Beside the house was a building big enough to hold an Olympic-sized swimming pool.

My heart beat faster and I couldn't help but smile. It was going to be no problem being Benny Spinks as far as I could tell. I wondered how he was getting on with being me.

My phone buzzed. I took it out and read the text message.

'On the bs!' it read. 'Nvr bn n a bs b4! Grt! Bny!'

So he was doing all right too. Him on the bus, me in the limo. Both nearing our destinations, and soon we would both be home, to the arms and to the bosoms of our families.

I wondered what would be for tea. I already knew what Benny would be having. Tuesday was fish fingers with chips and peas and a strawberry yoghurt for pudding. But what was I getting? I hoped it wouldn't be anything too posh.

The limo turned off the road. Joe stopped the car, wound down the window, and talked into an intercom by some electric gates. I noticed that there was a security camera mounted on a high post next to it. There was a buzz and the gates slowly opened. We drove on through.

The road led through a deer park. You could see

them, behind some fencing, bounding around and nibbling at leaves. We drove for ages past lush grass and beautiful lawns until finally we rolled to a halt with a satisfying crunch on the gravel driveway of the great mansion.

'Here we go then,' Joe said.

'Thanks, Joe,' I said and opened the door and got out.

'Bag!' he reminded me.

'Oh yeah . . .' He handed it to me. 'Thanks.'

'I'll go park up by the garages.'

The car moved off.

That was when I saw it.

How Benny could have overlooked it, I really do not know. Not even to this day can I imagine how he could possibly have failed to tell me about it. Maybe he was just so used to it. Maybe it was like part of the furniture. Maybe he had just grown up with it and took it so much for granted that he wasn't aware that he needed to tell anyone about it. Perhaps he assumed that everybody already knew.

Only I didn't. And I didn't know what to do. I just froze to the spot, with this mounting panic and a sudden sense of terror.

Bounding across the lawn towards me was the biggest, tallest, most enormous dog I had ever seen. It was heading straight for me at about fifty-nine miles an hour. Slobber was flying off its big floppy jowls like water coming out of a garden sprinkler. It had teeth the size of planks and ears that an elephant would have been proud off. It was heading straight for me.

Just then my phone buzzed. I had about three seconds to read the message, and then I'd be dead.

'Fgot abt dg. Nme Rudolph. Bny.'

Thanks Benny, I thought. Thanks for that. I'll know the name of the dog that killed me now. That'll be nice. As its fangs sink into my throat and I drift into unconsciousness, I'll be able to think to myself, It's good old faithful Rudolph who's doing this. And that'll make it all a whole lot better.

Then there he was – about half a ton of dog meat, coming at me like a rocket. He skidded to a halt, shook his head, sprayed everything around him with a coating of slobber, opened his mouth to bark something, then stopped and stared at me with perplexity and unconcealed hostility as if something were seriously wrong.

As if I were some kind of an impostor.

He walked around me, growling and snarling.

'Good boy,' I said. 'Good boy. There's a good Rudolph.'

He snarled even louder when I used his name.

He had me rumbled. He knew I wasn't Benny. I tried to get friendly with him. I reached out to pat him on the head. He snarled again and snapped at my hand with the plank-sized fangs.

What should I do?

Somebody would see us. Joe would appear from the garage. Or somebody would look out of a window. They'd see me standing there, afraid to move, with Rudolph the enormous dog basket case standing there, getting ready to rip my throat out. And they'd know I wasn't Benny too.

'Here boy.'

The bag. I slipped it off my shoulder and held it out slowly.

'There you go, Rudolph. It *is* Benny, you see. Because this is Benny's bag, isn't it? There. Have a little sniff of Benny's bag. Never mind me. You just stick your nose into that. And Benny's blazer too, see. Have a sniff of Benny's blazer.'

He did. He looked puzzled. But he looked less hostile. Then after a few more sniffs, he seemed positively friendly. Too friendly really, because he got all sort of pally then and slobbered over my trousers. I patted him on the head.

A voice called from a distance. I lifted my hand to my eyes to shelter them from the sun. It was a woman on a horse – and it was a face I recognised. It was my dad's favourite singer – Mimsy Tosh.

I waved to her.

'Hi, Mum!' I called.

'Hi, Benny!' she said. 'Good day?'

'All right!' I said. 'What's for tea?' I shouted.

'Ask Alice,' she said. 'Probably what we always have on Tuesday.'

Caviare and champagne, I supposed.

Then she cantered away, calling, 'Why don't you go and have a swim, and then you can do your homework?'

'I might,' I said. 'Will do.'

Rudolph had found a ball from somewhere and he wanted me to throw it for him, which I did, even though it was covered in slobber too – like everything else within two metres of him. I pitched the rubber ball as far as I could, right into the bushes. While he ran off to look for it, I walked over to the front of the mansion and opened the door. I walked into a great hall, full of high staircases and beautiful carpets. The door swung closed behind me.

I was home.

The young master himself was back from school, feeling a bit peckish and wanting a snack, and then maybe a nice relaxing swim afterwards, in his own Olympic-sized swimming pool.

'Hello!' I called. 'Anyone in?'

(It was what Benny always said. He'd told me.)

'Hello, Benny,' a voice called. 'In the kitchen.'

For a second I had a mental blank. I lost the map in my head, the one of Benny's house. Kitchen, kitchen, kitchen. Left or right or down the corridor in front of me? Then somebody dropped a pan, which gave me my bearings. I followed the crash to the kitchen, pushed the door open and went in. A woman was making jam. It had to be Alice.

'Hi, Benny.'

'Hi, Alice.'

'Good day?'

'All right.'

'Milk and biscuits?'

'Wouldn't mind.'

'On the table.'

'Thanks. When's tea?'

'Usual time.'

'Is it the usual?'

'Usually is.'

'Thanks Alice.'

'You're welcome.'

'See you.'

'Bye.'

I left the kitchen and took my milk and biscuits upstairs. I'd had to struggle not to stare when I'd gone into the kitchen. It was unbelievable. The stuff! The size of it! The goodies in the fridge!

How the other half live, I thought. I could tolerate a bit of this. This was the kind of life I could put up with for a few years, with absolutely no trouble at all. I could tell I'd been born to luxury, really. I just took to it, like greenfly to roses, like a duck to water. I just felt in my element.

A man came down the stairs as I was going up. It wasn't Benny's dad, I knew that much. He had a shaved head and big shoulders and looked tough. So it had to be one of the full-time security guards, there to protect the family from unwanted autograph hunters and publicity seekers and to make sure that intruders didn't get in. Intruders like me. There were two full-time security men, and Steve was the one with the hair.

So . . .

'Hi, Tony.'

'Hi, Benny. Good day?'

'All right. Might go for a swim later. About half an hour?'

'OK. I'll be there.'

He went on down the stairs.

Benny had told me that he wasn't allowed in the pool on his own. Somebody else always had to be there and Steve or Tony were usually happy to double up as lifeguard.

I called to him.

'Oh, Tony . . .'

'Yeah?'

'Dad home yet?'

'Nah! Of course not! He's playing tonight, remember?'

'Oh, of course, yes. I forgot. Is it on telly?'

'Yeah. But with the time difference, it'll be past your bedtime, mate.'

'Can you record it for me?'

'Yeah. Sure.'

'OK, thanks.'

He hesitated.

'Here – something wrong with your throat?'

'Think I might have a slight touch of laryngitis.'

'Yeah. I thought you sounded a bit different. You want to take some throat pastilles for that.'

'Yes, I will, thanks.'

'You think you ought to go swimming with a sore throat?'

'Oh, it's not a cold – it's just . . . I probably got it from shouting – at school – we were messing around.'

'OK. Half an hour, you said?'

'Yeah.'

'OK then.'

He disappeared and I found the door to my room. My own, very own room that I didn't have to share with anyone.

I bet that Benny wouldn't have a dent in his ceiling from suddenly sitting up in his bunk bed and almost bashing out his brains.

Turn right at the top of the big staircase, walk along, left into the first corridor, right into the next corridor, second door on the right – my room.

That was what he had told me, and now here it was. I turned the handle of the door. Benny Spinks was back to his own home turf, after a long hard day at school, and his room was no doubt dying to see him. So I opened the door and I went in, to see in even finer detail exactly how the other half lived.

12

The Other Half

Well, you could have parked a couple of fire engines in there, and still have had room for the bulldozer, the executive jet and the hippopotamus. And the stuff! Benny Spinks had so much stuff that his room looked like some kind of stuff store. He didn't just have wardrobes for his clothes, he had wardrobes for his stuff too, and chests and dressers, all full of stuff. (He probably had wardrobes for his wardrobes if I could have found them.)

I opened all the doors and drawers and peered in at all this stuff. There was the latest of everything; he had gadgets galore and a flat-screen TV about the size of a small wall.

I didn't know if his mum and dad had bought all this stuff for him, or if half of it had been freebies which had been given to his dad and he had passed them on.

My dad says rich and famous people never have to buy anything. People are always giving them stuff for free – like cars and clothes, so that they'll be seen driving them and wearing them, and everyone will want to be like them and will go and get the same thing. It's cheap publicity, I suppose. But it seemed strange to me that the people with most money had to buy the least, while those who hardly had any money never got given anything.

I just gawped at all of Benny's stuff. He'd said that I could use anything I wanted to, but I didn't feel like it, not straightaway. It was a bit overwhelming. It was like being locked in a sweet shop – there was all this delicious stuff around you, but you just didn't know where to begin.

Instead, I went exploring and opened the door to Benny's own private bathroom. The bath was enormous and it had gold taps and was sunk into the floor, like a little pool. And it was just for *him*. We didn't have a bathroom a patch on this at home. I felt a bit jealous then, which I hadn't done once so far. But now it didn't seem fair that some people should have so much. In fact, I had half a mind to be Benny Spinks for ever, and not swap back with him at all. But I knew that was impossible, and the moment soon passed. I quickly ate my snack, then I used the loo – which had a gold-plated flush – and then I went to borrow a pair of Benny's swimming shorts to get ready for the pool. He'd said I could, so it was no problem. He must have had a dozen pairs, all brand new and still in their wrappings. I knew his dad got loads of sports stuff as he endorsed a brand of sports gear and all the shorts must have been free. I chose a pair, found a towel, and headed for the pool.

The upper part of the house was quiet. I decided to do a little exploring before my swim. I walked the length of the first floor, quietly opening doors and peering into rooms. There were so many bedrooms you lost track of them, and each one was furnished in a different way, along some kind of a theme – like an oriental bedroom in the tropics, for example. There was even a bedroom fitted out to look like the inside of an old railway carriage.

I didn't meet anyone. I could hear faraway voices from downstairs. I tried to imagine Benny, coming home from school to this every day. It was luxurious all right, but it didn't half feel empty. I could picture him rattling around in his enormous bedroom, wondering which bit of stuff to get out of the stuff cupboard.

It was the silence though. That was what got me. It was never like that in my house. There was always somebody talking or arguing or Kevin asking where his shirts were or Elvis on the phone or Mum talking about what had happened at work or Dad shouting at the television or Debs bashing something with a spoon. But here, all the sounds were muffled and distant. It was like being behind thick glass.

I headed back downstairs. The heavy carpets swallowed the sound of my footsteps. The house was connected to the swimming pool by a covered walkway, so that you wouldn't have to get wet if it was raining. Even though getting wet was the whole point of going to the pool.

I found the changing room, changed and went to the pool-side. Tony was there, to act as lifeguard. He was sitting on a chair at the far end of the great long pool. I waved to him, and he waved back. He seemed a mile away. The surface of the water was flat, with not a ripple on it. I jumped in and the ripples spread out, then I started swimming.

It was strange to have it all to myself, and once again it was the silence which was the eeriest thing of all. No kids yelling and laughing, doing handstands and playing chase, or diving for locker keys, or jumping in and bombing the other swimmers while the attendants blew their whistles and shouted at them to pack it in or they'd be out.

Just me, swimming along, like a little lonely boat on a great flat ocean, pushing the water aside as I headed towards the distant shore. Then there I was at the other end. There was Tony. He nodded, I nodded, then I was off again, back the other way. Mine all mine, it was. Every drop and inch and Italian tile of it. I was a little Neptune, king of the swimming pool. King for a day.

I got out at the deep end and climbed up on to the lowest of the diving boards. I bounced and dived. It wasn't a bad one. Not great, but not a belly flop. I got out and tried the next one up, until eventually I was on the very top one, looking all the way down, right through the placid, limpid water to the very bottom of the pool, which made the drop seem even further.

'You be careful now, Benny!'

It was Tony, watching from where he'd parked his chair.

I wasn't a good enough diver to dive from here. I'd have belly flopped like a great, flat fish. So I put my hands by my sides and jumped. It was horrible – fantastic but horrible, both at once. It was like being on one of those theme-park rides where you leave your stomach behind you for a while and then it catches up with you later.

Ker-splash!

My feet actually touched the bottom of the deep end, then I sprang back up to the surface.

I gave Tony a thumbs-up to let him know that I was all right. He gave me one back, as if to say, 'Good one.' But maybe he was just being kind. After all, I was the boss's son. He was hardly going to tell me I was rubbish.

I did a couple of widths then – two of them underwater. When I tried to do a length underwater I couldn't manage it; the pool was too long – though

190

I could do a length underwater in our local pool, no trouble, and still have some breath to spare.

I decided to get out. It was great to have the pool all to yourself, but it hadn't been quite as great as I had expected. In some ways I preferred our own pool, even though people were always splashing you and getting in your way. I wasn't used to having anything all for me and me alone. I was so used to sharing. I'd never done anything else.

'I'm going now, Tony. Thanks!'

He waved from the other end of the pool, stood up and folded his newspaper.

'OK, Benny,' he said. 'I'll see you later.'

I went in search of the showers. They were power-showers, which pumped out hot water at a tremendous rate; if you put the dial to the correct setting, it hammered out like nails, thumping you on the back, giving you a bit of a shoulder massage to make the tensions of the day flow away.

Then I took one of the big, white dressing gowns, put it on, and headed back to my room to do Benny's homework and to get ready for dinner.

His homework wasn't much different from mine and he seemed to be at about the same place on the syllabus. I managed to finish his Maths – though I wasn't sure about some of the answers. I thought I might have got one or two wrong, but at least I'd done them and shown my workings, so he'd get some marks for that.

I flicked back though the book to see what he had got for his other Maths homeworks and so as to try and copy the way he did his numbers. He was about the same standard as me – a seven or eight out of ten usually, with occasional lapses down to three or four when he'd been in a rush or just wasn't trying.

I didn't bother with his Russian homework; there was no point in me touching it. The only Russian word I knew was vodka. It was practically a foreign language to me.

As I was finishing Benny's Maths off the phone rang – Benny's land-line. I was a bit hesitant to pick it up, but in the end I did and said a tentative, 'Hello?'

'Hello, Benny. My, you do sound as if you've got a bad throat.'

'Nothing serious,' I said. 'I'm sure I'll be back to normal in a day or so.'

'What time did you want tea?'

It had to be Alice, phoning from the kitchen.

'Eh – any time really.'

'Twenty minutes?'

'Fine.'

'Just come down then.'

'OK, thanks. I will.'

'I think your mum's got a do tonight so it'll just be you.'

'Yeah, OK.'

'See you soon then. I'll do the Tuesday usual.'

192

'Lovely.'

I hung up.

I didn't dare ask what the Tuesday usual was, as I was plainly supposed to know. It was probably going to be caviare and lobster washed down with fine wines. I just hoped I liked caviare. I had no idea what it tasted like. I just knew that rich people ate it, so Benny Spinks probably had it all the time, even in his sandwiches – if he took a packed lunch.

It came as no surprise to me that his mum was off to a do. She was always off to dos as far as I could tell. Every time my mum brought home a copy of *Okey-Dokey Weekly* there Mimsy Tosh would be, standing about at another do. Maybe it was the opening of a new restaurant, or the opening of an art exhibition or a new night club or a new film.

'She'll go to the opening of anything, that woman,' my dad said. 'I bet if you sent her an invitation, she'd go to the opening of a jar of pickled onions, just as long as a photographer was going to be there and she was going to get her face in the papers.'

I thought that was a bit unfair, as she was a pop star, after all. But she did seem very keen on getting her photo taken, that was true enough.

I watched a bit of big, flat-screen telly for a while then I strolled down the stairs towards the kitchen, acting casual as if I owned the place. I pushed open the door and went in.

'Hi, Benny.'

'Hi, Alice.'

'I've put you in the dining room tonight, is that all right? Your mum's got people round tomorrow and I've a lot of cooking to do in here.'

'Yeah, that's fine.'

'If you go and sit down, I'll bring it in.'

My mind went blank and for a second I couldn't remember where the dining room was in relation to the kitchen. I went and confidently opened a door, and found myself staring at a load of tins and packets.

'What did you want, Benny?'

'Just wondering if we had any ketchup. I thought I might have some on my caviare.'

Alice started to laugh.

'There you go,' she said. 'Always joking.'

It was news to me.

'I'll bring the ketchup in with me,' she said. 'You go and sit down.'

Fortunately the next door I opened was the dining-room one. It was more of a banqueting room really. I sat down at the end of a long, enormous table, which had one single, solitary place setting on it – mine.

Alice brought my tea in.

It was fish fingers and chips. With peas. Plus a glass of milk. And ketchup. For pudding, it was a raspberry yoghurt.

It was home from home.

I tucked in, a little disappointed that there wasn't any caviare, but relieved to get something edible.

Alice left me to it, and there I sat, on my own at the end of this dining table, which was about as long as the trailer of one of those lorries you see on the motorway.

It was a lonely life being Benny Spinks, I thought. It was all right having the chauffeur-driven limo and the gadgets and the stuff and the Olympic-sized swimming pool with power-showers, but you weren't half on your own a lot. I supposed you got used to it and didn't notice after a while. It was nice too, to be able to sit and eat a meal without having to listen to Elvis make sarky remarks about you and not to be banged on the head with a spoon by your sister.

Yes, it was nice and quiet and peaceful. It was just so—

Then the door opened.

'Hello, Ben.'

It was his mum – my mum – my mum for now: Mimsy Tosh herself, in person. I didn't have a clue what her real name was. I'd forgotten to ask Benny and he'd never thought to tell me. I could hardly say, 'Hi, Mimsy! How's it going, my old Tosh?' so I played it safe and said, 'Hi, Mum.'

She came and ruffled my hair and gave me a kiss.

I went bright red.

She pulled up a chair and sat down next to me.

'So how was your day?'

'Eh – not bad . . . Mum.'

'Got a bit of a throat?'

'Just a little.'

'You shouldn't have gone swimming then.'

'I'll be all right.'

'Pinch a chip?'

'Sure.'

She leaned over and took a chip from my plate. She wasn't like she seemed on the telly and the magazines. I mean, her clothes looked enormously expensive and she was all made-up and her hair was piled up on her head but – in a way – she was quite ordinary really.

'Since when have you been having ketchup, Benny? I thought you preferred the brown sauce?'

I'd forgotten that. Benny had told me too, that he had the spicy stuff.

'Just thought I'd try it. For a change.'

'Like it?'

'It's all right. Take another chip, if you like,' I offered.

'No thanks, darling. I'm eating out.'

'Where're you going?'

'Record company do. Promote the new single.'

'Ah, right. Back late then?'

'Afraid so. Alice will get you anything you need.'

'I'll be all right.'

'Not too late to bed now, Benny.'

'No. When'll Dad be back?'

I wondered if I'd get to meet Derry Spinks himself before I had to go.

'Not sure, darling. Tomorrow morning, hopefully. Depends on the flights, really.'

'Will he be back before I go to school?'

'Might be. Maybe. Ben . . .'

'Yes, Mum?'

'Are you all right, darling?'

'Yeah, I'm fine.'

I felt myself go cold. I was terrified that she had rumbled me, that she knew that I wasn't her son.

'I just worry about you sometimes.'

'Oh. Why?'

I didn't feel good about this. This wasn't right. Not me, in the guise of Benny Spinks, having heart-to-hearts with his mum.

'I just feel you're on your own too much, darling . . . I'll try and arrange things so we can all spend some more time together – you, me and Dad.'

'That'd be nice,' I said.

'Everything all right at school?' she asked.

'Fine,' I said, stuffing in some chips.

'Benny . . .'

'Yes?'

'I know you don't see much of your dad, but he has to make the most of it while he can. You do understand, don't you, darling? Anything could happen – injury, anything – it's a short career. You can't be a footballer for ever. He just has to make the most of it. He's probably only got a couple of years left at the top, even now.'

'It's OK. I know.'

'You don't mind?'

I was going to say no. But then I thought that maybe I ought to stick up for Benny a bit, and maybe say the things he wouldn't say, as he was possibly too shy and too polite.

'I don't mind, Mum, but I do get a bit lonely sometimes.'

'Oh, darling . . .'

'Maybe I could have friends round more often . . .'

'Well, yes, OK, I'm sure we could arrange that. You mean – from school?'

'Yes. And some other friends. Like people I know to chat to – you know – on the internet. Ordinary kids – from ordinary houses.'

'Well, as long as we can vet them first. We can't just have anyone round . . . they might be *rough*, darling.'

'I know, but there's like this boy I know, called Bill – he's not rough . . . well, not that rough – perhaps I could invite him round some time?'

'We'll see, darling.'

'He's all right.'

'I'm sure he is. We'll have to arrange something.'

'Thanks.'

A car horn tooted in the distance.

'That's Joe,' she said. 'He's brought the car round. I'd better go then, Benny.'

'OK, Mum.'

She gave me another kiss and I blushed again – but she didn't seem to see it.

'Mum,' I said, as she left the room.

'Yes?'

'You look nice,' I told her.

'Why, thank you,' she said.

'And I like your singing,' I said. 'Even if some people don't.'

She gave me a funny look and then she laughed.

'Thank you, Benny, darling. I'll take that as a compliment.'

'It was,' I quickly assured her.

I felt I had to make it up to her in some way for all the rotten things my dad had said about her sounding like a rat stuck up a drainpipe being poked with a sharp stick. Not that she knew he'd said that, but he had, and the words were out there somewhere, floating around the universe, maybe like bees, waiting to sting.

She gave me a smile, blew me a kiss, and then she was gone in a small cloud of perfume and a rainbow of designer clothes. She wasn't actually any prettier than my mum, but my mum's clothes came from the chain stores and her jewellery from a stall at the craft market.

What I'm getting at is that Mimsy Tosh was

probably wearing about half a million pounds' worth of diamonds and clobber, just to wander about the house; but she was still only somebody's mum at the end of the day. It wasn't as if she was that different or important. She was still only somebody's mum.

After dinner, I went for a wander outside. It was still light so I got Benny's quad bike from one of the garages where he had told me it would be, and I went riding all over the estate. That was fantastic, to have your own quad bike. I got the hang of it in no time. I rode all over the grounds for ages and I stopped off at the stables to look at the horses. There was a girl in there looking after them and grooming them. This had to be Tania, who Benny had told me about. She was foreign and didn't speak a lot of English, which was fine by me. She let me help her brush down the horses, then I got back on my quad bike and rode back to the house with the bike's lights on now, as the sun was sinking and it had started to get dark.

I parked the quad bike in the garage and then went to have a look at all the cars they had. There were a dozen of them – big expensive limos and small, even more expensive sports cars. There were Porsches and Ferraris and Jaguars and all sorts. I wondered when they got the chance to drive them all.

Then I went back to the house and Alice offered to make me some hot chocolate. So I got a mug of chocolate which I took up to my room with a couple of biscuits on a plate, and I sat there in front of the enormous telly with the remote control and I thought, Well, this is the life.

But whether it really was or not, I didn't know. I mean, it was *a* life – a kind of life – a different life. But whether it was the definitive life, well, who could be the judge? It made a nice change though, that was true enough.

I watched an episode of *The Simpsons*, then decided to brush my teeth and get ready for bed. I just couldn't get used to being on my own and having my own room, that was the really extraordinary thing. I kept expecting Elvis to appear at any moment and take a swipe at me with a towel. But he didn't.

I got ready for bed and put on a clean pair of Benny Spinks's pyjamas. He had dozens. I lay back and looked up at the ceiling. It was far, far away. There was no chance of me banging my head on that.

I wondered how Benny was getting on round at my house and how he was coping with having to be me, and how he was surviving having Elvis for a brother.

I only had two pairs of pyjamas. I'd told him where the clean ones would be, so he wouldn't have to put on the old pair. I could just picture him getting the fresh ones out of the drawer and Elvis saying, 'My, my, changing our pyjamas already, are we? Aren't

201

we getting clean and fussy in our old age? Why, if we're not careful, we'll actually be having a wash next.'

To which I would have replied, 'What do you know about washing, Elvis? In fact I've seen cow pats that have a bath more often than you.'

But how would Benny cope? Would he be able to stick up for himself? Would he be able to survive? I just hoped that a night with Elvis wouldn't do for him completely and the morning find him a gibbering wreck, at the top of the bunk bed, gently banging his head against the ceiling.

Then it crossed my mind that maybe he had already sent me word of how he was doing. He might have sent me an e-mail to my Yahoo address, using our computer. So I got out of bed, went and turned on his computer and got on to the internet. I logged on to my e-mail provider and tapped in my password.

Sure enough, there was an e-mail for me. The sender was Benny Spinks.

13

At Home

Hi Bill.

How are you getting on round at my place?

I'm afraid there's been a small spot of trouble here.

I'm typing this on your computer.

Your brother is lying unconscious on the floor.

I don't think I've actually killed him though, so please don't worry.

I'm afraid I had to strangle him, but it's only temporary. He should come round in about twenty minutes. It was a special hold they taught me at self-defence classes.

Mum and Dad thought I ought to know a bit of self-defence, just in case.

Is this what you do when he starts to annoy you? If not, I would recommend it. I don't want you to take this the wrong way, but I feel that your brother Elvis can be a bit of a pain.

First off though, everything went to plan. After we did the old switcheroonie, I went off and got the bus back to your place.

Imagine that! Me! On the bus! All on my own! I'd never been on a bus before. Not like that. Not where you pay when you get on. It's great, isn't it? You're lucky you can do that every day if you want to.

(Oh yeah. You wait until you've been standing at a bus stop for half an hour in the rain and then the next bus to arrive is full up.)

I was a bit nervous when I got back to your house, I don't mind telling you. As I walked up the back path – like you'd said to do and not use the front – and came to the kitchen door, I almost turned round and fled.

I nearly rang you up right there and then and said, 'Bill – the whole thing's off.' Which would have been stupid and no point anyway by that time, as you were probably already round at my house, pretending to be me.

So anyway, I plucked up courage and went in.

Your mum had just got back from the shops with your little sister and was unpacking groceries on to the table.

I don't want to be rude, Bill, but your kitchen seemed so tiny. I mean, it's a nice kitchen, it really is, I liked it, and don't take this the wrong way, but after my place, it all seemed so small. Almost like a toy house in some ways. (Hope that doesn't seem rude.)

So anyway, in I go and say, 'Hi.' I tried to sound like you as much as I could, but I don't think I did such a great job of it as your little sister gave me funny looks and your mum asked if I was all right.

I just said that I maybe had a slight throat infection. She told me to go and gargle with some stuff in the bathroom which I said I would later on.

I went to go upstairs then, to your room. But as I did, I realised that your mum was giving me a really odd look. She looked surprised about something – almost shocked. Then I realised. You told me in your information that you always

205

head straight for the biscuit tin when you get home. And I'd forgotten to do it! I tried to cover up and said, 'Whatever am I thinking of? I've forgotten my biscuits.'

'Yes, Bill,' your mum said, 'I thought maybe you were sickening for something or going down with the flu.'

But then something even worse happened. I had an even bigger blank. I couldn't remember where you'd said the biscuit tin was!

So I just had to stand there, like a great big lemon, with your mum and your sister staring at me, waiting for me to go and get my biscuits when I didn't know where the tin was.

There was only one thing for it – bluff.

So I went and pulled a door open.

'Bill,' your mum said. 'Why are you looking in the broom cupboard?'

I tried to make a joke of it.

'Just a joke,' I said. 'Ha, ha.'

So I closed the broom cupboard and opened another door. This turned out to be the one to the utility room.

'Do stop messing about, Bill,' your mum said, and she went and opened the right cupboard and got the biscuits for me. So I took a couple and went up to your room – but they were still giving me funny looks. I almost decided to give up and tell them who I was and what we'd done. The strain was something terrible. But I decided they wouldn't believe me, and once I was on my own up in your room, it wasn't so bad anyway.

To be honest, I'm so used to being on my own at home most of the time, I find other people to be quite a strain, even when they're not.

Well, your room Bill . . . I mean – it's quite a nice room – but it's not all that big, is it? Not even if you were on your own. But having to share it with your brother . . . and to be on the top bunk as well! Did you know that you've got a big dent in your ceiling? I reckon that it must be where you've banged your head over the years, when you've suddenly woken and gone to sit up and not remembered where you were. Maybe you never noticed you were doing it, but you've definitely got a big dent there all right. You have a look when you come home. You can't miss it. Honest.

So anyway. I sat down with my biscuits and made a start on your Maths homework. I don't think I did too bad a job – you ought to get reasonable marks and I tried to disguise my numbers to look like yours. I didn't even attempt the Spanish though, as I thought it would be a waste of time.

So anyway, there I am, sitting quite happily finishing off your Maths homework, minding my own business, nibbling at my biscuits and enjoying being you for a while in a different house, when I hear the door slam downstairs and then these big heavy footsteps come stomping up and the next thing I know somebody kicks the door open with a bang and your big brother Elvis walks in.

Do you know what he said to me, Bill?

He said, 'What's up with you, pig face? Don't you know you're supposed to stand up and curtsey when royalty enters a room?'

I mean, what did he say that for? And it was totally unprovoked. I mean, 'pig face'! It's a bit much, Bill. I don't know how you put up with it.

Anyhow, I remembered you saying that your brother had to be stood up to or he just gets worse, so I tried to give him a sort of nasty look, like he was some kind of slug or something and said, 'Get lost, mallet head. And on your way out open a window, as it seems that a big stink just walked in.'

I dare say that you would have come out with something a good deal better, but I didn't think that was too bad an answer at short notice to be honest, as I am really just a beginner at that sort of thing.

What surprised me though was the way your brother Elvis reacted, because he didn't really react at all. It was like water off a duck's back to him. He just changed his shirt, threw the dirty one down on the floor and said, 'Put that in the laundry basket, will you, pie brains?' To which I answered, 'Do it yourself you big fat blob of puss. I'm not your servant.' So he said, 'If that shirt's still on the floor when I come back, you're a dead man.' So I said, 'Go and stick your shirt up your nose and I hope you choke on the buttons.'

Off he went then, slamming the door behind him. But he didn't seem in the slightest bit suspicious that I might not be me. I mean, you that is. You know what I mean.

It wasn't half strange, Bill, being you,

in your house, with all these people around me all talking and arguing. It takes a lot of getting used to. I know there are more people in my house, but they aren't family really, they work there, and they're usually quiet, and they seem spread out over a wider area. And maybe you're so used to it that you don't even notice, but most of the time, in your house, it's like there's a riot going on.

Dinner was the time which was worrying me the most. I kept thinking that if anyone was going to rumble me it would be when we all sat down to eat. But when it came to it, everyone seemed more interested in their food. (It was fish fingers, by the way. We usually have that on a Tuesday too.) Your eldest brother Kevin doesn't say much, does he? He just stuffs it down and clears off. Your brother Elvis, though, kept trying to pinch my chips when your mum wasn't looking and then denying it, while your little sister – and I don't know if you know this – has developed a habit of hitting people on the head with a spoon, making out that they're boiled eggs. It's all right for a joke the first time it happens, but it soon wears thin.

Crisis time came with the pudding. It
was choc'n'nut ice cream with sprinkles.

(My favourite too. I've missed out on the
choc'n'nut! It was usually strawberry yoghurt on
Tuesdays! Nobody had told me that we were having
that, or I'd have done the swap with Benny Spinks
on a different day.)

Of course I couldn't risk eating it, not with
my peanut allergy, so I had to say, 'None
for me thanks, I'm full,' and nobody could
believe that you were refusing your ice
cream.

(No, I bet they couldn't.)

Even Elvis looked surprised.

(No, you didn't give it to him, did you?)

In the end I gave half my ice cream to
Elvis and half to your sister.

(Well, at least he didn't get all of it. That would have
been madness.)

After tea we sat down and watched a bit
of telly. My mum was on, singing her

latest single, but your dad doesn't like her much, does he? He said that he'd heard better singing at the wolf enclosure down at the zoo.

(Oh my parents – cringe, cringe. Sorry, Benny.)

I thought that was a bit uncalled for and I stuck up for her and said that in my opinion she had a really good voice. But your dad said in that case he'd have to take me down to the doctor to get my ears syringed as there was obviously something wrong with my hearing.

So anyway, the trouble started when I began to get ready for bed. I got up on to the top bunk in your other pyjamas (which I found where you said) and I was lying there reading one of your books when Elvis came in. He lay down on his bunk under mine, started reading a magazine and then put his feet up and began to kick me up the mattress. This really got on my nerves. I politely asked him to stop but he didn't pay any attention and just kicked me up the mattress worse than ever. So I asked him to stop again. But still he wouldn't. So I asked him a third time and now he said he'd stop when he felt like it and what was I going to do about it?

Well, I felt I had to be fair with him and give him a bit of warning, so I told him that if he didn't pack it in I'd come down and give him the secret stranglehold I knew and he wouldn't wake up for half an hour. He said something like, 'Ha ha, I'd like to see it,' and, 'What stranglehold is that then, bogey face?' and, 'You couldn't strangle the air out of a paper bag,' and so on.

So he kicked me up the mattress again, and I'm afraid to say that I lost my temper. I got down from the top bunk, really riled. He lay there smirking at me, so I gave him the special squeeze, and the next thing, he was out like a light. He seems to be starting to wake up now, so I'd better sign off. I just thought I would take advantage of the lull to send you this e-mail to let you know that everything's going fine and that the great switcheroonie has been a big success so far. I hope it's going well with you. See you tomorrow at 4.40 for the swap back. Maybe next time we can swap for three or four days. Or maybe a whole week. Hope you're OK, Bill, and that you like

my room. See you. Must go. Don't forget
to feed my fish and a locust for the gecko.
Elvis is waking.
     Yours,
     Benny (alias Bill)

I must admit that I was a bit stunned. Rich, spoiled, pampered, overprivileged Benny Spinks had sorted out my brother in just one evening. He'd succeeded where I'd tried and failed for years. I bet that Elvis wouldn't know what had hit him.

I just wished that I'd been sent off on private self-defence lessons to learn secret strangleholds, but I guess we'd never had the money for that sort of thing, and I'd just had to make do with basic throttling and the odd punch in the head. I supposed I was just self-taught, really, but you can only go so far on your own and there's no real substitute for a good teacher. It is hard when you are like me though and have to make your own way in the world without any advantages.

There was a knock on the door of Benny's room.

'Benny . . .'

It was Alice's voice.

'I saw your light was still on and just thought I ought to remind you that it's past bedtime. Your mum asked me to make sure you weren't up too late.'

'Yeah, OK, Alice. Putting it out. Just got to feed the fish.'

'OK. Night then.'

'Night.'

I switched the computer off, fed Benny's pets, then turned off the light. The room was full of big shadows. I went to the window and looked out. There wasn't a sound, except for the rustling of the wind in the trees. No cars, no sirens, no police helicopter circling overhead, chasing joy-riders and car thieves; no sounds of people singing as they came back from the pub. Nothing like home at all.

I wondered how Benny would sleep in my house or whether the usual racket out in the city streets would keep him awake.

As I was getting into bed, my phone buzzed with a text message. I opened it and read it.

'Ur brthr snring smthng trble,' it said.

Which I took to mean 'Your brother is snoring something terrible.' But what else was new?

'Pls advise. Bny.'

I sent him a text back.

'Ear plgs undr pllw,' I said.

Of course, he could have tried another stranglehold, I supposed, but if Elvis was already asleep, that probably wouldn't have helped.

I lay in the great big bed that belonged to Benny Spinks, in his great big room in his vast, huge house. To all intents and purposes I was Benny Spinks, living the Benny Spinks life in the grand Benny Spinks style. I'd ridden his quad bike and met his

215

mum and swum in his pool and been chauffeur driven in his limo, and I'd seen his horses and all his wardrobes of stuff.

Tomorrow morning, if his dad got back on an early flight, I might even meet him too – Derry Spinks, in person, the most famous, richest, possibly even the best ever footballer in the entire world. Then I'd get to go to Benny's posh school and meet his rich, posh mates and eat posh lunch and sit though posh lessons – maybe even lessons in being posh . . .

And yet . . .

I felt strangely . . . disappointed. As if I still hadn't got to it, to the real core of being Benny Spinks. Because in some ways, despite all the money and everything, his life didn't actually seem all that different from mine. And that couldn't be true, could it? Because he was rich and famous and I – well, I was nobody. Just Bill Harris, Benny Spinks look-alike, and that was the only claim to fame I had – that I looked like somebody else.

I lay back on the pillows. They were big and soft. Real feather pillows, I guessed. The ceiling was miles away above me. No fear of banging my head on that. It was great, it was marvellous – all the space and the quiet – it was sheer, absolute luxury.

And yet . . .

I was missing something. I just couldn't seem to get to sleep. I tossed and turned for what seemed like ages. Then I realised what it was.

I missed . . .

(Don't laugh.)

I missed . . .

Elvis.

And the sound of him snoring, a faint drone, even with my ear plugs in. It was hard getting off to sleep without him. I missed the sound of him tossing and turning and the creak of the bunk bed.

I missed him not being there to say, 'Good night then, fat face,' just before we turned off the light. I missed not being able to say, 'Fat face yourself, cheese feet. And try and keep your mouth shut or you'll end up swallowing your pillow again.' And him saying, 'Never mind those ear plugs, don't forget to stick a big cork in your bum, or you'll stink the place out.' And me saying, 'A cork wouldn't be big enough for yours, you'd probably need welding equipment and a bung the size of a bucket.'

Then he'd kick me up the mattress.

It was really odd. So many times I'd lain there on the top bunk, wishing I had my own room, that Elvis would just disappear and never come back again. Now, at last, I had my own room, and everything I could have wanted. But was I happy? No, I wasn't.

I was lonely, and I wished Elvis was there.

Stupid, isn't it? I mean, who'd have thought it?

Sometimes I think that maybe one of the worst things in life is getting exactly what you want, because a lot of the time, for all sorts of reasons, it's nothing but a big disappointment.

Tiredness got the better of me in the end though, as it always does. After all, it had been a long, exciting, and a pretty adventurous day. And we had got away with it!

That was the most incredible thing. We'd planned the whole thing and actually put it into operation. We'd done it – the great switcheroonie, the greatest switcheroonie there had ever been. We'd fooled them all and we'd got away with it.

I began to look forward to posh school tomorrow and to fooling them all there as well. This was the kind of adventure you could talk about to your grandchildren, when you were an old man of fifty or something. You could tell them all about the great switcheroonie and how you'd fooled the world.

So I mellowed out a bit then, and I drifted away into darkness.

I was woken by somebody knocking on the door, saying, 'Time to get up, Benny. You've slept through your alarm.'

For a second I didn't recognise my surroundings, then I remembered where I was and I called back, 'I'm getting up. Coming. Thanks, Alice.'

So I got up to face another day.

Me. The one and only Benny Spinks.

I made my way to the enormous bathroom, had a wash in the enormous sink, frizzed up my hair to ensure that I still looked like Benny Spinks, then I got dressed and packed his books into his backpack.

Alice called from downstairs.

'Benny – don't forget it's Games today.'

'Okay, thanks.'

I saw a sports bag in a corner of his room, picked it up and looked inside. There was some kit and a pair of boots in there, so I presumed this was what I had to take. I shouldered the two bags and headed down to the kitchen for breakfast. I took a last look at Benny's massive bedroom and all his reams of stuff.

Well, Benny, I thought, it was nice to be you for a while and to stay in your house, but all things considered, even with all the stuff you have, I think I'll be happy to go home this evening. It's what I'm used to, and I guess I prefer it there – even if I do sometimes bang my head on the ceiling when I wake up.

Then I closed the door on his room, never expecting to see it again, and went on down the wide, elegant staircase.

But if I thought that I would only have to be Benny Spinks for a few more hours and then be free to be myself again, I was gravely mistaken.

I was doomed to be Benny Spinks, Esquire, for a while longer than that.

14

Russian . . .

I sat on my own in the enormous kitchen, munching on a bowl of Weetabix.

Alice came in and made me some toast. She said that Mimsy Tosh was still in bed. She'd got home in the small hours and was having a lie-in.

'Usual on it, Benny?' she asked when the bread popped up from the toaster.

'Please,' I said.

The usual turned out to be one Marmite toast and one honey toast. Not *my* usual, but it was all right.

She stared at me when I went to pour myself an orange juice.

'Are you drinking orange juice now?'

Benny had left a few gaps in his information sheet (maybe I had too, in mine). He certainly hadn't told me anything about not drinking orange juice.

'Eh . . . thought I'd give it a go.'

'There is apple, if you want it.'

'Well, I would prefer apple, actually . . .'

She brought it over and I had some apple juice –
just like Benny would have done.

Tony, the security guard, came into the kitchen,
reading the morning paper. I presumed the other
guard, Steve, had been on duty throughout the
night.

'Hiya, Benny.'

'Hi.'

'We won then.'

'We did?'

'Three-one, and your dad scored two.'

'Great!'

'Soon be fit then?'

'Nearly ready.'

'The car should be outside in five. Joe's just on his
way back from the airport.'

'OK.'

He went out. I carried my dishes over to the sink.
Alice gave me a funny look.

'Why, thank you, Benny, but I'd have done that.'

I guess, unlike me, Benny was used to being waited
on. I hoped he didn't try that at my house. Waiting
for somebody else to put your dishes in the sink
around there was not a good idea. There was a very
strong chance that if you waited for someone to do
that, you might end up in the sink yourself.

I said cheerio to Alice, picked up my stuff and

headed for the hallway. Light was streaming in through tall, elegant windows. As I walked across the marble floor the front door opened, and in strode somebody I had seen a hundred, if not a thousand, times before. I'd seen him on the telly and on the front and back pages of the newspapers.

In walked Derry Spinks himself.

I almost asked him for his autograph.

'Benny . . .'

I felt awful. It hadn't been so bad with Benny's mum for some reason, but I just felt terrible: awkward and embarrassed and a total fraud. I just felt that he had to know I wasn't the real Benny, that he would see right inside of me and know the truth.

Maybe he was just too tired. He must have caught a very early flight to get home already and he looked pale and exhausted.

'Hi . . . Dad!' I managed to say.

He gave me a funny look.

'What's up with your voice? You sound different.'

'Just a sore throat. Nothing serious.'

'It's good to see you, Benny. Mum up?'

'Not yet.'

'Having a lie-in, eh? Bless her.'

'Good game, Dad? Tony said you scored two.'

'Yeah. Bit scrappy. But we won. Did you record it?'

'Tony said he would.'

'Good. OK, son.'

He took a few steps nearer. He was right by me now. He seemed taller and bigger than he looked on the telly. He reached out and ruffled my hair.

'You need that cutting, mop head.'

'Get the number-one clippers out, eh?'

'Yeah. Have it like I used to. Down to the bone!'

He grinned down at me.

'How's school, Benny?'

'Fine.'

He squatted down, so that we were more or less the same height.

'How's the rugby problem? Any better?'

I didn't know. Benny hadn't said anything specific about any rugby problems, just that he wasn't great at Games. I didn't know anything about rugby. Even less than I knew about football. I'd never played it in my life. All I knew about rugby was that the ball wasn't round.

'Eh . . . coping,' I said. I couldn't think what else to say.

'Well, don't worry,' Benny's dad said. 'It's just the one term and then you'll be playing something else.'

'Yes, Dad,' I said. 'Right. Better go then—'

'C'me here!'

He dropped his bag and gave me an affectionate kind of bear hug.

I started to cough. Fortunately he let me go. He ruffled my hair again, grinned and said, 'Push off then. See you when you get back.'

'See you . . . Dad,' I managed to say, then I got out, as fast as I could.

It was him being so famous which had unnerved me. That and being right there, in person, in the flesh, standing in the hallway, doing ordinary stuff – like breathing, and talking, and wearing clothes and carrying a bag.

I could hardly cope with it.

Things improved once I was in the car. Joe, the driver, obviously wasn't much of a morning person. He was a bit baggy-eyed anyway, from having had to get up so early to drive to the airport and pick up Dad. (Benny's dad, of course; the only stretch limo with driver my dad had ever been on was a bus.)

I looked at my watch. Eight-thirty. Nearly sixteen hours since the start of the great switcheroonie. Sixteen gone and eight more to go. So far, so more or less good. We'd both got away with it. But how was it going to be at school?

Maybe the most difficult people of all to fool aren't the ones who know you the best – in the sense of being your family and living in the same house. Maybe the ones who are hardest to fool are your contemporaries, your friends and enemies, the ones you sit in class with. They seem to know all your foibles and all your weak spots and are able to home in on them like guided missiles locked on to their targets.

I was still an impostor, and I didn't want anyone

twigging on. For all I knew, I might get lynched.

Now Benny had warned me about one or two of his school friends (if 'friends' was the word). They sounded on the nasty side to me. He had told me to be especially wary of Jeremy Poret and Roland Smythe as they had it in for him.

So in that respect posh school didn't seem much different to any other school. Everywhere you go, somebody has got it in for someone.

Joe dropped me at the gates of Cheadlehulme College for the Sons and Daughters of Gentlefolk (Established 1532). I said cheerio and he said he'd see me at twenty to five in the same place. I waved and entered the grounds and followed the other pupils down the driveway towards the school.

'Hi, Benny!'

'Hi!'

I didn't know who she was but Hi was Hi even without a name coming after it. Some faces I did recognise and could put names to. Benny had scanned and e-mailed me his class photo. I'd committed a few names and faces to memory. I'd sent him a copy of my class photo too, and I'd put a circle round Vicky Ferns and had drawn an arrow with Dangerous next to it.

'Hi, Ben.'

'Hi, Piers.'

I knew it was Piers from the colour of his hair. Ashwin was easy too – he had on a turban.

'Hi, Ashwin.' (Take the initiative, I thought.)

'Hi, Benny.'

Easy as pie.

'Oh look who it is. It's useless Spinks!'

These two had to be Jeremy Poret and Roland Smythe. They were mooching along together and they must have seen my limo draw up.

'Useless yourself,' I said, for something to say, keeping it low key to start with.

'Hey, Spinksy,' Jeremy Poret (the blonde one) said. 'Was that your old man kicking a football last night?'

As soon as he said that, I knew instantly what was wrong with them – they were jealous. They were envious that Benny's dad was famous.

'What about it?' I said.

'When's he going to get a proper job?' Roland Smythe sneered. 'What sort of a job's that for a grown man – that's what my father says – running round in shorts! Ha!'

'What, your dad says that when he's pushing his dustcart about, does he Roland?' I said.

They stopped dead, both of them, their mouths hanging open.

'What did you say?'

'You heard.'

I immediately realised. The reason Benny Spinks had been having a bad time with these two was because he wasn't mouthy enough. But I'd never had that problem. I'd had years of experience with Elvis, who was a sort of training course in survival and self-defence. A few more days with Elvis – and he seemed to have made a great start, judging from his e-mail – and Benny Spinks would be eating these two for breakfast.

'Are you trying to imply that my father is a dustman?' Roland Smythe said, shocked.

'What makes you think that?' I said, all innocence, and I carried on past them towards the school.

I didn't think they'd try anything, and they didn't either. They just gawped a while then I heard Jeremy Poret say, 'And who does he think he is?'

Well, right at that moment, I thought I was Benny Spinks. But I wasn't telling him that. It was all too complicated to explain.

I followed the other pupils into the school. Benny had told me where his classroom was and which was his desk. I left my stuff and went with the others to the great hall for morning assembly. It was a magnificent place, nothing like my school – there wasn't a single bucket out to catch the drips.

In my opinion, though, if you've seen one school assembly, you've seen them all, and the person who invents something new to say at school assemblies will probably make a fortune.

There was all the usual stuff: a bit of news, a bit of hymn singing, a bit of praying, a bit of 'we'll all pull together and do our best', a bit of 'keep off the flowerbeds in future' kind of thing and a bit of

227

special announcements, then it was off to class.

It was a nightmare.

Benny hadn't bothered to tell me that the first lesson of the day was Russian. I didn't know any Russian, not a word of it. And I hadn't done the homework.

I explained this to the teacher and said that I was sorry but I had left my homework at home and would have to hand it in tomorrow.

'OK, Benny,' she said. 'Just this once. Now, see if you can say what you just said to me again. Only this time – in Russian.'

I think I went the colour of a well-boiled sheet.

'Eh . . .'

Everyone in the class was looking at me.

'Have a try, Benny,' Mrs Winweed (the Russian teacher) said. 'You're normally so very good.'

'Eh . . . I – I'm – sorry-ski,' I said, 'but . . . I 'ave forgotten-o-vitch my – eh – homework-ski and I'll try-omov to bring it in-ski . . . tomorrow-o-vrod.'

Mrs Winweed's mouth fell wide open, as if she was waiting for someone to shovel coal into it.

'And what was *that* supposed to be, Benjamin?' she said. 'Are we trying to be funny?'

I knew it was bad. If it was Benjamin, it was bad.

'This is no way to behave and certainly no way to start the day. I am giving you a de-merit card. Right now. Two more, and it'll be detention!'

I tried to look humble and ashamed. Jeremy Poret

and Roland Smythe were sniggering fit to burst.

Mrs Winweed wrote out the de-merit card and handed it to me.

'Now get your book out – if you haven't left that at home, and if you have, share with Letitia – and don't let me hear another squeak out of you for the rest of the lesson. Just keep your head down and pay attention.'

She did me a favour there, saying she didn't want to hear another squeak. But it was a long forty-five minutes, listening to this language I didn't understand.

Halfway through, I had a bad twinge of conscience. I remembered that Benny didn't know any Spanish, and I'd forgotten to warn him that I had Spanish on a Wednesday morning, same as he had Russian. I wondered if he'd got me into detention yet. Still, even if he had, it wouldn't have been the first time.

15

. . . *And Games*

Nobody wanted me.

I couldn't believe it.

It was just like home.

There we all were, standing on the sports field of Cheadlehulme College for the Sons and Daughters of Gentlefolk (Established 1532), and the two appointed captains were picking sides. And nobody wanted me. Nobody wanted Benny Spinks to be on their team.

I just stood there with all the others; with the uncoordinated kids and the two-left-feet jobs and the ones who were off to fat camp in the summer and the ones with milk bottles where their glasses ought to be and the skinny ones who had to hold on to heavy objects when high winds started to blow. Benny hadn't mentioned anything about being among the great unwanted. Maybe he'd simply forgotten, or he'd been too embarrassed about it.

Benny Spinks, son of Derry Spinks, the country's most famous footballer – not wanted on the team. It was rugby, admittedly, and not soccer, but all the same, it seemed unbelievable that they wouldn't want Benny Spinks.

'OK, Corin, we'll have you.'

I looked to see who Corin was. He was standing just behind me. I don't know if you've ever actually seen a baby rhino wearing boots and rugby kit, but that was what he looked like. He went off to join his side. In the back pocket of his shorts he had what looked like a cream bun. He probably kept it there for emergencies. Next to go was Peregrine, who was about seven feet tall and had the physique of an under-nourished matchstick.

I glanced over to the far field where the girls were warming up for a game of hockey. I wondered if they might have me, but guessed not. They were probably a bit fussy as well.

'Lionel – have to be you then, I suppose.'

Lionel went off. He'd already lost one of his contact lenses and so was operating with one eye shut. He looked as if he might start going round in circles at any minute.

There were only two of us left now – me and a pear-shaped boy called Rupert. He looked a bit like that bear in *The Jungle Book*, the one with the narrow shoulders and the big middle. I also had the impression that his knuckles were dragging on the ground.

It had to be me now, I thought. I surely wouldn't be left until very last. If it was a choice between Benny Spinks and Rupert the pear-shaped knuckle dragger, then it had to be Benny, no doubt about it.

'Rupert!'

Off he went to join his side, his knuckles leaving tramlines in the damp grass as he dragged them along behind him.

'OK, Spinks. Blue team. Isn't much choice, is there?'

I went to join the blue team. The red team seemed greatly relieved. The other players in the blue team looked a bit depressed as I walked over to join them; some of them were shaking their heads and sighing, as if they were all doomed.

'No chance of winning now,' someone muttered.

I guessed that Benny Spinks wasn't just *bad* at rugby; he was absolutely terrible, a liability of the first order.

'OK, quick warm up, then we'll get started,' the sports teacher, Mr Dibbick said, and he blew his whistle; more for effect than for anything else.

We ran around, passing the ball to each other. People tried to keep me away from it, and it away from me, but finally it had to come my way.

'And don't drop it this time, Spinksy!'

Well, I was hardly likely to drop it. You couldn't

miss it. It wasn't exactly small. I caught it and passed it on. The boy I passed it on to was so surprised, he dropped it himself.

'Flipping heck,' he said. 'Spinksy caught it! And they say that miracles can't happen!'

I couldn't see what the problem was. I mean, I'd never even played rugby before, but I couldn't see what was difficult about it, I mean, *you could pick the ball up*!

I'd always wanted to do that during football. I could never get it to go where I wanted it to when I kicked it. The number of times I'd thought to myself, If I could only pick this ball up and run with it, I'd be a real star! But whenever I tried it, I got whistled and jeered at and the other team got a free kick.

'OK! Let's get started!'

They put me on the back line. I guess they thought I couldn't do too much harm there, stuck at the back, out of the way.

A whistle blew and the game started – reds against blues.

There seemed to be a bit of violence involved. It wasn't like football where you were only allowed to jump on people in the other team as long as the ref didn't see you doing it. In rugby you could do it all the time. You could grab people round the legs and trip them over to get the ball off them.

I'd always wanted to do that. I was never any good at getting the ball off anyone in football, they were always too fast and too tricky for me. But I'd often thought, If only I could just jump on them, or trip them up, I could get the ball while they were lying on the ground and be away with it.

It didn't look too bad at all, this rugby business. You could pick the ball up with your hands and you were allowed to trip people up as well.

It could have been made for me. It was right up my street.

'Spinksy! Stop daydreaming! Catch it!'

The ball came flying through the air. I was all alone at the back of the field, near to our goalposts. I didn't see where the ball had come from or who had thrown it. But I reached out and caught it, and it landed with a thud in my arms. I stood there, wondering what to do next.

Then I saw them coming.

There must have been about a hundred of them.

The whole of the other team were charging down the pitch, coming to get me.

'Run, Spinksy! Run!'

I didn't need telling twice. I ran. And if there's one thing I'm good at, it's running, especially in straight lines. But I'm not bad at wavy lines either, and even though I say so myself, I'm no slouch at the old dodging.

They were almost on me before I got started, all two hundred and fifty of them – or however many there are in a rugby team – I'd not had the chance to count them all, but it was quite a lot. I ran past them, dodging and weaving, desperate to get away. If I fell to the ground, they'd all pile on top of me, and I'd never have got out alive.

'Go, Spinksy! Go!'

What else did they think I was going to do? Stand there and get trampled to death?

I tore on up the field. I made it to the halfway line and then to the three-quarters. I'd dodged most of the opposition, though there were still a few to go, while the ones I had avoided were turning round and running up behind.

But my team had stopped running completely. They were all just standing there, with their mouths open, as if they'd just seen a UFO hovering over the tennis courts. I wondered what they were gawping at, but I was too busy sprinting to stop and look.

Then there I was. Right at the end of the pitch, standing under the other goalposts, with the ball in my hands.

What was I supposed to do now? Run back again?

Everyone on my team started shouting, all at once, as the opposition charged up to get me.

'Touch it down, Spinks, you idiot! Touch it down!'

Touch it down?

What was that then?

I didn't know what they were on about, but I was fed up with holding the ball by now anyway, so I put it down on the ground. The other team could have it now if they wanted it. There was no sense in my getting killed.

The ref blew his whistle and shouted, 'Try!'

Apparently I'd scored.

My team went mad. They all started cheering. I'd scored some kind of a goal. They all came over and slapped me on the back and said, 'Well done, Benny,' and 'Nice one,' and 'What a run,' and stuff like that.

One of the others got to 'convert' the ball then – which meant kicking it over the posts from a standing start. He did all right and the ref blew his whistle again.

Apparently we were five points ahead already.

They gave me the ball all the time after that.

I mean, I just couldn't see what the problem was, or what the big deal was either, come to that. It was all so simple. All you had to do was run in a straight line, do a bit of dodging, and then touch the ball down at the other end.

To be honest, it was so easy I got bored with it. We were winning thirty-nine nil at half-time. It hardly seemed worth playing the second half.

People were coming up to me all the time, slapping me on the back and saying, 'We never knew you could do that, Benny!' and 'Has your dad been giving you lessons?' (But he played soccer, not rugby, so I don't know why they said that.)

I tried to be modest about it and make out it was nothing much and anyone could do it. I just had this modest talent, I suppose, for running very fast in short, straight lines.

The only thing that worried me was the real Benny Spinks. It was all very well me being hero for a day, but what about when he got back and they expected him to do the same thing all over again next week, and he couldn't?

I'd have to warn him when we swapped back round at four-forty by the gates. Maybe he could throw a sickie next week, or get a note from his mum saying he had a sprained ankle. He could give that to the sports teacher.

But even if he never played rugby again, I felt that at least today would always be remembered. I hoped that it maybe made up for the de-merit card in Russian.

I scored another ten tries in the second half. I could have made it more, but I didn't like to push it. There was no sense in showing off.

After games, it was lunch. They had pretty good lunches at the Cheadlehulme College for the Sons and Daughters of Gentlefolk (Established 1532). They were better than ours. There was a wider choice too. I had my usual though – pizza and chips. I didn't want to take any chances. There were a lot of vegetables and salads on offer, but you have to be careful with that kind of thing or you can easily upset your stomach.

I sat in the canteen, eating my pizza slices. I looked

around me at all the rich kids, the Sons and Daughters of Gentlefolk, as the sign outside the school said. I wondered if they all lived in big houses with Olympic-sized swimming pools. I bet myself that none of them lived in a house like mine.

I felt like a spy who had infiltrated some enemy headquarters, afraid that one false move would give him away. Yet nobody appeared to doubt for a moment that I wasn't the real Benny Spinks.

Except for one person – a girl, who kept looking at me. Maybe she had some sort of deep personal interest in Benny Spinks. Maybe she had a soft spot for him, or maybe he'd even confided in her and had told her all about the great switcheroonie, and she was keeping an eye on my performance and holding the cards up, giving marks out of ten.

Her name was Bella, and she had dark brown eyes. Whenever I glanced up, she was looking at me, and her whole expression seemed to say, 'I know you're not Benny Spinks, Bill Harris. I know what's up and I'm on to you. But you don't have to worry, because I won't tell anyone. In fact, I think it's quite funny really that you're getting away with it, and that everyone else has been fooled. But I haven't, not me. I just want you to realise it, that's all – your fate is at my mercy. I could blow the whistle on you any time, if I wanted to. But I don't, so I shan't, so you're all right.'

But even if she had spilled the beans, who'd have

believed her? What if she'd gone up to the form teacher and said, 'Excuse me, but I have reason to believe that the boy who says he is Benny Spinks is in fact an impostor and that in actual fact great switcheroonies have taken place right under our very noses.'

They'd have thought she was mad.

I wanted to find out a bit more about her, so I texted Benny when no one was looking.

'Bella? Hu she?'

'Bella Wilton. Mum fms ballet dncr,' came the reply. 'I'm OK. U OK? C U 4.40.'

So Benny was surviving too. I studied Bella from a safe distance. You could see a ballet dancer in her. Or maybe I was imagining it from what Benny had told me. I wondered if maybe she was his girlfriend, but he'd not mentioned it. Everyone's entitled to a few secrets, after all. Even when they're you.

The rest of the afternoon dragged a bit. First it was Geography, then it was History, then there was a Biology lesson.

School's school, I suppose, posh or not, and lessons are lessons and they're pretty much the same everywhere. Some are interesting and some are boring and some seem as if they're never going to end.

I made a note of what Benny would have to do for homework that evening, after we had switcheroonied back round again, and I hoped he was doing the same for me, and guessed that he probably was.

Finally the clock got to four-fifteen, and then, after another interminable five minutes, the bell rang. It was time to pack up and go, to return to being Bill Harris, to go back to the bunk bed and the dent in the ceiling and getting mistaken for a boiled egg.

One day Debs would grow up and get too old for that game.

I wondered if I'd miss it.

I packed Benny's books into his backpack. I remembered to take his sports kit too. I said cheerio to a few people and began the walk up to the top of the driveway, to where the gates were, and the big weeping willow, with its canopy of branches going down to the ground.

It was four-thirty-three.

Someone caught up with me. A boy called Matthew Timms. He didn't seem all that popular really. His father was a rich merchant banker; Benny had told me that in his info sheet.

I think he just wanted someone to talk to.

'Hi, Benny.'

'Hi, Matt.'

I wanted him to go away. I had to duck in under the willow, to meet Benny, who might already be there. I couldn't afford to walk out of the gates. The limo would be parked there, with Joe at the wheel. If he saw me . . .

'Your dad playing football on Saturday, Benny?'

'Eh . . . yes – should be – guess so. Look – I need a wee, Matt. Forgot to go . . . I'm going to have to nip behind the tree there . . .'

'Oh yeah, sure, Benny. No problem. Right you are. See you tomorrow then.'

'Yeah, see you, Matt.'

'Bye.'

Thankfully, he walked on. I nipped in under the willow. Nobody saw me, as far as I could tell.

It was four-thirty-seven now. Benny wasn't there yet, but should be at any moment. Any moment now.

I loosened my tie, ready to take it off and hand it back to him. I took my things from his blazer and put them into my trouser pockets, so I wouldn't leave anything behind when we changed coats back round again.

Four-forty exactly. It said so on his expensive Rolex watch.

Should have been here by now. He wasn't late exactly, not yet. I'd just more or less expected him to be here on time, possibly even a bit earlier.

Maybe he'd got a bit lost. Maybe he walked slower than I did. Maybe he'd decided to take the bus and was stuck in a bit of traffic.

Maybe he liked being me so much he'd decided to stick at it.

No, I didn't think so, somehow.

Maybe he'd murdered Elvis and gone on the run.

Maybe Elvis had murdered him.

241

I decided to call him on his mobile. It rang, but he didn't answer. Maybe it was on mute and he didn't hear it; maybe it just wasn't possible for him to answer it right then; maybe he'd lost the flipping thing, or left it behind at school, in my locker. I left a voice message.

'Hey, Ben, it's me. I'm waiting. It's getting on for four-forty-five now. Just wondering where you are.'

I tried to be patient, but it was starting to gnaw away at me – impatience at first, then anxiety. I looked at my watch again. It was four-fifty.

Where the heck was he?

The anxiety turned to panic. Why wasn't he there? What had happened to him? Why hadn't he turned up? He should be here. This wasn't fair. An arrangement was an arrangement, a deal was a deal.

I got an idea. I rang home. Maybe Benny had simply forgotten who he was. Maybe he'd had a blow to the head. Maybe he'd gone back to my house, with concussion and amnesia. Kevin answered. I disguised my voice.

'Hello, can I speak to Bill, please? It's a mate of his from school.'

'Sorry, he's not home yet. Want to leave a message?'

'No, I'll ring later. It's all right. Thanks.'

Then I saw something.

A pair of feet. Big ones, in big polished shoes. I could see them shuffling and pacing up the path on the other side of the willow. Then I heard a voice, and someone muttering to themselves.

'Where is he? Where's he got to?'

It was Joe. Benny's limo driver. Fed up with waiting, he'd come to see what was up, to look for some sign of Benny, dawdling down the drive. He walked around in a little circle, then disappeared. He was probably parked on a yellow line and was worried about the traffic wardens.

Where was Benny?

What was I to do?

I couldn't walk out of the school gates; Joe would see me. He'd be there at the wheel of the limo, silently fuming and trying not to show it, as I was the boss's son, and he had to be polite to me, even when he didn't much feel like it because I'd kept him waiting.

What could I do then? Run for it? Just go home? Or tell Joe I wasn't Benny Spinks and that the real Benny Spinks should have been on his way, but hadn't turned up yet?

It was five o'clock now. Something had happened. Something, somewhere, had gone wrong. This wasn't just a bit late, or slightly overdue. Benny knew that Joe would be waiting, that I would be waiting. He knew how important it was to be here on time.

Something had happened to him. Maybe he'd had an accident? What was I going to do? How was I going to tell his mum and dad – *my* mum and dad – anyone's mum and dad?

What if he'd been killed?

Five past five.

It had all gone wrong.

I didn't like this any more. I wished we'd never started it. I wanted to be home, lying on my bed, staring at the dent in the ceiling and trying to think of sarky remarks to make to Elvis when he came in and started making sarky remarks of his own.

Come on, Benny – where are you?

Where was he? How could he do this? He knew the deal. Why was he late? We had to swap back, be ourselves again. I didn't want to be him for ever. That wasn't the arrangement at all.

I couldn't just stay here though, under the willow, hiding like a deer from the hunters. I had to take the initiative. I had to move.

A car horn blared out on the street. Joe, I guessed, venting his impatience, wondering where I was.

I stepped out from behind the canopy of branches. Nearly everyone had gone. I looked back down the driveway towards the school; some stragglers were making their way up the path; some children were heading for the tennis courts; some had stayed behind for extra-curricular activities; others were probably doing homework in the late-room.

What now? I checked my phone for messages –

nothing. I rang Benny's number again, but still no answer.

All right. I knew what I had to do. I had to walk out, go to the car, tap on the window, say, 'Look, Joe – this is difficult but . . .'

Then I'd have to explain. I'd have to tell him that I wasn't Benny Spinks at all, that I was only pretending to be, and that the real Benny Spinks had gone walkabout and had apparently disappeared.

There was no choice. I couldn't go on waiting. I had to act. So I turned and walked away from the willow and up towards the gates. Stone lions sat guarding the masonry, but they were no use to me. They didn't know where Benny Spinks had got to, and that was the only important thing just then.

It had all gone wrong. The great switcheroonie had turned mouldy and sour, full of lumps and clots, like gone-off milk. I didn't like it, I wished I'd never got involved in it, I didn't want to play this game any more. But I didn't have a choice. I had to see it all the way through to the final whistle.

I walked out of the gates of Cheadlehulme College for the Sons and Daughters of Gentlefolk (Established 1532). I walked past the fine columns and the big stone lions, standing ever vigilant to protect the school.

There was the limo. There was Joe at the wheel, drumming his fingers on the dashboard, looking fed up and bored and a big bit angry. He saw me. He looked relieved. He reached across and opened the door for me, so I wouldn't have to do it for myself.

'Benny! Where have you been?'

'Hi, Joe. Sorry. Look, the thing is—'

'Well, never mind, you're here now. Hop in. We've got to pick your mum up from the shops on our way back. I'll just ring her, tell her we'll be a bit late.'

I was already in the car. The words – 'The thing is . . .' were all jumbled up – wouldn't come to me.

Then I had it, a better idea.

I shouldn't tell him. I should wait. I should go on being Benny Spinks a while longer. Go on pretending and wait for Benny's call. Maybe it was just some minor hitch, that was all. He'd let me know on my mobile, and then we could rearrange the great switcheroonie back again for tomorrow, same time, same place. Or maybe do it at the school gates in the morning.

Yes. I was panicking, I decided, for no reason. It was just a matter of being Benny Spinks for another day. I could manage that, and he could be me. No worries.

So, rightly or wrongly, I got into the car next to Joe the limo driver, and I pulled the door shut.

'Seat belt, Ben.'

'OK.'

'OK?'

'Done it. Can we have a different radio station?'

He put on the indicator and pulled out into the traffic, then he took the next left, as I think he always did, taking a short cut down an empty, quiet road, which avoided the roundabout and the build-up of rush-hour traffic.

Then it happened. So fast it was almost over before it had started. We were halfway down the road when a car pulled out from the kerb, right out into the centre of the road.

Joe stood on the brakes and started swearing. I felt my seat belt lock tight around me and pinion me to the seat. The next moment there was a second car, blocking the road behind. Then there were people running and heading for us. Joe reached for a switch on the dashboard, one which would have locked all the doors. But before he could get to it, his door was wrenched open and a hand reached in – with a gun in it.

The gun was pressed right up against Joe's temple. I saw his jaw tighten, and the look of surprise, and perhaps fear on his face.

'Don't move,' a man's voice said. 'Or you'll have serious brain damage.'

Then he shouted to some other men who were running for my side of the car.

'That's him,' he said. 'Get him. Get the boy!'

The door was pulled open and hands reached in. Someone pressed something smothering over my face, some kind of rag, soaked in a sickly sweet liquid.

247

And they did the same to Joe. I struggled and fought, but I had no choice than to inhale it.

It was nice really, a lovely kind of feeling. You felt you could just let go and surrender, and not have to worry about anything, ever again. It felt like all my troubles were over, as everything around me span like a top, and then suddenly went completely black.

16

Ear Ring

'One word out of you, and you're dog biscuits.'

I opened my eyes, and for a moment thought I was back at home, lying there on the top bunk with the ceiling just above me, and Elvis being rude and unpleasant, same as usual. I tensed and waited for the kick up the mattress.

Only if this was my bedroom, it seemed to be driving up the motorway at a very high speed. And the kick up the mattress didn't come.

'You hear me?'

I nodded. From where I lay I could see two hard-looking faces and four dark, menacing nostrils. One set of nostrils had a deep scar running alongside, and the other pair of nostrils had smoke coming out of them. One of my abductors was smoking a cigarette. His colleague didn't approve and fanned the smoke away with his hand.

I was on the floor of the car, by the back seats. It wasn't a very dignified position to be in. Also, they both had their feet on me, which I didn't think was very nice.

'You keep your mouth shut, you'll be all right, kid – got it?'

I nodded, my mouth hanging open with – to be honest – sheer terror. Who were these men? What did they want with me? Where were they taking me? What was the stuff on the cloth they had put over my face? Was that why I now had such a thumping headache? Or was that due to the motion of the car and to being trapped on the floor?

'Hey, Vinny – not so fast. If you top the hundred they'll pull us over. Keep it down to seventy.'

A voice grunted and I felt the car slow down. All I could see from where I was lying were the two faces, the nostrils, and some blue sky. I didn't recognise any of them.

A third face appeared, peering over and looking down from the front passenger seat. This face didn't look any more attractive than the other two. It had a stubbly chin and an ear ring. The new face cracked a smile.

'All right then, Benny, old son?' it said. 'Don't you worry, boy. You'll soon be back home and splashing round your swimming pool. It is an Olympic-sized one you've got, isn't it?'

I nodded, remembering what Smoky Nostrils had said about keeping quiet.

'That's right, thought it was. Well, don't you fret none, Benny boy, just as soon as your dad comes across with the money – as I'm sure he will, you being his pride and joy and all—'

'Apple of his eye,' Smoky Nostrils said. 'The jewel in his crown, the—'

'Yeah, all right,' Ear Ring said. 'No need to make a meal of it. Anyway, Benny, my old son, just don't you go fretting none or wetting the old pantaloons.'

I was a bit miffed at that one. I had absolutely no intention of wetting the old pantaloons, as he put it. Quite the contrary. I was very determined to keep the old pantaloons as dry as possible for as long as I could.

'Soon as your old man coughs up with the pennies, you'll be well on your way home, and back tucked up in your beddy-byes. OK?'

I decided to risk a few words.

'You don't go to beddy-byes at my age,' I said. 'You go to bed.'

Scar Face poked me with his foot.

'Oh, highty-toighty!' he said. 'Who's the spoiled little rich kid then? Bringing down a peg or two, that's what you need, Benny, my son.'

'I'm not your son,' I snarled. 'And I'm not spoiled.'

He dug his foot into me again.

'Oh, highty-toighty,' he repeated.

I thought about sinking my teeth into his ankle, but decided against it for two reasons: one, it might not taste very nice, as he didn't seem like the sort of person who changed his socks a lot; and two, I was in a vulnerable position, lying on the floor, and there was no sense in making things worse for myself.

Ear Ring looked over from the front seat. He seemed to be the one in charge.

'Oi,' he said to Scar Face. 'Don't bruise the apples.'

'He was being lippy,' Scar Face said.

'Let him,' Ear Ring said. 'He won't be lippy long.' He grinned at me. 'Will you, my son?' he said.

Well, I still wasn't his son, but there was plainly no point in making an issue out of it. So I changed tack and tried a different approach.

'Look,' I said, 'I don't know what you all think you're doing, but do you have any idea who I am?'

They all started chortling then, even Vinny, who was driving the car.

'Know who you are, boy? I should hope we do! You don't think we go napping kids for the fun of it, do you?' Smoky Nostrils said. 'Know who he is indeed! Funny man!'

Ear Ring looked down from the front seat and smiled. When he smiled, he looked even more sinister than when he was scowling. In fact I wished he would go back to scowling, it was less scary.

'Oh, we know who you are all right, Benny boy. We know all about you. 'Cause we've been casing

252

you on and off for weeks. We know all your little ways and your comings and goings and your little routines. We worked out just how to nab you and just when to do it. And it couldn't have gone smoother, boy. It was like pouring melted chocolate – eh, boys?'

The others grunted in agreement.

'So don't you worry, my son, we know who you are all right, Master Benny Spinks . . .'

So they didn't know who I was at all then. They knew who they *thought* I was. But I wasn't. I was Bill Harris.

'And we know just who your dad is . . .'

That's right, I thought, Tom Harris, who works for Inter-Netty, installing broadband.

' 'Cause, let's face it, everyone and his dog knows who Benny Spinks's dad is!'

'And his mum,' Nostrils said.

That's right, I thought. Mrs Jenny Harris; she works part time for social services as a helper, three afternoons and two mornings a week. She's well known for that. Almost internationally famous.

'Not that she can sing much!' Nostrils went on. 'Though I dare say she's pretty good at cracking wine glasses.'

'Ah ha ha!'

They all had a good laugh at that.

'So we know who you are all right, Benny. And what you're worth. At least what you're worth to your old man. Though you probably ain't worth much to anyone else. So we were thinking of, well . . .'

Ear Ring looked at Scar Face and Nostrils and said, 'Do you think we should tell him what we want for him? Or do you think it'll make him big-headed?'

'I should think he's big-headed already,' Nostrils said.

'Yeah,' Ear Ring agreed. 'He probably is.' He looked down at me. 'Well, Benny boy,' he said. 'The going rate for you today – what we thought we'd ask for – is a nice, round, three million.'

Three million? I gulped and swallowed.

'Your old man should be able to afford that no trouble, shouldn't he? I mean, three million; he earns that in a couple of weeks, doesn't he? What with his deals and his sponsorships. Yeah. I'm sure he could fork out three million to get his boy back, and not even notice he'd spent it.'

I thought I ought to say something defiant. I couldn't think of anything original, so I said what people say in films when they find themselves overpowered and outnumbered in difficult situations.

'You'll never get away with it,' I said. (I think another thing that they often say is, 'We're running out of time!')

Ear Ring looked at me, cool as an ice box full of cucumbers.

'I don't see why not, Benny. I don't see why not at all. Yeah. Three million. Or maybe even four. Or is that being greedy? Three million four ways. How's your sums, Benny? I bet you must be good at sums. I bet they teach you all that at your posh school, eh?'

'Seven hundred and fifty thousand each,' I said.

'Clever boy,' Ear Ring said. 'And he didn't even need his calculator. Just what I made it too. Seven hundred and fifty thousand apiece. Of course, your old man can make that in five minutes by advertising bootlaces, can't he?'

I didn't really think so. I thought the only way my dad could ever make that much money would be if he robbed a bank, won the lottery, or went out and kidnapped Benny Spinks.

Benny Spinks.

Where was he? Where had *he* got to? Why hadn't he turned up at the willow at the appointed time, for the great switcheroonie back again? Or what if he had finally arrived there, a few minutes after I'd left, to find me gone?

But if he had, he'd have found the police there too, and some great commotion, and Joe the limo driver would be there, recovering from the cloth over the face with the smelly stuff on it, giving a statement. And as soon as the police saw Benny – the *real* Benny – walking down the road in my school uniform, they . . .

They wouldn't know what to make of it at first. They'd stand there scratching their heads, trying to figure out what had happened. But then Benny would explain all about him and me and the great switcheroonie and how I was him and he was me for a day, and how I had obviously now gone and got kidnapped in his place, and it was all a big mistaken-identity case. Then, when all that got out on the national news, and when these four crooks in this car got us to where we were going, and when they put the telly on to find out what the world was thinking about Benny Spinks being kidnapped . . .

And when they discovered that instead of being worth three million quid . . .

I was worth – absolutely – nothing.

They weren't going to be very happy about it.

I wondered if I ought to tell them right now exactly who I was – so as to avoid subsequent disappointments. But then, they wouldn't believe me. They'd think I was just trying to talk my way out of it.

It was best to just play along with things, I decided, and do the explanations later, after we'd stopped at their hide-out and they'd got the telly on, and had found out the truth.

Then I thought of something else.

What if Benny Spinks *hadn't* turned up, on his way to the weeping willow? What if he'd had an accident, or fallen down a hole? There'd be nobody to say who I was. And what about my mum and dad? Or what if Benny Spinks decided to be me for ever? Surely he wouldn't? He'd never want to do that. I wasn't even sure that I wanted to be me for ever. It surely wouldn't appeal to him, not after the luxuries he was used to. He'd be bound to miss his own mum and dad, just as I was, and want to go back home in the end.

'What's up with you, Benny boy?' Scar Face said. 'Dog got your tongue?'

'It's cat,' Nostrils said, but Scar Face ignored him and prodded me with his shoe. 'Well?' he said. 'Not speaking?'

Typical, I thought. One minute they tell you not to open your mouth or you're a dead man, next minute they want to know why you're not speaking. This is adults all over for you – totally inconsistent and never able to make their minds up.

'Next exit,' Ear Ring said.

'OK,' Vinny answered.

There was the click of the indicator and the car turned off the motorway. Our speed dropped and we stopped for a few seconds, maybe waiting at a roundabout, and then we were moving again.

We drove in silence. After another twenty minutes, we turned off the road and went over a bumpy track. A while after that the car stopped. Vinny turned off the engine.

'Here we are then,' he said. 'Home sweet home.'

'You two bring the boy,' Ear Ring told Scar and Nostrils. 'Hide the car,' he told Vinny. 'But wait till I get the stuff out of the boot. And where's the laptop?'

'Here,' Nostrils said. 'Next to me.'

'Pass it over.'

Nostrils handed him a small lap-top computer.

'Let's go.'

'And no funny business,' Nostrils told me. 'Just don't try anything, Benny boy. Got me?'

They clambered out of the car and waited for me to follow. I was so stiff and cramped they almost had to pick me up. There was no chance of my running away; at that moment I could hardly walk.

I was just grateful they hadn't put me in the boot. If there's one thing I don't like, it's dark, confined spaces. They bring me out in the heebie-jeebies.

I didn't get much of a chance to look around before they hurried me into the house. We were in the country, I could see that. I made out an old garage with a corrugated iron roof, a wooden shed and an ancient summer house. Then we were inside, into an old whitewashed, black-beamed cottage. There didn't seem to be much furniture, and it smelt of damp.

'Put him in the back room, the one with the little skylight, and keep the door locked.'

They'd obviously got the place ready well in advance. The room they put me into was reasonably comfortable, with a bed and a telly and some books.

'Keep yourself amused, kid,' Ear Ring said. 'And just shout if you want the bathroom. Vinny'll be cooking us all some tea soon, won't you, Vinny?'

Vinny grimaced, as if he were doing it under protest and sufferance.

'Oven chips are his speciality, aren't they, Vin?'

'With fish nuggets and tinned peas,' Scar Face added.

'Gourmet cooking, see,' Ear Ring said. 'Jamie Oliver, eat your heart out.'

'But make sure you cook it properly first, ha ha,' Nostrils added.

Then they locked me up.

I turned the little telly on and fiddled around with the aerial on it to get a better picture. There was the blurry face of Bart Simpson. Homer was chasing him round the garden, while Ned Flanders peered over the fence.

I switched channels.

'And now, the news.'

I could hear a second television, on the other side of the door. Vinny, Scar Face, Nostrils and Ear Ring had fallen silent. They were watching the news too, on the same channel as me. I could tell from the announcer's voice.

'In a dramatic abduction today, Benjamin Spinks, the son of the England and international footballer, Derry Spinks, was snatched from outside the exclusive Cheadlehulme School.'

A big cheer went up next door from the kidnappers.

'Derry Spinks and his wife Mimsy – formerly a singer with the Ketchup Girls, before leaving to pursue a solo career—'

'If you can call it a career . . .'

'If you can call it singing . . .'

Be quiet, will you, I thought at them. I turned up the volume on my set.

'– are said to be deeply shocked at the abduction and have issued a plea to the kidnappers not to harm their son.'

'As if we would,' I heard Ear Ring say, on the other side of the door. 'We're nothing but pussy cats.'

The news reader went on.

'The police believe that the abduction was the work of professionals. They have declined to go into details, but Chief Inspector David Tremlenson, who is in charge of the case, confirmed that a ransom demand has already been received, and the police are investigating to ascertain whether it is genuine. And now, the news abroad.'

Next door went silent. They'd put their set off. I turned mine off too, so as to be able to hear what they were saying.

They sounded perplexed.

'What's going on?' Vinny said. 'How can they have got a ransom demand? We've not even sent one yet.'

'It's a bluff,' Ear Ring said. 'Has to be.' But his tone wasn't quite as confident as his words. He was rattled, you could tell.

'It's the cops, trying it on,' Scar Face said.

'Trying what on?'

'I dunno – something. Trying to faze us or something.'

'It doesn't make sense,' Nostrils said. 'Why would they say they'd had a ransom demand when we've not even sent one?'

'They're up to something.'

'What?'

'How do I know?'

'Gimme the lap-top. And go and get the chips on. All this kidnapping's made me hungry.'

'All right, all right!'

'And get the kid.'

I heard the door being unlocked. Nostrils looked in.

'You're wanted.'

I followed him out into the kitchen where the other telly was. Vinny was putting the oven on and then shaking a big bag of oven chips on to a metal tray.

'I hope someone brought ketchup,' Scar Face said. But it didn't seem as if anyone had. (Not that it mattered to Benny Spinks – he didn't like it.)

'Come here, Benny,' Ear Ring said. He was setting up his lap-top, plugging it into the phone connection. He fired it up and went on line. He got into some anonymous, and I guessed untraceable, e-mail account he must have already set up. I saw that he had called it Kidnap@Yawwho.com.

'What's your e-mail address, kid?' he said. 'Your private one? Your mum and dad's?'

I didn't know. I knew what Benny's was, but not his dad's. I took a guess that the second part would be the same as Benny's and the first part would be D.Spinks instead of B.Spinks. So I told him what I thought it was, hoping I'd guessed right.

'Right. Let's get a little dialogue going.'

He began to type. He saw me watching him and grinned.

'Ransom demands have come a long way, eh, Benny?'

I saw him type £4,000,000. He'd decided to go for broke then.

'Of course, in the old days, it was cut-ups,' he said. 'Ever seen the old films, Benny?' he asked me. 'They'd snip letters out of a newspaper and stick them on a postcard to make words out of them, and then send it to the grieving parents inside an envelope. Nice and anonymous. No handwriting to trace.'

I watched him type the e-mail: Once the sum has been agreed, details of drop-off and pick-up will be given. Reply to sender at this e-mail address.

'Untraceable, see, that was, the old cut-ups. No handwriting. No finger prints. They knew a thing or two, those old cons, eh?'

He typed something else. I didn't see what it was. He'd moved around so that his back was between me and the screen of the lap-top.

'Trouble was, it all took time. You had to post your letter, they had to read it, they had to get back

262

to you – and what if it went astray, or got lost in the post? Problems, problems and troubles, troubles. But today – well . . .'

He'd finished typing now, and seemed to be re-reading the message for any mistakes.

'. . . today, we have the technology, Benny boy. Instant response. No hanging about. You just send off your totally anonymous and completely untraceable ransom demand at the flick –' he hit the Send key, '– of a button.'

Off the e-mail went. They hesitated a few moments, eyeing me suspiciously, waiting to see if an 'undeliverable mail' message would ping back. But it didn't. I must have guessed the right address.

'That seems OK then,' Ear Ring said, sounding satisfied. 'We'll leave it with them to read and digest for a couple of minutes, and look forward to their response. How are those chips, Vinny?'

'I'm doing them, I'm doing them.'

'Good. Gives you an appetite, this kidnapping business. That and thinking what you might do with your share of four million quid.'

'Sunny Spain, mate,' Nostrils said.

'Beautiful Bahamas,' Scar Face told him.

'South America for me,' Vinny said.

'You don't even know where South America is,' Ear Ring sneered.

'Yes, I do,' Vinny said. 'It's near America – only a bit south.'

'Well, it's Oz for me,' Ear Ring said. 'The great down under. Just me and the kangaroos and a cool million quid's worth of Derry Spinks's money.'

The lap-top pinged and a pop-up came on the screen.

You've got mail, it said.

'Here we go,' Ear Ring said. 'We've got mail. They've got back to us already.' He grinned at me. 'Your dad'll be counting the cash up,' he said. 'Not much for him, four million. He carries that much around in the back pocket of his jeans, doesn't he? He always keeps a few million in his wallet, I dare say, for tipping waiters and incidental expenses. What it must be to be rich, eh, Benny boy? You don't know how easy you've had it, kid. But you will.'

He clicked with the mouse to open up the e-mail.

'Let's fix the where and when then. How we get the money and where we hand you over.'

But the answer he got wasn't the one he had expected. He read it with increasing perplexity, as Vinny, Scar Face and Nostrils watched him, looking every bit as puzzled as he was.

I got a bit worried about the chips.

'You won't let the chips burn, will you?'

Vinny didn't seem to hear me though. Nobody did. The four of them were staring at the computer screen.

'What the hell's going on?' Ear Ring said. 'Are

they trying to be funny? Is this some kind of a joke? 'Cause if it is, someone's going to live to regret it.'

I didn't like the way he looked then; nor did I like the direction he was looking in.

He was looking at me.

Accusingly.

I edged forwards to see what was on the screen.

> How did you get this e-mail address? Please do not use it again. I do not find this very funny. We have already received a ransom demand from the genuine kidnappers who are holding our son, and who have proved as much by means which I certainly do not intend to reveal to hoaxers such as you.
>
> I really don't understand why the abduction of our son is some kind of a joke to people like you and a reason to send hoax e-mails pretending that you have him.
>
> Kindly don't send any further e-mails to this e-mail address. We need to keep the channels of communication open with the real kidnappers and can well do without junk mail cluttering up the inbox from sick-minded jokers like you.
>
> D.S.

They all stared at each other and then they stared at me – as if I had something to do with it; which I suppose I had.

'What the— what's going on?' Nostrils said.

'I'm thinking,' Ear Ring said. 'I'm thinking. It doesn't make sense and yet there has to be an explanation . . .'

There was. And I knew what it was. I was one step ahead of him. But then I knew something that he didn't.

He didn't know that there were two Benny Spinkses, one genuine, and one a forgery.

Two different Benny Spinkses?

Then why not two different kidnap gangs?

That would explain it – why Benny hadn't made it to the willow.

He'd been abducted, maybe outside the school, by another gang, who'd had exactly the same idea. They'd probably nabbed him on his way to the great switcheroonie-back, maybe ten or fifteen minutes before I'd been nabbed.

Two Benny Spinkses.

Two kidnap gangs.

Two ransom demands.

'It's all getting a bit confusing, you know,' Vinny said. 'There's something going on here that I don't understand.'

I noticed there was smoke coming out of the oven. He'd gone and burned the chips.

17

The Litmus Test

It was a long night. We were quite far out in the country, and the country wasn't a place I was used to. The only night I'd spent in the country was round at Benny Spinks's house, pretending to be him. It hadn't been so bad there, but here it was a different matter. For a start I was locked up. And then there were the owls.

'Birds of bad omen, owls are,' I heard Vinny say. 'It's a bad sign, is owls.'

Ear Ring told him not to be so stupid, but Vinny wasn't at all happy. He kept saying that he had a bad feeling about it now, and it was all wrong, and they should call the whole thing off and scarper and leave me in the house, then ring someone later to tell them where I was.

But the others weren't having it.

'You can turn your back on four million quid if

you want to, mate,' Nostrils said, 'but I'm not showing it my shoulder blades. And if you clear off that's four million three ways instead, which is all the more for us.'

So Vinny stayed with them, as he didn't want to miss out. But he went on saying that he had a bad feeling about everything and that the owls weren't helping either, until finally Ear Ring told him to shut up and give it a rest or he'd stick his head in the oven along with the burnt chips.

Vinny came to my room to see how I was. I think Ear Ring had sent him. Ear Ring was Mr Nasty and Vinny had been elected as Mr Nice. He came into my room and sat on the end of the bed.

'You all right, Benny boy?' he asked.

'Fine,' I said.

'You don't have to worry none, son,' he said. 'Soon as the money comes, we'll let you go and you'll be back home. No one's going to harm a hair on your head – not when they're worth four million quid – get it?'

'Yes,' I said. 'Right.'

'One thing, boy,' he said. 'You might have noticed that everyone calls me Vinny but nobody else gets called anything as we don't want you knowing anyone's name and telling them to the coppers once you get freed.'

'Yes, I had noticed.'

'Well, there's no point in you telling them that my

name's Vinny as that's not my real name, see.'

'Ah. Right,' I said.

'My real name's Pete, see. So telling them my name's Vinny won't do you no good at all.'

'Right.'

He didn't appear to notice that he had just told me his real name, so I decided not to mention it.

He went off and left me alone then. I lay on the bed, with my hands under my head, looking up at the dent-free ceiling and trying to work out what must have happened – and hopefully work it out before Ear Ring did, as I had to stay at least one step ahead of him.

At school, in Science, Mr Fowler had told us that in the past, several people had thought of the same thing at more or less exactly the same time.

'An idea whose time has come!' was how he described it. 'It was almost in the air. Electricity, flight, radio, television, cars; despite what the books say, and the way they like to give credit to one person for a particular invention, often several people had the very same idea at exactly the same time. So it was inevitable that someone should make the discovery. It was an idea whose time had come.'

Like kidnapping Benny Spinks.

There was an idea whose time had come. No doubt about it. Kidnap the son of the richest footballer in the country, hold him to ransom, get a few million out of it, and then let him go. Easy pickings, a great modern invention; up there with the mobile phone and the digital camera.

Only it wasn't just Ear Ring and his friends who had thought of it, there'd been another kidnap gang of great minds, thinking the same thing too.

They'd probably both sat outside Benny's school, in separate cars, unaware of each other's existence, maybe parked around opposite corners, watching his comings and goings, timing his arrivals and departures, calculating his most vulnerable moments and deciding how they were going to snatch him off the street.

So there they were, the two kidnap gangs, each oblivious to the other, seeing each other's cars every day perhaps, but thinking they belonged to parents.

They'd maybe sat outside the school for weeks on end, one parked in Church Street, the other in Dean Lane, each watching the entrance, waiting for their chance to nab Benny, each blissfully unaware of the other.

Then they'd seen Benny (the other gang that is, not Ear Ring's), they'd seen him making his way along the road to meet me under the willow behind the wall. He was wearing my blazer, of course, but our blazers were the same colour and one school crest looks much like another.

So without bothering too much about why he was walking *into* the school at that time of afternoon instead of coming *out* of it, they'd grabbed him –

easy as scoring in an open goal – and they'd gone off with him in the boot, tearing off down Church Street. And Ear Ring's gang hadn't seen anything.

Then I came out – late. The coast was clear. Most people had gone. I got into the limo. There was only Joe the driver to take care of. So Ear Ring and his mates, watching from Dean Lane, sprang into action and I got kidnapped as well.

Two kidnap gangs, two Benny Spinkses, two ransom demands.

Problem was, who was who? Who was the real Benny Spinks? Which kidnap gang was going to get the money? And what was going to happen to the Benny Spinks who wasn't Benny Spinks – i.e. me?

I didn't like to think about it.

I thought of my mum and dad. They'd be worried now, wondering why I hadn't come home. They'd have phoned around and gone looking, and when I still didn't turn up, they'd have gone to the police.

All right, my disappearance would be overshadowed by the bold and fearless abduction of Benny Spinks in broad daylight, but I was still a missing person and I had to be looked for too.

How long, I wondered, before Ear Ring worked it out? As soon as it came on the news, I guessed, that one Bill Harris – whose most distinctive feature was that he was the spitting image of Benny Spinks – had gone missing and not come home. He'd know at once. He'd be unlocking the door and shaking me awake, saying, 'All right then, kid, which one are you? Are you the real Benny Spinks?'

What was I to say to that?

If I told him that I wasn't the real Benny Spinks, he might let me go. Or he might not believe me. No, he wouldn't believe me. Of course he wouldn't. Because that was exactly what the real Benny Spinks would say – that he wasn't Benny Spinks, so they'd set him free.

But even if I did convince them that I was plain, ordinary Bill Harris, they still might not let me go. Because I knew all their faces and could identify them. They might decide to get rid of me.

Then there was Benny himself. What was best for him? Surely it was best to keep them confused, so they didn't know who they had.

That was what I decided to do. No matter what happened, I would go on claiming that I was Benny Spinks. It seemed to be my best chance of surviving.

I fell asleep on the bed. I didn't bother taking my clothes off, I just lay on top of the duvet. As I drifted off, I wondered if Elvis was missing me, or was worried about me, and how he was coping all alone in the bunk bed, with nobody to kick up the mattress.

'Oi! You! Get in here!'

It was early morning. The news was on. They turfed me off the bed, dragged me into the kitchen and sat me in front of the telly. I missed the tail end of it, so they switched channels to find the news on another.

There I was.

'Police are appealing for assistance in discovering the whereabouts of William Harris, a Norris East schoolboy who failed to return home yesterday afternoon. William – known to his friends as Bill – was said to have left school at his normal time and to have set off to walk home alone. The police have issued this picture of the missing boy. He is described as friendly, cheerful and a good student. He was not believed to have had any problems, either at school or at home. Bill's parents have issued an appeal for their son to get in touch with them if he is in any kind of trouble, or for anyone who may have seen him, or have any information regarding his whereabouts, to come forward. Bill is dark-haired, of average build and height, and he occasionally liked to take harmless pleasure in the fact that he was often mistaken for Benny Spinks – the son of Derry Spinks, the footballer – to whom he has an uncanny resemblance.'

Ear Ring turned the set off. He sat there at the kitchen table, along with Nostrils, Scar Face and Vinny.

'Well, boy?' he said.

'Well what?' I asked, trying to look innocent and wondering if Vinny was likely to be putting any toast on soon, as I was quite peckish and could have done with a bite of breakfast.

'Well what? It's ******* obvious what!' Ear Ring said. (He was getting a bit angry by then.) 'There's two of you, isn't there? There's Benny ******* Spinks and there's Bill ******* Harris! And they've both been ******* kidnapped! And one of them's worth a cool four million, and the other one's worth **** all. And the only thing of the slightest ******* interest to us right now, old son, is which ******* Benny Spinks are you?'

Personally I didn't think it right that Ear Ring should be using the sort of language that you have to blot out with little stars when you write it down. I felt that this was giving a bad example to young and impressionable people like myself, who might be tempted to use such words themselves and think that it was big and clever to say that kind of thing.

'Well? Are you the real Benny Spinks or aren't you?'

'Of course I am,' I said.

'Prove it,' Nostrils said.

'How?' I asked him.

'What's your dad's name?' Nostrils asked.

'Don't be ******* stupid!' Ear Ring said. 'Everyone knows his dad's name! There's little kids living in jungle villages who know his dad's name. That won't prove anything.'

'Your mum's name, then?'

'Will you shut it for a minute, while I think?'

Ear Ring went over to his lap-top. He typed an

e-mail and sent it off. Then we waited. A reply pinged in shortly afterwards.

'All right, kid,' he said. 'I've just e-mailed your home. They have a question for you. That only their boy could know. So tell me – what colour's the wallpaper in your bedroom?'

'Blue stripe,' I said. 'With a darker blue border. There's also a big picture window, overlooking the grounds. To the right of the window are some fitted cupboards, to the left—'

'All right, all right. Blue stripe will do.'

He typed another e-mail then waited for an answer. By the time it came, the others were all clustered around the lap-top, peering over his shoulder.

'Well?' Nostrils said.

'Right answer,' Ear Ring said.

A cheer went up. But Ear Ring didn't look happy.

'What's wrong?' Vinny said. 'It proves we've got him, doesn't it?'

'No,' Ear Ring said. 'Not if you read the rest of it. The other kid, grabbed by the other gang, gave the same answer. He got it right too.'

They all looked pretty unhappy at that. Then Vinny seemed to brighten up; his brow unfurrowed itself and his lights seemed to go on.

'I got it,' he said.

'What?'

'There's two of them,' he said.

'We know there's two of them,' Ear Ring said

between gritted teeth. 'That isn't the difficulty—'

'No,' Vinny said. 'I mean there's Benny Spinks and then there's his twin brother – say, Joey Spinks—'

'Joey Spinks?'

'Yeah. And when they were born they were identical twins. Only Joey turned out to be a bit strange – and uncontrollable – and so they kept him a secret . . . and they have done ever since, and they've kept him locked up in this room in the attic, for years and years – chained to the bed—'

'Chained to the bed?'

'Yeah. With a potty.'

'A potty?'

'And they put his meals under the door.'

'The door?'

'Yeah, but then one day, he escaped – because he has this phenomenal strength . . . or really strong teeth maybe – and he bit through his chains—'

'Bit through his chains?'

'Yeah, and escaped through a window and went on the run. And then he headed for Benny's school – dressed in one of his old uniforms – and he waited outside for him; maybe wanting to be revenged because Benny had had all the advantages while Joey, his twin brother, had been kept in a poky room all these years, chained to the bed—'

'With a potty?'

'Yeah, with a potty . . . and his meals under the door.'

'Vinny . . .'

'Yeah?'

'Vinny, we hear what you're saying, but quite frankly . . .'

'Yeah?'

'I've never heard a bigger load of rubbish in my life. We know some other kid's gone missing. They said so on the telly this morning. Some kid who was always getting mistaken for Benny Spinks. Not his twin brother, Boris, who they kept in the attic. So just do us all a favour, Vinny, and leave the thinking to other people and go and make some toast!'

'Well, I was only trying to help!' Vinny said, and he went off in a sulk to put some bread into the toaster.

Ear Ring sat deep in thought. You could almost see it, getting deeper all around him, as if he were sinking down in an ocean of thought in a one-man submarine.

Then he snapped his fingers with a loud click and said, 'Got it!'

The others looked at him expectantly.

'The Fingles!' he said.

'Fingle?'

'The Fingle mob. Has to be. Who else would do it? Everybody else is into other things – banks and security vans and all the rest. But Fingle – it's her kind of thing.'

'Babs Fingle, you mean?' Scar Face said.

'Babs Fingle and Co,' Ear Ring nodded.

'What'll we do?' Nostrils asked.

'Pass us your mobile,' Ear Ring told him.

'My mobile?'

'If I use mine, they might trace it.'

'Ah. But they might trace mine too,' Nostrils pointed out.

'Not to me they won't,' Ear Ring said. 'What's her mobile number?'

'I dunno,' Nostrils shrugged.

'Home number then. We'll get the answering.'

'I might have that,' Scar Face offered. He took out a small pocket address book and passed it over.

Ear Ring dialled a number. He listened to a message, waved his hand for a pen, noted a number down on the wooden kitchen table, then rang it up.

'Hello? That Babs Fingle? It's me. Yeah. You know who. Listen, I think you and me have got a problem, would that be right?'

The others looked at him. He gave a thin smile and nodded his head.

'Thought as much,' he said into the phone. 'So how about we sort it? I suggest we split everything in equal shares. You happy with that? How much are you asking? Really? Well, we were asking for four.'

'How much are they asking?' Scar Face wanted to know.

Ear Ring held up three fingers.

'We'll keep it to four then,' he said. 'Or maybe up

it to five. How many of you are there? Four? Same here. So five million between eight, that's . . .'

'Five-eighths of a million each,' I chimed in. 'Which is, approximately, six hundred and twenty-five thousand each. Not bad for a day's work.'

'Shut it, will you?' Ear Ring said. Then he spoke into the phone again. 'No, not you Babs,' he said. 'The kid here. Having a bit of trouble with the brain box. OK look, we'd better have a meet. We can come to you or you can come here. OK. You'd better come here then. It sounds safer. Get here as soon as you can and bring him with you. Then we'll find out who's who and get it sorted. I'll tell you where we are . . . Oy, Vinny – take the boy to his room so he can't earwig.'

I grabbed some toast and they locked me up in the room again. I put the TV on for a while and then turned it off. I heard them all talking, out in the kitchen. Their voices were low, as if they didn't want me to hear. I tiptoed over and put my ear to the door.

'I know how to do it,' Ear Ring was saying. 'It's sheer litmus paper, mate. You dab it into the real Benny Spinks and it turns red. You dab it into the phoney one, and nothing happens. I remember reading it somewhere. You don't have to ask no questions or nothing like that at all. It'll tell us who the real Benny Spinks is and no trouble at all. But it's drastic, so we'll only use it as a last resort. Vinny . . .'

'Yeah?'

'You get in the car, find a shop, buy some and then bring it straight back here.'

'OK then.'

'When the Fingles get here with the other kid, we'll get it sorted.'

'What'll we do with the wrong one? When we know which is which?'

'Take him and dump him somewhere and let him go home. We don't want two flipping kids. One's more than enough trouble. We just want Benny Spinks – and now we know how to tell who he is.'

The outside door banged and shortly afterwards I heard a car being started up and driven away. I lay on the bed and looked at the ceiling, trying to make sense of what I'd heard.

What had they meant? What was the litmus test? What was this infallible method that Ear Ring had dreamed up of telling who was the real Benny Spinks?

Then I knew. I just knew. I could see it all. I knew exactly and precisely what they were going to do. I knew it down to the last detail.

Only I wasn't going to let it happen. I was starting to make plans of my own. I was one step ahead of them, and with luck that one step might turn into two, then three, then several thousand.

The first thing was to convince them that I was Benny – and then the real one would be free to go.

Then once he was safe and home, I could reveal that I wasn't Benny, that I was worthless, and they'd have to let me go too. Nobody in my family was going to pay four million quid for me, not even if they wanted to, they didn't have the money. The most money we had was the holiday money, and the change in the big jar that we used to keep the kitchen door open.

So that was the plan. Convince them I was the real Benny. Get Benny freed. Tell them who I really was, get freed too.

Surely the best laid schemes of mice and men and Benny Spinks look-alikes couldn't always go wrong? Surely they had to go right occasionally?

I heard the car return, then I heard Vinny come into the kitchen.

'I got it,' he said.

And I knew, even without seeing it, what he had been to the shops to buy, and what at that precise moment he was putting down on the kitchen table.

'Good,' Ear Ring said. 'That'll do it. But keep it out of sight.'

A cupboard door creaked and then banged.

'OK. Hopefully they'll soon be here.'

About twenty minutes later there was the sound of another car drawing up outside the house. It had to be the Fingle gang. I heard a woman's voice saying, 'Bring him in. And don't take the tape off till we're in there.' I could imagine them bundling Benny in, with duct tape over his mouth and a blindfold over his eyes, maybe with his wrists and ankles bound.

Maybe he'd even had to travel in the boot.

There were other voices and there were doors opening and closing, followed by hellos and how are yous and all the sounds of birds of a feather flocking together – criminal, thieving-magpie, cuckoo-in-the-nest sorts of birds.

Next I heard Ear Ring's voice say, 'OK. Bring in our one and let's sit them down together and take a look at them both.'

A key turned in the lock. The door opened and Nostrils stood there, blocking the light. He had a packet of cigarettes in his hand. A message on the packet read Smoking Kills. But it didn't seem to bother him. Maybe he thought he'd kill the packet first, before it killed him, and he'd do it by setting fire to the contents.

'Come and join us, kid, why don't you?'

I followed him into the kitchen. There they all were – Ear Ring, Scars, and Vinny – and seated with them around the table was a woman who had to be Babs Fingle and three hard-looking men – her associates.

And Benny. The real, original, accept-no-substitute, one-hundred-per-cent genuine, unique and authentic Benny Spinks, wearing my school blazer.

He looked at me and I looked at him.

'Sorry, Bill,' he said, 'about what's happened.'

'That's all right, Bill,' I said. (I couldn't have them thinking he was the real Benny.) 'Not your fault. Don't worry about it.'

Then I saw them, right there, slap bang in the middle of the table, there on a nice white plate.

There they were. The sandwiches. Freshly cut and ready for the eating. The litmus test. The deciding factor. The means of detecting the real Benny Spinks.

I knew what was in them. But Benny didn't.

It was simple.

It was peanut butter.

18

Will the Real Benny Spinks Please Throw Up?

Whether they had intended to, or whether they hadn't, the Fingles had all sat down on one side of the table; while Ear Ring's gang faced them from the other. Benny and I were in the middle, one on each side. I guessed that one – if not all – of the kidnappers must have read in *Okey-Dokey Weekly* or somewhere about Benny's peanut allergy. Hence the peanut-butter sandwiches sitting on the plate. If all else failed, this would be the litmus test, the decider, the penalty shoot-out. But I acted as if I hadn't even seen the sandwiches, and had not the slightest interest in them.

'All right,' Ear Ring said. 'The truth, and no messing. Who's Benny and who's Bill?'

'I am!' Benny and I both said.

Ear Ring looked annoyed and started again.

'OK, let me rephrase that, as you're finding it so difficult. Who's Bill?'

'He is,' we answered.

A muscle in Ear Ring's face began to twitch.

'It might be better if I handled this,' Babs Fingle said.

Ear Ring gave her a nasty look, as though she were trying to muscle in on his territory and to undermine his authority and make him look small in front of his mates. But then he smiled and gave her a condescending look, as if to say, Let's see you do better if you think you can, and said, 'Be my guest.'

'OK,' Babs Fingle said. She was quite pretty in a tough-looking way and had a tattoo like a bracelet around her arm. 'One at a time. You first.' She pointed at me. 'Who are you? Benny or Bill?'

'Yes,' I said.

A muscle in Babs Fingle's face began to twitch too.

'Let's start again. Is your name Benny Spinks?'

'Yes,' I said. 'It is.'

She turned to Benny.

'So you're Bill Harris?'

'That's right,' I said. 'He is.'

'I wasn't asking you,' Babs Fingle said, 'I was asking him. I'm sure he doesn't need you to tell me who he thinks he is.'

'He might have forgotten,' I said.

'Will you shut it?' Nostrils said. 'Or I'll shut it for you.'

'Only trying to be helpful,' I said.

'If we all do the talking we'll never get anywhere!' Ear Ring said. 'Babs – you carry on.'

She looked at Benny again.

'What's your name?'

I tried to kick him under the table, to let him know that he ought to say he was me. That way they'd let him go, then when he'd gone I could tell them who he really was, and then they'd have to let me go too as I wouldn't be worth any ransom.

Only I missed him and kicked one of Babs Fingle's gang instead.

'Ow!' he said. 'Who did that? Who kicked my ankle?' He stared across the table at Vinny. 'Was that you? You do that again, I'll come over there and tear your ears off and stick them up your nose.'

Vinny started to get to his feet.

'Oh, you will, will you? Well I'll tear your nose off and stick it in your ear!'

The Fingle bloke got to his feet too.

'You – me – outside – any time!' he said.

Babs was getting annoyed.

'Do sit down, will you, Chainsaw,' she said. 'We're trying to have a serious discussion here, and all you two can do is play footsie under the table.'

'Well, he started it,' Vinny said.

'Did not,' Chainsaw said. (I would have liked to have known why he was called Chainsaw, but didn't feel it was the right time to ask.)

'Well, stop it anyway. Now then.' Babs fixed Benny

with a hard, menacing stare. 'We want to know what your name is – your real name.'

'It's B-Benny S-spinks,' Benny said.

(And if Babs Fingle and Ear Ring had known just a little bit more about Benny Spinks, they would have been able to tell right then and there who the real one was. If they had known that the real Benny Spinks began to stutter when stressed out and under pressure . . . But they didn't.)

'OK,' she said. 'So you're both Benny Spinks?'

We nodded. Everything was nice and quiet for a few seconds. It was quite restful really. Then she brought the flat of her hand down on to the table.

'You can't both be Benny Spinks!' she yelled, so loudly that everybody jumped. 'One of you is lying. Now which one is it? Which one of you is a liar?'

Benny and I pointed at each other.

'He is,' we said.

'I'm starting to lose my patience,' Babs Fingle said.

'I've already lost mine,' Ear Ring said. 'I think it's time to move on to other strategies.' He glanced at the plate of sandwiches.

'In a minute,' Babs Fingle said.

She plainly only wanted to use the peanut-butter sandwiches as a last resort. Obviously, they had to be careful. For all they knew, Benny's allergy might have been a really severe one. A mouthful of peanut butter might do more than bring him out in a rash – it might kill him.

Benny Spinks alive was worth millions. But Benny Spinks dead, what was he worth then? And what about the two gangs of crooks? Kidnapping was one thing, but murder – and it would have amounted to murder, too . . .

'Look,' Ear Ring said. 'I say ours is the real thing. When we knocked him off, he was in the limo. He was with the driver. He was wearing the right school blazer. Where did you knock yours off? Round the corner, wasn't it? And what was he wearing?'

'It looked like the real thing at the time.'

'It don't look like it now.'

We were still both in school uniform. Nobody had thought to get us any other clothes.

'Ours is the real deal,' Ear Ring said. 'Anyone can see he's the genuine article. Or why else would he be in Benny Spinks's limo, wearing Benny Spinks's blazer? Nah. You slipped up there, Babs. You went and nabbed a dead ringer all right, but you didn't get the real McCoy.'

Babs Fingle's gang looked a bit downcast at this, while Nostrils, Scars and Vinny cheered up no end, and started nodding and saying, 'Yeah, what about that then?' and similar sounding things.

But Babs Fingle wasn't put out at all.

'If your Benny is the real Benny,' she said, 'how come his eyes are the wrong colour?'

She took a rolled-up magazine from her coat pocket and threw it down on the table. It was a copy of *Okey-Dokey*, and the main feature was Derry Spinks and Mimsy Tosh at Home – a Marriage Made in Heaven?

There was a photograph of them all together, and there was Benny, staring out at the camera. His eyes in the photo were greeny-brown, but mine were more greeny-blue. It was such a tiny difference no one had noticed it before.

Ear Ring studied the magazine picture, but not for long. He snorted and threw the picture back down on the table.

'That's just the printing,' he said. 'Or a trick of the light. That doesn't prove anything. You pick up a different magazine, his eyes'll be different again. It's like the controls on the telly, you fiddle about with them, you can make the picture any colour you want.' Then his eyes narrowed and he looked cunning. 'How about birthmarks?' He turned to me and Benny. 'Who's got the Spinks birthmark, eh? Which one's got that? That'll sort it.'

'What is the Spinks birthmark?' I asked.

'You should know.'

'There isn't one,' I said.

It went a bit quiet again. I saw Ear Ring wink across the table at Babs Fingle. Here it comes, I thought. The peanut butter. I had to make it look convincing. I got ready – mentally prepared.

Ear Ring sat back in his chair.

'Well, no hurry,' he said. 'Why don't we have a

289

little refreshment and then sort it out after. Cup of tea, Babs?'

'Lovely,' she said.

'Vinny, put the kettle on.'

Vinny looked irritated, as if he were cheesed off with always being the one who had to burn the chips and scorch the toast and put the kettle on, but he stood up anyway, and went to the sink.

'How about you boys?' Ear Ring said. 'You must be peckish.'

'Not particularly,' I said.

'Not much,' Benny agreed.

'But I insist,' Ear Ring said, pushing the plate of freshly-cut sandwiches forwards. 'Eat it while you can. You don't know when the next meal will arrive. There you go, lads – Benny and Benny – tuck in.'

The plate was slap bang between us.

'There's honey, there's Marmite, there's cheese.'

No mention of peanut butter. There was probably just a smear of it, in each one. So small you wouldn't even notice it – unless you had an allergy.

'Glass of squash with that, boys?'

'Please.'

'Thanks.'

'Vinny!'

Vinny (resentfully) got the squash.

All eyes were on us. We sipped our squash. Benny pushed the plate towards me a little.

'Sandwich, Benny?'

'After you, Benny,' I said. (Though I didn't want him to be first – I had to be first. I just wanted it to look good.)

'No, after you, Benny,' Benny insisted. (As I'd anticipated he would.)

'OK, Benny, thanks very much.'

'Not at all, Benny. There you go.'

I reached out. Picked up a sandwich. Brought it towards me. Opened my mouth. Bared my teeth. Inserted sandwich into gob. Bit. Chewed.

And then . . .

It was spectacular, even if I say so myself. You've never seen a fit like it. I was especially proud of the way I managed to froth at the mouth, without benefit of any accessories, such as whipped cream or shower gel.

The moment my teeth touched the sandwich I went into spasms; I writhed and squirmed and threw myself across the table, drumming with my fists and kicking with my heels.

'Mind him! Don't let him hurt himself. Hold him down!'

They grabbed me from all sides. I went on drumming my heels and shaking uncontrollably (well, they thought it was uncontrollably; it was all beautifully choreographed, in my opinion). I made terrible moaning noises and was especially proud of the way I made my eyeballs disappear. This was an old party trick I had, and which I sometimes used to put Elvis off his dinner.

'His eyes have disappeared!' Nostrils shouted. 'They've gone to the back of his head!'

'Keep hold of him,' Ear Ring said. 'It's just a spasm.'

I decided it might be a good idea to have an asthma attack as well. So I did. I started to wheeze something terrible and to claw the air. I let my eyeballs roll back into place for a second, so that I could see what was going on.

'He's suffocating!' Babs Fingle yelled. 'What have you done? What a stupid idea!'

'I knew the real Benny Spinks was allergic to it and this was the way to tell them apart!' Ear Ring said.

'Not much use telling them apart if you kill him in the process.'

'A bit of peanut butter's not going to kill him!' Ear Ring said. 'Is it?' he added uncertainly, as I started to make choking-on-my-tongue gurgles. He had the look on his face of a man who sees five million quid slowly slipping from his grasp.

'Fetch a spoon and stick it down his throat!' someone shouted. 'Vinny! Get a spoon!'

'Why's it always me who has to get the spoons?' I heard Vinny say. 'I filled the kettle and got the squash and I cooked the chips last night—'

'Burned them, you mean.'

'And I did the toast this morning, and I cut the sandwiches, and now, on top of all that, I've got to go and get the spoon to stop him choking. Well, why doesn't somebody else do something for a change?'

'Ahhhhhh!' I went. 'Ahhhhhh! Ahhhhhhh!' And then I made an awful gurgling noise, like someone trying to flush a football down a toilet.

'Just get a spoon! He's swallowing his tongue!'

'What does he need a spoon for anyway? What's he going to do with it? Eat a bowl of cornflakes?'

'I need the spoon to get his tongue back out from down his throat you stupid— never mind, I'll get it myself.'

Ear Ring yanked out a drawer from one of the kitchen cabinets. Cutlery spilled everywhere. He picked up a huge serving spoon from the pile of silver on the floor and headed for me, as I lay on the table, writhing, gurgling and frothing at the mouth.

I didn't like the look of that spoon at all. I certainly didn't want him sticking it down my throat. I decided to make a partial recovery.

'Ahhhhh – gnnnnnnnnn!'

'It's all right!' Babs Fingle said. 'His tongue's out! But his eyeballs have gone again.'

I let my tongue loll out of my mouth. I rolled my eyeballs a while longer, then allowed them to go back to their usual place.

Out of them I saw the real Benny Spinks, at the other end of the table, looking at me with an expression of horror, as if he thought that I really did have a peanut allergy, just like him.

I gave him a wink, then had another spasm to disguise it, so it would all seem like part of the convulsion. In doing so, I kicked the sandwich plate clean off the table.

'Watch him! He's having another fit!'

I had a few more for good measure, then gradually let them subside. I rolled my eyeballs around a couple more times and did a bit more foaming at the mouth. I tried to get eye contact with Benny once more and to give him a nod of reassurance. I hoped he saw and understood that it was his chance now to get out of the place and that he wasn't to worry about me; that I'd be all right.

My feet stopped drumming on the kitchen table. I let myself go limp. I eased off on the frothing, and just blew one nice big final bubble for effect.

'I think he's over it now,' Nostrils was saying. 'He's going to be all right.'

'Yeah,' one of Babs Fingle's henchmen said. 'He's pulling through.'

'Amazing,' Scars said. 'You'd never think it, would you, that a little dab of peanut butter could cause that sort of reaction.'

'Yeah,' Ear Ring said. 'Sort of reaction *you* get, isn't it, mate, when faced with an honest day's work?'

Everyone laughed at that except Scars, who went red and glared at Ear Ring. But he didn't dare say anything, as Ear Ring was the boss.

'Well, Babs,' Ear Ring said: 'Looks like you

kidnapped the ringer after all, and the genuine article's ours.'

'And what about what we agreed on? You'd better not go back on that.'

'OK. A deal's still a deal. We split the money eight ways.'

'And what about him?' Babs said. 'The other kid?'

'Get rid of him,' Ear Ring said. 'I don't think he's going to be worth anything. Not Bill Harris here. What are you worth, son? All of fifty quid or something? Ha ha.'

I caught Benny's eye. No heroics, please Benny, I thought. Just go along with it and get out. I'll be all right. Just go.

'OK, Billy boy. You come with me.'

'Where you taking him?' asked Babs.

'Somewhere we can get rid of him, of course,' Ear Ring said.

For a sickening moment I thought he really meant to get rid of him . . . for good.

'Put a blindfold on him, we'll take him for a spin then kick him out the car and he can make his own way after that. He won't know where we are or be able to tell anyone nothing.'

'OK.'

'Then we'll send Benny's mum and dad another little e-mail – telling them we've got their Benny here, the real one and only, and there's no doubt about it.'

Off they went. I slid from the table and sat slumped in a chair while Vinny stood by with the large serving spoon in his hand, just in case I should have a sudden relapse. He gave me the impression that he was looking for any excuse to use it.

They blindfolded Benny and took him outside, then drove away in the car. Scars and Chainsaw took him. Babs Fingle and Ear Ring sat hunched over the lap-top, sending off new ransom demands and assuring Derry Spinks at the other end that there was no duplication any more and they had the real Benny Spinks at their mercy.

I decided to give it a while before I told them the truth. I could see that they might be a bit annoyed about my deceiving them. I didn't want to tell them too soon or they might ring up Scars on his mobile, and tell him to turn the car round and bring Benny back.

Scars and Chainsaw returned in about an hour.

'Well?'

'We dumped him on the outside of town. I stuffed a bit of money in his pocket so he can make a call and get a bus or a cab or whatever. He'll be all right. We left the blindfold on and his hands tied, but the knots were loose. He'll get out of them in ten minutes.'

'No one saw you?'

'No one. How's it going this end?'

'They're coming round to it. First they said five

million was impossible. Then they said they still didn't believe we had him. So I suggested that I send them a bit. Maybe chop an ear off and put that in a nice little envelope.'

My hand went instinctively to my ear.

'What's up, son?' Chainsaw said. 'Getting worried? Yeah, so you should be. We're going to cut your ear off and send it off in a box. So if you want to get the wax out of it with your little finger, you'd better do it now. Haw, haw!'

'Please, don't cut my ear off,' I said.

'All right. We'll cut your finger off instead then – but I wouldn't do that for everyone.'

'But I don't want to lose a finger either.'

'A toe then. But it's special favours now.'

'But I don't really want you to cut anything off.'

'Oh, my, my, aren't we just too picky.'

'Not if you cut my finger off I won't be.'

They seemed to think it was all a big joke.

'I'm hungry,' I said. I was. Breakfast had been hours ago and it burned up a lot of calories, having fits. 'Could somebody make me a sandwich?'

They all looked at Vinny who looked at me and said, 'The stuff's all there. Make your own.' He muttered something about 'spoilt little rich kids' and something else about 'trying to look pathetic' and 'don't give me the poor little rich boy stuff. It cuts no ice and it melts no hearts round here.'

So I made my own sandwich. None of them was

paying any attention. Both gangs were gathered around the lap-top as Babs Fingle and Ear Ring negotiated with whoever was at the other end of the e-mails – maybe it was Derry Spinks, maybe it was the police, probably it was both.

I made myself a nice chunky sandwich. A great big doorstep, it was. Two thick, tasty slices. We always had wholemeal at home, so a nice farmhouse white was a real treat for me.

Then I got the jar and I slapped it on. Then I got the other jar and I slapped some of that on, too.

It isn't to everyone's taste, I grant you. In fact some people think it's pretty disgusting. But personally, it's always been a great favourite of mine.

Big doorstop sandwich. With jam.

And peanut butter.

Mmm.

Lovely.

I took a bottle of milk from the fridge and poured myself a long, cool glass. Then I took my enormous sandwich and my glass of milk and sat down at the far end of the table for a good stuff.

I think I must have been chewing rather loudly, because the sound seemed to distract them. One by one they looked up and stared, all gradually falling silent, until all you could hear was the slurp of my milk and the chomp of my sandwich.

Ear Ring was staring at me. He looked from me to my sandwich to the kitchen cabinet where I'd left the jars. I hadn't put them back yet, as I might have fancied another sandwich. There was the knife, there was the jam, there was—

The peanut butter.

The jar open. The lid off. Over two-thirds of it gone.

Mmm. Yum, yum, yum.

' 'Ere!' he said. 'What are you eating?'

I went on chewing. I felt it was the better answer. As our English teacher, Mrs Campbell, was always saying, 'Actions speak louder than words.'

There was an awful, eerie silence, as the actions went on talking and as everybody listened to them, spellbound. Then there was the sound of pennies dropping and of cogs, clicking into place.

19

Escape

I continued chewing. They went on staring. From somewhere far away, there still came the sound of pennies dropping and machinery whirring, of light bulbs going on, and of jigsaws being put together – the final pieces slotting into place.

Nobody spoke.

I realised then that perhaps this had been a bad idea. Maybe I shouldn't have made myself that peanut-butter and jam sandwich and so blatantly sat down to eat it. Maybe I had slightly miscalculated their reaction when they realised that I was not the real Benny Spinks and that they had let the genuine one go free, an hour and a half ago.

They watched, waiting for me to have another peanut fit, or for big red blotches to suddenly appear. My sandwich tasted dry in my mouth. It needed something to wash it down. But my glass was empty.

'Drop more milk would be nice,' I said. As nobody offered to get me one, I went and poured my own.

The silence went on building, like a skyscraper going up. I refilled my glass and returned from the fridge, heading for another bite of my sandwich. The silence by now was up to the thirty-seventh floor. Suddenly I noticed that my feet weren't on the ground, and that things in general had gone a bit pie-shaped and tight around the collar.

It was Ear Ring. He'd grabbed me by the shirt and had lifted me clean up into the air – with one hand.

'You little—'

'Exguse me, but you're gilling my gilk . . .' I managed to gurgle.

But he didn't care if he was gilling my gilk or got.

'I'll spill your ******* brains!' he said. (He was back on the little stars again, which is always a bad sign.)

Babs Fingle was on her feet too, looking at me from about a centimetre away. 'You devious little—' she said. 'You crafty little— What you've done, it's practically criminal! You're a bad one, you are. Why, I've half a mind—'

'Yeah, so have I and all,' Ear Ring said.

He was opening and closing his free hand, as if it was hungry to give something a good punch; as if it hadn't done so in a long time and was suffering from withdrawal symptoms.

It was difficult for me to get any words out, due to being half throttled, but I managed to gurgle

301

something in a wheezy whisper, which I hoped would appeal to their better natures.

'Why gon't we all just git gown,' I gasped. 'And galk about gis like givilised geople?'

Ear Ring's grip around my collar got even tighter. I noticed too, with some dismay, that a large dollop of peanut butter had slipped out of my sandwich and had landed on his shoe.

'You little *******!' he said. 'You ******* little *******!'

He let go of me so abruptly that I fell down on to a chair. Vinny came over and waved a finger in front of my face.

'We ought to do for you, you know that?' he said. 'We trusted you, we did! We kidnapped you in good faith, and let you ride in the car, all nice and comfy on the floor, when we could easily have trussed you up and chucked you in the boot instead, along with the spare wheel. Then we brought you here and gave you your own little room with a bed and a telly, and I made you toast in the morning, and cooked you chips – even if they were a bit well-done – and this is how you repay us. You're an ungrateful, selfish boy! People like you don't even deserve to be kidnapped and that's the truth! It's your parents I feel sorry for. Especially your mother.'

He sat down, looking fed up and thoroughly disgusted; he folded his arms, turned his head away and refused to look at me.

'Kids,' he said. 'Who'd have them?'

Nostrils, who'd been sitting there glowering in silence, kicked the table with anger and frustration. Everyone turned towards him.

'Well, this is great, isn't it?' he said. 'Now what do we do? We've been taken for suckers by a ******* kid!'

(They were all pretty big on the little stars by now. I was even thinking of using a few of them myself.)

'Sixty minutes ago we had one worth five million. Now we've got this useless twerp who's probably not even worth his weight in horse ****.'

(Which I thought was a bit uncalled for, personally. I mean, all right, I wasn't Benny Spinks, but I still had my uses.)

'That's just tremendous, isn't it?' Nostrils went on. 'All the time and money we spent on planning this. Now, instead of getting half a million apiece or whatever, what we get is a big slice of nothing! On top of that, we've still got the poor man's Benny Spinks here to get rid of, and the coppers sniffing about everywhere by now, more than likely. Well, that's just ginger peachy, isn't it? In fact, I've not had a day as good as this since I went down the dentist for a root filling and they ran out of anaesthetic! Just great!'

Nostrils seemed to speak for all of them. Babs Fingle's associates, in particular, looked very dejected; and they were eyeing me up with unveiled hostility.

'We'll have to get rid of him,' one of them said. 'So there's no clues.'

'Yeah,' another of them said. 'How about a nice little snooze . . . with the fishes?'

'Yeah,' the first one agreed. 'Stick his feet in a bucket of cement and chuck him off a bridge soon as it gets dark.'

'Or maybe we could fit him into a nice motorway fly-over somewhere. Or use him as house foundations,' Chainsaw suggested. 'Chop him up nice and small and mix him in with the concrete.'

'Wait a minute,' Ear Ring said. 'We're forgetting something.'

'What?'

A broad smile spread across Ear Ring's face.

'Think about it,' he said. 'Nothing's changed.'

'Yes it has,' Scars said. 'An hour ago we had a kid worth millions. Now we've got Lavatory Brush here, who's probably worth about fifty pee and whose dad would need a bank loan just to raise that!'

(I didn't think calling me Lavatory Brush was very necessary. There was no need to get personal.)

'No, no,' Ear Ring said. 'You're looking at it all wrong, mate. No. What we have here is the brave little soldier who so cunningly and cleverly stuck his own head into the old crocodile's mouth, to stop it biting Benny Spinks's head off. He's been a brave boy, hasn't he? He's used his noddle. He's made the big sacrifice and carried on like a hero. He's saved

Benny Spinks. Now then – what are Benny Spinks's mum and dad going to think about that?'

'Well, they'll be grateful,' Scars said.

'That's right,' Ear Ring said. 'Grateful and glad and something else beginning with G and all. Know what?'

'Happy?' Nostrils said.

'That begins with H not G, you stupid— Not happy – *guilty*! Guilty that someone else's son is still being held hostage while their Benny got away. Him staying behind was the price of their boy escaping. Right?'

'So?'

'So when we ask cheapo-boy here's mum and dad for five million in ransom or he gets the chop, and when they can't pay it, well, who's going to pay it for them?'

'Yeah – Derry Spinks!'

'Exactly. Because if he doesn't, what're people going to say? That there was Derry Spinks, letting some poor kid make the big sacrifice to let his own kid go free, but when it came to that kid going free, he wouldn't even put his hand in his pocket.'

Babs Fingle gave a smile.

'He's right, you know,' she said. 'They still have to pay. They can't not pay.'

'So it's still on?'

'It's still on. Let me get at the lap-top there.'

Ear Ring moved his chair and sat down at the computer. I don't know what he typed in it, but it seemed to get admiring glances from those who were watching over his shoulder.

'– and twenty-four hours to do it –' Ear Ring said as he typed, '– or we'll send a little token, in an envelope, to show we mean business.'

'Like a couple of toenails,' Scars said.

'Yeah,' Vinny said. 'Or a couple of toes!'

They all had a good long laugh about that, though it made me feel quite queasy. I had the feeling that even though they were laughing, underneath it they were perfectly serious.

I looked down at my shoes. I wondered if they were thinking of two toes on one foot, or one toe on each. Either way didn't seem very appealing.

'Finish your sandwich, kid,' Nostrils said. 'What's the matter? Don't you want it no more?'

I didn't. So they carted me off to the little room with the skylight in it and locked me up again.

I lay down on the bed and looked at the dent-free ceiling and I thought about things, about the present and the future, and especially the past. I thought about me and Elvis, and me and school, and how I'd always been last at getting picked for the football teams and then how everything had changed quite by accident, all thanks to the big fan in the changing room, blasting out warm air, and how it had frizzed my hair up and altered my whole life in a moment, by turning me into Benny Spinks.

Suddenly I'd had friends everywhere and even

Vicky Ferns – who'd never given me so much as the time of day before – was all over me like a cheap tracksuit and wanting to be seen with me. Then there I was, down at the Green hanging out with cool skateboarders who'd never even acknowledged my existence before. Soon I was going to the cinema with Vicky Ferns and getting invited to join her and her mates for smoothies in fashionable drinking establishments (even if I did have to buy them). Yes, there I was, with Vicky on one arm and a whole bevy of beauties trailing along behind, just like I was a film star or something. And it was all down to a new hairstyle and to Benny Spinks.

Benny Spinks. None of it would have happened without Benny Spinks. If he hadn't ever existed then you know what would have happened when the fan in the changing room frizzed my hair up?

Everyone would have laughed.

That's right. They all would have laughed at me and said I looked like an old rock star from way back when frizzed-up hair was all the rage. They'd have sniggered and taken the mick and I'd never have heard the end of it, and I'd have gone straight home and had another shower immediately just to flatten the frizz down and get rid of it.

But because I looked like Benny Spinks and Benny Spinks was rich and famous and all the rest . . .

And then, I thought about how I went and cashed in on my look-alike qualities and how that had, in turn, led me to actually meet the real Benny Spinks and to find out that he wasn't such a bad bloke really when you met him, even if he was rich and famous.

Next came the great switcheroonie and the discovery when I got to his house and got a taste of his life that rich and famous wasn't all it was cracked up to be and that not so rich and a bit hard up and not famous at all had its plus points as well. I went to his school, pretending to be him, and I found out that just like me, he was chosen last for the team and he'd been too embarrassed and ashamed to mention it in advance – yes, even Benny Spinks, round at rich and posh school, was among the last. Even Benny Spinks had his troubles.

After that had come the double kidnap and my great bit of acting with the peanut butter, so that Benny could get away and so that when they discovered I was just a big nobody they would let me go as well.

Only it hadn't quite worked out like that. Those best laid schemes had gang a-gley, just like Rabbie Burns and Mrs Campbell had said they would.

Here I was now, far from home and held hostage by a vicious bunch of kidnappers (well, two vicious bunches, to be precise) who wanted five million quid from Benny Spinks's dad or they'd start to chop my toes off and put them in a Jiffy bag and send them off (probably first class and marked Fragile: Toes) to show that they meant business.

And if the money didn't come – what then? Maybe they'd cut a few more toes off, or make a start on my fingers, or chop off an ear, or something else that I could ill afford to lose as I might only have one of them, or two at the most.

And why? For what? What was behind it all?

Me, that was what. And my stupid idea that life would be better and I would be happier if only I could be Benny Spinks.

I wanted to go home.

I wanted my dent in the ceiling back.

I wanted Elvis back, kicking me up the mattress. I wanted Debs banging me on the head at breakfast, pretending I was a boiled egg and sticking toast soldiers in my ears. I wanted Kevin, whom I hardly ever saw except for going out and coming in, and Mum, telling me off for not keeping my room tidy (though it was Elvis who messed it up) and Dad in his Inter-Netty jacket, coming in after a hard day of broadband installation, saying what a tiring life it was and how about putting the kettle on.

I didn't want to be Benny Spinks any more.

I wanted to forget all about him and chauffeur-driven limos and Olympic-sized swimming pools and Mimsy Tosh and the Cheadlehulme School for the Sons and Daughters of Gentlefolk (Established 1532).

I wanted to be me. Yes. That's right. For maybe the first time in my life I was absolutely sure of what I wanted to be.

To be me. And nobody else.

And while I wasn't entirely sure who 'me' was exactly, I was willing to work on finding out. And if I didn't get picked for any teams or invited to the Green or to go for smoothies with Vicky Ferns, then so be it. Just as long as I could have Mum and Dad and Debs and Kevin and even Elvis. That was all I wanted, to go home now, and not be Benny Spinks. I didn't want to play the Benny Spinks game any more.

But I couldn't go home. I was still the substitute for him, his stand-in. Until his dad came up with a cool five million, I wasn't going anywhere – unless you count the little bits chopped off me and stuffed into Jiffy bags and sent off by special delivery to show that Babs Fingle and Ear Ring meant business.

I think it was the lowest point in my life. I'd quietly longed for ages to be popular and cool and sought after, just like Benny Spinks. Now here I was, miserable as sin.

If only I could be Bill Harris, I thought. I'd be happy, if I could be him.

He didn't seem such a bad bloke really, with such a bad life; there was a lot to be said for him, I realised that now. He was all right, was old Bill. He had many good qualities, in his way.

'You may as well have the rest if it.'

It was getting dark outside. Vinny was at the door,

carrying a glass of milk and a plate. On the plate were two sandwiches.

'Dinner,' he said. 'Your favourite. Peanut butter and jam. And don't choke on it.'

'Have they paid the ransom yet?' I said.

'You wish,' he sneered, then without further explanation he slammed the door shut and locked it.

You wish? What was that supposed to mean? That they'd refused to pay? That they'd made a lower offer?

What did five million pounds look like, I wondered? How many suitcases would it fill? Wouldn't the police try to mark it in some way, and set a trap for when Babs Fingle and Ear Ring went to collect it? And wouldn't the kidnappers be aware of this and do all they could to avoid it?

Well, they obviously weren't going to tell me anything. The less I knew the better, as far as they were concerned. I could sit there and stew with my milk and peanut-butter sandwiches until the cows came home – or until Chainsaw came in with something hidden behind his back and said, 'Right then! Time for the little piggies to go to market!'

I winced and curled up my toes. I couldn't eat the sandwiches and left them on the plate. I lay on the bed as the room grew darker, not even bothering to turn the light on, staring up at the ceiling and the skylight. It was the kind of window you couldn't even open to let air in. It was held in place with some wooden batons screwed into the plasterwork.

Wooden batons. Screwed in.

I put on the light.

I felt in my blazer pocket – well, strictly speaking it was Benny Spinks's blazer pocket. If only he had a Swiss Army knife or something like that. But no, there was nothing. Just his fountain pen. We'd had to swap pens as it would have looked funny for Benny not to be using his usual pen.

I unscrewed the cap and looked at it. It was a really expensive pen, just as you would have expected Benny Spinks to have, made from some kind of costly metal like titanium. There was a little clip attached to the cap for holding it in place in your breast pocket. The clip was tapered and came to a kind of arrow-head at its end. A bit like the tip of a screwdriver, I thought. Quite a lot like the tip of a screwdriver.

I stared up at the skylight and back at the pen clip. I was sure it would do the trick. I just needed to bend the clip out.

Only how was I to get up there? It was so near, and yet so far away. If only I'd been six feet taller. But then, if I'd been six feet taller, they'd never have dared kidnap me in the first place. If I'd been six feet taller, they'd never have mistaken me for Benny Spinks, who would have been six feet shorter than I was. None of this would have happened at all if only I'd been six feet taller. I'd heard it before and I could see that it was true – taller people have an easier life.

There was a chair in the room. I dragged it over, then I stood up on it, but the skylight was still miles away above me. I set the chair on the bed, but the mattress was too soft and wobbly. It was impossible to stand up on the chair without toppling over. So I gave up. I put the chair back and then I got into bed, turned off the table lamp and lay looking up at the moonlit ceiling. I could hear voices from the kitchen. It was Ear Ring and Co, probably discussing what they were going to do with their five million.

I wondered if the police would find me. Maybe Benny Spinks would be able to lead them to the hide-out, but then, as he'd been blindfolded and driven here in the boot of a car, maybe not.

Or maybe they'd be able to track where we were from the e-mail address the gang was using. Maybe my dad would come into his own and he'd be able to locate it using all his broadband expertise, and then Mum would have to change her opinions about his overalls with Inter-Netty on the back. Or maybe the e-mail couldn't be traced at all. I guessed not. Ear Ring wasn't stupid. He'd have set up his e-mail address behind a complicated web of servers. He might even be setting up new addresses for each message and reply.

Then there was the five million. Surely Derry Spinks would never pay it. I wasn't his son. And it was a load of money, five million quid, even to someone as rich as him. Perhaps he'd try and beat them down. Maybe he'd simply refuse to pay and tell them to do their worst. Then they'd start cutting my toes off.

The police wouldn't want him to pay it anyway. Or they'd want to mark it in some way so that the kidnappers could be traced. Or they'd try and arrest them at the pick-up. Or maybe Ear Ring had already thought of that, and he'd devised some risk-free way of picking up the money.

I remembered seeing how it was done in a film once. The kidnappers told the victim's husband to get on a train with the money in a briefcase and to throw the case out of the window when he saw a prearranged signal – someone with a red scarf. So, of course, he had no idea where the drop-off would take place. It could have been anywhere between London and Scotland. And when the signal finally did come, it was in the middle of nowhere. There was somebody standing there, out by the track, waving a red scarf. The man threw the case out of the window from the train corridor and that was it.

Of course the police could have followed the train in a helicopter, but the kidnappers had already thought of that, and had said that if they saw a helicopter, they wouldn't make the pick-up and the whole thing would be off.

Next I thought of Benny Spinks and wondered how he was getting on. He should have been home by now, safe and sound. I wondered about my mum and dad and how they'd be all worried and how Mum would be saying that she'd give five million to get me back if only she had it, but she didn't, and what could they do?

Then I fell asleep. When I woke there was daylight trickling in through the skylight window. That was when I got the idea. 'Sleep on it,' my dad was fond of saying. 'If you've ever got a problem, sleep on it.'

I could see how to get up to the window. It was so absolutely obvious, I didn't know why I hadn't thought of it before.

Quietly as I could, I stood up and began to move the bed. It was only a single one and not all that heavy. I turned it around, then I picked up the end and stood it upright.

It made a sort of ladder. The base, which held the mattress, was made out of wooden slats. It was very unstable, but I could just about walk up it, and then there I was – on top of this wobbly ladder-bed (or bed-ladder) using the pocket clip on Benny Spinks's pen to undo the screws holding the batons around the skylight.

It took me ages to do it: I almost fell off a dozen times and my arms were aching. I kept thinking that someone was at the door and about to come in and they'd catch me taking the last of the screws out and removing the glass.

It turned out not to be glass at all, but some kind of Perspex. I carried it down and placed it on the floor. Then I looked up. There was freedom. All I had to do was to climb up the bed, through the window, on to the roof, drop down on the ground outside, and away.

Only what if they saw me? What if they caught me?

So I didn't do anything like that at all.

I went and I hid in the wardrobe. I sat there, crouched and cramped and afraid to make a sound. I waited for somebody to come to my room with a plate of toast and a mug of tea for my breakfast.

I waited and waited. My foot went to sleep, then my other foot, then my legs, then I started getting cramp. Then I got an itch on the back of my neck, but I didn't dare move to scratch it; I couldn't have reached it anyway. Finally, after about an hour or more of being stuck in the wardrobe, I heard the lock turn and the door to the room being opened.

'All right, kid! Here's your breakfast! Rise and—'

It was Vinny's voice. He never got as far as the '– shine'. The next thing I heard was a plate hitting the floor and a cup smashing. Then Vinny was shouting at the top of his voice, 'He's gone! The kid's gone. He's got out the window!'

A stampede of feet came running, all at once, and a whole lot of voices were shouting loudly and there were quite a few '*******!'s in the air.

'He can't have gone far,' I heard Ear Ring say. 'Fan out and start looking for him. Get him and bring

316

him back! That's five million quid gone missing, and we'd better ******* find it!'

The feet ran out, but I didn't move. I stayed where I was, nursing my cramp and listening. It was a good job I did. Because after a few minutes I heard movement. Somebody had remained behind in the room, maybe standing there, staring up at the glassless skylight and the upturned bed.

'Little *******!' a voice said. It sounded like Babs Fingle. It had to be. She was the only woman there. 'We should have thought of it,' she added. Then somebody called from outside.

'Babs! Are you coming? Or don't you want your share any more?'

She left the room. I waited a few minutes more before opening the wardrobe. I tumbled out on to the floor and lay there, trying to rub some feeling back into my legs. Then I stood up, limped out to the kitchen, took a piece of bread, and went to the exterior door.

The cars had gone. Some of the gang must have gone to look for me on foot, and others had taken the cars to check the nearby roads. I assumed that they would assume that my first instinct would be to walk back towards the town, to take the first road which might look like it was heading towards people and civilisation.

So I did the opposite. I headed out towards the hills behind me, keeping close to the hedges that separated the fields and clinging to the lines of trees.

I walked for what seemed like ages, but which was maybe no more than a quarter of an hour. I'd soon eaten the bread. I found a fast-moving stream which looked all right to drink from, so I scooped some water up into my hands and drank and washed my face.

I turned and looked back and I could see them searching for me, far down below. One of them looked up, and although I immediately ducked, I was too late. He pointed and shouted and the others looked in my direction. They started running, and so did I. I ran as fast as I could.

I came to a road. It was deserted, remote. I said a little prayer for a car to come – a police car preferably. But there wasn't even a farmer on a tractor or a horsey lady with a pony and trap.

I looked back and could see them all gaining on me, running up over the fields, the fit ones far ahead of the smokers. Nostrils was lagging well behind.

I jogged on along the road, then stopped to get my breath. As I did, I heard a horn toot and turned to see . . .

Well – I couldn't believe it. It was a van. A white and blue van with a familiar logo on the side – it said 'Inter-Netty'.

It was Dad. It had to be. He'd tracked them down. I knew he would. He'd found out the location they'd been using on the lap-top and he'd come, single-handed, to my rescue.

The van braked to a halt. I ran over to it. The window was sliding down. A face peered out.

'Hey, son, you can't tell me where Long Lane is, can you? I'm a bit lost.'

It wasn't Dad at all. It was Horace, a workmate of his. They sometimes went fishing together, down on the canal.

'Billy,' he said. 'What the heck are you doing here? I thought you'd been kidnapped!'

'I have,' I said. 'And they're after me.'

'Get in,' he said. 'In the back. On the floor.'

I did. Just as they got to the road. Horace revved the engine up and we drove past them. They acted friendly and called on him to stop, but he didn't, he just kept on going. I peered out at them through the back window. They didn't see me.

Horace stopped the van about a mile down the road.

'You can sit in the front now,' he said. 'And put your seat belt on.'

He was tapping a number into his mobile phone.

'Who are you ringing?' I asked.

But he was already through.

'Police,' he said, into the phone. 'That's right. Yeah, it is. Yeah. It's an emergency.'

20

History

The rest is history, I suppose. It was in all the papers and on all the TV channels. They got the gang – well, both gangs to be accurate – and they found the house Benny and I had been held in and they were all taken to court and sentenced to prison for 'a good long stretch' as the saying has it.

I felt a bit sorry for them actually. I didn't think they'd really intended to cut my toes off. But then, you can never be sure with desperate criminal types, especially when there's five million quid at stake.

I was soon reunited with Mum and Dad and Debs and Kevin and even Elvis sort of grunted and said it was a real pain to see me – which was his way of being friendly, I suppose.

Benny Spinks was round to see me that same day, and so were his mum and dad. There was a big to-do in our street when their limo, with Joe at the wheel, turned up and parked right outside our house. Mr Bancroft, who lives next door, came round and complained that the limo was blocking his path and he couldn't get his push-bike out. I think he just wanted to get a look at Derry Spinks in the flesh, to be honest.

There were loads of reporters outside too, with so many flashes going off it was like a firework display. The Spinkses came in and Mum got the best cups out and put the kettle on and kept saying things like, 'You'll have to excuse the place, Mrs Spinks, as I've not had a chance to tidy properly, what with the kidnapping and everything.'

But Benny's mum was all right and she said, 'Not at all, really, it's absolutely spotless! And please – call me Mimsy.'

So she did. And Mum told her how much we all loved her singing and that we'd bought every one of her records. She said Dad was especially fond of her performances and had always been a big Mimsy Tosh fan, even from her Ketchup days. She also gave Mimsy Tosh her own personal recipe for marmalade, which Mimsy thanked her for and said she would be sure to make some the moment she got home to the mansion. (Though personally I didn't think she was even all that sure where the cooker was.)

Dad, meanwhile, said that Derry Spinks didn't want to be messing round with any cups of tea, and what he really needed was to taste a drop of Dad's home-made beer, because beer was good for you, as it had plenty of iron in it, and that was just what a professional footballer needed to keep himself in trim.

So Dad took Derry down to the shed and showed him his bottles of home-made beer. They were gone a good half an hour and when they came back they were making stupid jokes and laughing at them, though nobody else found them funny.

Well, Benny and I had to tell them all the truth, the whole truth, and nothing but the truth. It all had to come out because the police needed to know everything to build up the case against Ear Ring and Babs Fingle.

So we told them the lot, all about how we'd met when working on the ad for Nicka Nacka bars and how we'd kept in touch and had then organised the great switcheroonie, and how we had put the plan into action and how nobody had noticed a thing.

Elvis was more than a mite surprised when he discovered that the person he thought had been me had really been Benny Spinks and the Spinkses were equally astonished about the vice-versa.

I think Elvis was a bit mortified to learn that Benny Spinks had given him the nerve pinch of death and also that he had shown himself up for the big bully he was by kicking Benny Spinks up the mattress, thinking he was me. But he pleaded for a second chance and so we gave him one.

Mimsy Tosh was amazed at the resemblance between me and Benny and she could barely believe that she had not noticed anything strange about me and that I had passed myself off so thoroughly as Benny himself.

Dad and Derry Spinks had brought some bottles with them from the shed and they had a bit more of Dad's home-made beer, and Derry Spinks said it was a good drop and that he hadn't tasted as good as that in a long time.

Dad insisted he have some more then, though Mum (and Mimsy) tried to discourage it, and Dad had a bit more too, and then he asked Derry Spinks if he could say something to him and speak frankly and Derry Spinks said, 'Sure thing, mate. Go ahead.'

So Dad gave Derry Spinks a couple of tips and pointers as to how he could improve his game.

'I've noticed on the telly,' Dad said, 'that you need to work on that left foot a little, Derry. If you did that, you'd be stronger in the cross.'

Derry Spinks thanked him very kindly for his advice and said he'd be sure to work on that and would have a word with the coach about it during his next training session. Then they had some more beer.

It was quite something really – though I say so myself – to have the world's most famous footballer round at our house. It was hard to believe it was happening. You almost had to pinch yourself. There was a big crowd out in the street too, trying to see in through the window. Mum wanted to draw the curtains but Dad said, 'Let them look! Let them! Let them all have a good flipping gawp!'

Anyway, after a while, it was time for them to go, for, as we knew, Derry Spinks and Mimsy Tosh were a busy couple with many commitments and demands on their time. But before they left Derry said he had a few words to say and Mimsy Tosh agreed with him.

It was me he had to say the words to. He said he wanted to say how grateful he and Mimsy were to me for helping Benny escape from the kidnappers and for pretending to be him with the old peanut-butter ploy. He said that it was bravery beyond the call of duty and stuff like that. But I just got a bit embarrassed as I'd never really thought of it in that way and I just said that anyone would have done it – which they would, I was sure – and that anyway I thought of Benny as a good friend really and I'd only wanted to help him out and I knew he'd have done the same for me if I'd been rich and famous and worth five million quid, only I wasn't.

Well, Mum got a bit sort of tearful then – even though she hadn't been down to the shed where the home-made beer was – and she said she was just glad to have me back, as she was sure that Mimsy was to have Benny back, and that only a mother really knows what heartbreak there is when one of your own is taken from you and goes missing. Mimsy got a bit tearful too, and she said that was right, but Dad just rolled his eyeballs and poured out the rest of the home-made beer.

Then Derry Spinks reached into his pocket and took out an envelope and said, 'Bill, I can never really tell you or show you how grateful I am to you for what you did in helping save Benny from those kidnappers, but here's a little something with our best wishes, from me and Mimsy and Benny.'

'That's right, Bill,' Benny said. 'It's from all of us.'

I didn't like to open the envelope then, as it would have been a bit embarrassing, but I opened it later, and as you may have guessed, it was a cheque, made out to me.

I'm not going to tell you how much it was for. But I'll tell you one thing – I'll never be short of the wherewithal for a few smoothies down at Starbucks. Not ever. Not even if I live to be two hundred and ten.

But that wasn't all. There was more to come.

'I'd also like to invite you all to sit in the directors' box for the Cup Final,' Derry Spinks said. 'Only if you'd like to come, of course. I don't know if you'd be interested—'

'We're interested!' Dad said. He didn't say it on his own either. Elvis and Kevin and me and Mum and even Debs said it too.

'And seeing as you've been so hospitable with your home-made beer, Tom,' Derry Spinks said to Dad,

325

'maybe I can offer you a few bottles of champagne to have while you're sitting in the directors' box watching that match.'

'Now that,' Dad said, 'would be champion.'

Derry also gave me a signed football and a pair of his old boots. (New ones might have been nicer, but who was I to complain?) But that still wasn't all. Oh no. There was more. Here's the good bit.

Derry Spinks fixed it for me to kick off the Cup Final. I don't know how he managed it, but he did. Maybe when you're the most famous footballer in the world you can fix absolutely everything – apart from broken legs.

I got to run out there, in the team strip. Just me. Bill Harris. Who never got chosen for anything, who was always last in the team, always. The crowd was roaring and the atmosphere was as charged as storm clouds. There was so much excitement around you could have pulled it out of the air and chewed it.

Someone shouted my name and the crowd picked it up. They all knew, you see, about what had happened. It had been in all the papers by then.

'We want Bill. We want Bill. We want Bill!'

I was sure I'd never do it. I'd always messed it up. Everybody knew I was useless at football. I was sure I'd miss it and it would all go wrong.

Derry placed the ball on the spot.

'Go for it, Bill,' he said. 'You can do it. Think of everything else you've done. You can do this too.'

The crowd fell silent. The pitch and the stadium seemed enormous. They seemed to go on for miles. I measured my steps, took a few paces back, tried to concentrate. I remembered all those times they'd never wanted me, all the times I'd been left for last, all the times they'd said, 'Oh no! Not Bill Harris! We don't have to have him, do we?'

But those times seemed a long way away now and a long time ago.

'Here we go, Bill,' I told myself. 'Here goes for nothing. Here goes for bust!'

I ran, and I kicked, and then I heard the crowd as the ball soared high in a perfect arc and sailed into the afternoon air.

'Nice one, Bill,' I heard Derry say. 'I couldn't have done better myself.'

Benny Spinks and I are still mates. He comes round my house occasionally and I go round his. He's all right, is Benny. There's no swank to him. You'd never know from talking to him that his dad was the most famous footballer in the world.

He was able to fill me in on a few more of the details of what happened when he was me. And I told him a little more of what happened to me when I was him.

I won't tell you all of it, but there's one thing that stuck in my mind.

When Benny was at my school, pretending to be

me, he was standing in the playground when Vicky Ferns came up to him and said, 'Bill Harris . . .'

'Yes?' he said.

'I've been watching you,' Vicky Ferns said.

'Yes?' (He was getting nervous by now, thinking he'd been rumbled.)

'And you've changed recently.'

'Have I?'

'Yes,' Vicky said. 'You have.'

'In what way?'

'You don't look as much like Benny Spinks as you used to,' she said.

Benny gawped at her.

'Beg pardon?' he said.

'I said,' she said, 'that you don't look so much like the real Benny Spinks any more.'

'But—'

'But nothing,' she said. 'You just don't look like the genuine article. I mean, you still look a bit like him, but not close enough.'

'Oh,' Benny said, disappointed (but not particularly upset) to hear that he didn't much look like himself.

'So I'm afraid,' Vicky Ferns said, 'that it's all off.'

'What is?' Benny said.

'Our relationship,' she said. 'And going out for smoothies. It was nice while it lasted, but I'm sure you'll understand that I receive many offers of smoothies from other boys in the school and I can't really be seen hanging about with big nobodies whose only claim to fame is that they look like somebody else, especially when they don't really look like them so much any more.'

'Oh, right. Absolutely,' Benny said. 'I quite understand.'

'So no hard feelings,' Vicky Ferns said. 'And I'm sure that we can still be good friends, just as long as you stay out of my way and don't annoy me.'

'Right you are, Vicky,' Benny said. 'I'll try to do that.'

Of course, when I went back to school it was a different story then. Once I was a local hero and friend of the famous and had sat in the directors' box and kicked the big game off, Vicky Ferns changed her tune and was dead keen to go for smoothies again. She even offered to buy them. But I didn't make any promises. I was too young to commit myself.

Besides, I was otherwise engaged. I'd arranged to go to the pictures with Sandra – Sandra Debbings, if you remember, who sits at the back of the class and never says much, but who came up to me in the playground once and said that she liked Bill Harris just as he was.

It was Benny who gave me the idea to ask her out.

'There's a really nice girl at your school, isn't there, Bill?' he said. 'The nicest, best-looking one there, I reckon.'

I thought he was talking about Vicky Ferns again (though I wasn't sure about the 'nice' in relation to her).

'Her name's Sandra something,' he said. 'I thought she was really great. In fact I wouldn't mind asking her out for a smoothie one day.'

He did and all. They did go out together. Just as friends. But I didn't mind. I can afford to be generous and understanding about that kind of thing.

I've let my hair go back now to how it was. I've stopped frizzing it. I don't look much like Benny Spinks any more. I just look like plain Bill, old Bill Harris as was. I look like him.

Sometimes people say to me, they say, 'Bill, doesn't it worry you that Benny Spinks is a bit friendly with Sandra, who's your best and one and only girl?'

But I just smile and shake my head. You see, they don't understand really how it is with me and Sandra Debbings.

I mean, don't misunderstand me, I like Benny Spinks, he's a good mate. But to be honest, what has he ever done? Apart from have a famous mum and dad?

Whereas me, well, I reckon I've got one or two things to be proud of, even if I do say so myself. Things like foiling kidnappers and doing the old peanut-butter ploy, and then the hiding in the wardrobe plan, while working the pretending to have gone out of the skylight scheme, and generally thwarting criminals and saving the day.

So why should I be worried or jealous if Benny takes Sandra out for a smoothie once in a while? It's not Benny she's interested in. He knows that and she knows that and I know that too.

It isn't Benny. Not really.

I mean, he's a good sort and a great mate, and he's always turning up on the telly doing advertisements for Nicka Nacka bars.

Yes, he's a nice enough bloke in his own way.

But he's no substitute.

For the real thing.